Dear Readers,

Many years ago, when I was a kid, my father said to me, "Bill, it doesn't really matter what you do in life. What's important is to be the *best* William Johnstone you can be."

I've never forgotten those words. And now, many years and almost 200 books later, I like to think that I am still trying to be the best William Johnstone I can be. Whether it's Ben Raines in the Ashes series, or Frank Morgan, the Last Gunfighter, or Smoke Jensen, our intrepid Mountain Man, or John Barrone and his hard-working crew keeping America safe from terrorist lowlifes in the Code Name series, I want to make each new book better than the last and deliver powerful storytelling.

Equally important, I try to create the kinds of believable characters that we can all identify with, real people who face tough challenges. When one of my creations blasts an enemy into the middle of next week, you can be damn sure he had a good reason.

As a storyteller, my job is to entertain you, my readers, and to make sure that you get plenty of enjoyment from my books for your hard-earned money. This is not a job I take lightly. And I greatly appreciate your feedback—you are my gold, and your opinions *do* count. So please keep the letters and e-mails coming.

Respectfully yours,

William W. Johnstone

WILLIAM W.
JOHNSTONE

WRATH OF THE MOUNTAIN MAN

PINNACLE BOOKS
Kensington Publishing Corp.
http://www.kensingtonbooks.com

PINNACLE BOOKS are published by

Kensington Publishing Corp.
850 Third Avenue
New York, NY 10022

First Pinnacle Books Printing: December 2004

10 9 8 7 6 5 4

Printed in the United States of America

PROLOGUE

Sheriff Buck Tolliver set a bottle of whiskey in the middle of the rough-hewn table and took his seat. There were four other men sitting there, each as rough and weathered-looking at the old boards of the table.

Jerry Hogarth, known to friend and foe alike simply as Hog, both because of his great size and his rather slovenly personal hygiene, grabbed the bottle and splashed a generous amount into the tin cup in front of him. He also managed to pour about a third of a cup down the front of his already heavily stained shirt.

Bubba Barkley, sitting on Hog's left, gave him a rough elbow. "You gonna pass that bottle on over here or are you gonna try'n keep it all to yoreself, Hog?" Bubba was almost as big as Hog, but unfortunately had about the same mental ability—that is to say, very little.

Hog gave him a look, but shoved the bottle over with the back of a grimy hand as big as a ham.

Before Bubba was through pouring, Jimmy Akins, called the Kid by everyone because he favored fancy gunfighter attire and looked to be only about eighteen instead of his nearly twenty-three, shifted the toothpick around in his mouth and grunted, pointing at his own tin cup.

"You too lazy to pour yore own?" Bubba asked, but he poured anyway. "Or are you still trying to keep your gun hand free in case some desperado breaks in here and you have to fast-draw on him?" Bubba was referring to the Kid's rather irritating habit of trying to use his left hand for everything in order to keep his right hand hovering near the butt of his pistol. He'd read in a dime novel that it was something the real Kid named Billy used to do.

Buck ignored them and addressed himself to the remaining man at the table, Jeb Hardy, who unlike the others was well groomed and neatly dressed, and might almost have looked like an accountant, if you failed to notice his dead, cold, snakelike eyes, the way his pistol was tied down low on his right hip, and the way the wooden handle of the Colt was worn down from frequent use.

"How'd we do last week, Jeb?" Buck asked.

Jeb gave a half smile, reached into a leather case sitting on the floor next to him, and brought out a handful of papers. "We obtained the stake certificates to four new mines, and partnership agreements on three others," he said, his eyes smug.

"Any trouble?" Buck asked, meaning had they had to kill anyone to get the papers.

Jeb shrugged, his eyes again going flat, making it plain that he didn't appreciate being questioned like some lowly employee about how he'd done his job. "Not too much. A couple of miners fell and broke their arms, and one got a broken jaw, but we didn't have to plant any of them forked-end-up."

Buck nodded, pleased with the week's work. Before long, he and his band of men would own or control ninety percent of the best gold and silver mines in the county.

"I wanna know somethin', Buck," Hog growled, whiskey running down his chin, which he blotted with the tail of his shirt.

"Yeah, Hog?" Buck answered, turning to stare at the

man and wondering how in the world one man could attract so much dirt and grim without actually lying down and wallowing in it.

"How come we do all the dirty work an' you an' Jeb git to keep most of the profits?" He glanced at Bubba and the Kid, but both of them just lowered their eyes and pretended they hadn't heard the question. They, unlike Hog, were smart enough to know it wasn't healthy to question either Buck or Jeb about the split of their take. Better to just take what they were offered and be thankful they weren't really having to work for a living.

Buck put out a hand when Jeb's eyes flashed. He'd handle this, he signaled Jeb with a look.

"It's very simple, Hog, so even a dumb son of a bitch like you ought to be able to understand it." When Hog's eyes widened and his face turned beet red, Buck pointed to the sheriff's badge on his shirt. "This badge and my job as sheriff of this county is what is keeping all of our butts out of jail, and Jeb's law degree is what enables him to finesse these claim stakes and partnership agreements through the courthouse and, if they're ever challenged, through the courts so that we'll get our money without being hauled into jail and strung up for claim-jumping and murder."

He leaned across the table and glared at Hog and the others next to him. "All you bring to the table, Hog, is your muscle, which I can hire on any street in any town in this county for half what I'm paying you." He paused, not wanting to talk too fast for Hog's slow-witted mind to keep up. "Am I making myself clear?"

Hog pursed his lips and nodded reluctantly, the color still high on his cheeks and sweat glistening on his forehead. "Yeah, I guess so."

"No, Hog," Jeb said, his dead snake eyes fixed on the large man. "You'd better *know* so, because if you have any doubts at all about the fairness of this arrangement, Buck and I can change it in about two minutes flat, and you'll be back shoveling horseshit in the livery so's you can eat."

The mention of the livery put fear in Hog's eyes. He'd hated shoveling out the livery every day, but mucking stalls had been the only job he could get until Buck and Jeb had offered him this one. "No, no," he said, holding up his hands. "What you're payin' me is jest fine."

The Kid looked at Hog disgustedly, shaking his head. What a dumb ass, he thought. The Kid didn't particularly think his pay was so hot, but the job had other compensations for him: He got to bully, beat up, and draw down on men just about every day, and this fed his soul much more than any money ever could. No, he'd keep his mouth shut. Things were going along just fine as far as he was concerned, and to be honest, he wasn't all that sure he could outdraw Jeb in a fair fight if it came down to it.

"Speaking of money," Buck said, drawing a wad of greenbacks out of his coat pocket and throwing it down on the table. "Weekend is coming up, so take that and go on into town and live it up a little bit."

He got up from the table. "But be careful not to flash around the whole wad and draw attention to yourselves; and you'd better not cause any trouble in my town," he warned, pointing his finger at the men. "Remember what I said. Save the rough stuff for work."

Buck walked out of the old, ramshackle mining cabin where he always met his men and pulled a long, black cheroot out of his shirt pocket. He fired up a lucifer and put the flame to the end of the stogie.

Jeb walked out and stood next to him, making sure

he was upwind of the pungent tobacco smoke. "You think we need to worry about Hog?" he asked.

Buck blew out a stream of blue smoke and shook his head. "No, he's too dumb to try and go against us. Even he knows it'd be the end of a good thing for him."

"How about the others?"

Buck shrugged. "Same thing. Where else are they going to earn so much money for so little work?"

"That's for sure," Jeb said. "'Cause we are making a hell of a lot of money."

"And we're going to keep on making it, partner," Buck said, "as long as you keep any of the men we get the claims from too scared to go to the authorities."

Jeb's eyes again turned flat and hard and evil. "Any of them that do manage to grow the *cojones* to make a complaint won't live long enough to testify at a trial, that I'll guarantee you."

Buck shook his head. "Even so, I don't want any complaints to come to the attention of the governor, so make sure you step on anyone who might even be thinking about shooting off their mouths."

Jeb leaned over and spit on the ground. "You let me worry about that, Buck. You just keep on keeping the law off our backs and we'll have enough money to retire to St. Louis within a year."

"St. Louis! Hell, I'm planning on going to New York City," Buck said. He grinned. "I hear beautiful women are thick as fleas on a hound dog up there."

Jeb looked at him out of the corner of his eye. "Yeah, but if you're planning on going up there, we might want to work an extra year. Those New York ladies are mighty expensive to maintain, especially for somebody as butt-ugly and downright crude as you, Buck."

When Buck started to bristle, Jeb laughed and

slapped him on the shoulder. "Just teasing you a mite, partner. Don't take no offense now, you hear?"

Buck's eyes flashed. "Yeah, well if I did take offense at something you said, Jeb, you'd wake up with a bullet in your skull."

All of the amusement went out of Jeb's eyes in a flash and the grin faded from his lips. "Now don't let your mouth overload your ass, Buck, or someone might think you're good enough to take me down."

Buck smiled and tilted his head. "We may just have to find that out one of these days, Jeb."

"Any time, Buck, any time."

Buck rode back into what he liked to refer to as "his town" on his dun gelding, sitting high in the saddle, his chest thrown out, and a steely glint in his eye should anyone not know he was top dog in this kennel.

He'd come to the small mining camp known as Payday a few years back, when it was a typical lawless, anything-goes, wild and rowdy camp. Buck had seen his opportunity, and had bought himself a tin badge through a mail-order magazine and pinned it on. Anyone who had the temerity to question his authority found themselves looking down the barrel of his .45 Colt, or the twin barrels of the ten-gauge express gun he carried in a rifle boot on his saddle.

Buck was smart enough to not come down hard on the things the miners liked to do after working their claims all day, so he let the whores and the saloons and the gambling palaces stay in business, as long as they gave him a little cash on the side, "for security." He did, however, run off both the town's lawyers, not wanting anyone but himself deciding what was legal and what was illegal.

And when a drunk confided to all who would listen

in a saloon one day that he was not only a good barber, but that he was a better than average dentist and doctor to boot, Buck managed to convince him the town needed him and that he could do worse than make Payday his home.

Dr. Hezekiah Bentley had settled in, and if the townspeople could manage to get injured before five in the afternoon when Bentley went off the wagon every day, they had a fair chance of getting fixed up and surviving the experience. If, on the other hand, they had the misfortune to get shot or stabbed or break a bone after dark, they tried their best to survive on their own until Doc woke up the next day and was over his hangover before consulting him—it was much safer that way.

As Buck rode down the main street, he nodded and tipped his hat at some of the ladies of the evening as they passed, and waved and shouted hellos to some of the men, who waved back. Buck was pretty popular in town, having learned it was better to govern by giving the people what they wanted rather than enforcing a stricter interpretation of the law. So, in Payday, just about everything was legal, everything except making Buck Tolliver angry.

Every week, usually on Friday afternoons when most of the surrounding miners were in town to spend the dust they'd pried from the earth the previous week, Buck held court in the largest saloon in town. He would place a chair on top of the bar and any men with grievances against one another would come before him to argue their cases. Buck would nod sagely and then rule, usually for the man with the most money or the best mine, extracting his "fee" for legal advice later when no one was around to witness the transaction.

The few men who didn't appreciate Buck's wisdom

or his judgments would often later be found shot or stabbed to death. It didn't take long for the people of Payday to get the hint: Buck Tolliver, for better or worse, was the law in their town, and if they didn't like it, they should just move on—it was healthier that way.

After a few years of this, making a good living but not getting what he considered rich, Buck decided to expand his horizons. Payday was growing larger every day, and more and more people were coming up into the mountains of northern Colorado to make their fortune by mining. He remembered a friend of his brother's, a man named Jeb Hardy, who'd managed to get a law degree through the mail and was working minor swindles on people back in the big city of Denver.

He took a vacation, made a run over to Denver, and looked Jeb up. Over drinks, after sharing a toast to Buck's dead brother, Buck put his proposition to Jeb. If he'd come back to Payday and take care of the legal matters, Buck had an idea how they could both get rich, without having to work overly hard doing it.

Soon, they had a thriving business. Jeb and the hard cases they'd hired would locate isolated mines and then threaten or beat the men into giving them part of their operations in exchange for "security" to keep other claim-jumpers away. The fact that Jeb and his men were the only claim-jumpers in the area mattered not at all. There was no one, other than Sheriff Buck Tolliver, to complain to, and for some strange reason, that never seemed to do any good.

Most of the miners just gritted their teeth and gave Jeb and his men their percentage and kept on working their mines. The few who refused soon found they couldn't mine much gold or silver with broken arms or wrecked equipment. Those that still weren't convinced soon found themselves dead, shortly after signing over their claims to Jeb.

It was a neat scheme with very little risk, as long as Buck Tolliver was sheriff and as long as Jeb could find men willing to do whatever he wanted to make the plan work.

So far, neither had been a problem, and Jeb and Buck just kept getting richer and richer.

CHAPTER 1

The members of the Nez Percé tribe that made their home in far northern Colorado watched as the tall, broad-shouldered man with the salt and pepper hair walked among their young Palouse studs. He stood a bit over six feet tall, shoulders as wide as an ax handle, and even the loose cut of his buckskin shirt and trousers couldn't disguise the muscles that rippled and moved under the skins.

Some of the braves whispered among themselves, for they'd often heard their fathers sit around the campfire at night and sing songs of this man, a man known to them all as the Last Mountain Man. They sang of him and of his blood brother, a man who called himself Preacher, and how they'd stood alone against the High Lonesome itself and conquered it as no white men ever had before or since.

A few of the younger braves flexed their muscles and puffed out their chests and strutted around the camp as though the presence of this man who was a legend even among people other than his own did not impress them overly much. A couple even muttered derogatory comments, in their own language, of course, in the neighborhood of the big man to show him they weren't at all afraid of him or of the many guns on his belt or even the big knife in his belt.

A slight smile curled the lips of Smoke Jensen as he

finished his examination of the young Palouse studs he'd come up here to barter for. He spoke the language of the Nez Percé as well as the young braves, but he took no offense at their behavior, knowing it was a rite of passage among the Indians to show no fear when growing into manhood.

He ducked under the lariat rope that served the Indians as a makeshift corral and moved with long strides to stand next to the chief of the tribe, Gray Wolf.

As Smoke pulled two cigars from the breast pocket of his buckskin shirt and offered one to the chief, he said in a low voice, "You might tell Running Deer over there that even if by some miracle he was able to defeat me in battle and take my woman, she would break him over her knee as easily as I do this lucifer." Smoke demonstrated what he meant by snapping the match between his fingers after he'd lighted both their stogies.

The chief laughed, not at all embarrassed that Smoke not only overheard his braves, but that he spoke their language as well. The chief puffed out a large mouthful of smoke and said, "If I told him that, though it be true that you speak with straight tongue, for I remember your woman from last year, it would break Running Deer's spirit, which is high with the bravery of youth, my friend."

Smoke nodded, smiling, for the chief was correct; it would crush the young man to be confronted like that and be unable to defend his honor. "I know, old friend, so I'll handle it my own way," Smoke said.

He turned to face the group of young braves gathered near the fire and let his eyes seek out the one who'd said, just loudly enough for Smoke to hear, that if the chief would allow it he would whip the old man and take his woman into his teepee for the winter.

"Running Deer," Smoke called in perfect Nez Percé dialect, causing a surprised frown to appear on the young man's face and traces of fear on the faces of some of the others who had likewise spoke ill of the mountain man. "Would you show me how these young studs run? The chief tells me you are one of the best riders of green-broke horses in the tribe."

Running Deer's frown disappeared and was replaced by a chagrined smile. "Chief Gray Wolf has told the Mountain Man the truth, and all of these horses can run like the wind," he said as he handed his bow to a friend and moved toward the remuda. "But there is one who is faster by far than the others. I call him Blizzard," he said in the Nez Percé language—"because he is like the strong wind from the north in winter as it races through the mountains—unstoppable."

Smoke nodded, deciding he would name the horse Storm if he proved to be as fast as Running Deer claimed.

Cal and Pearlie, Smoke's two hands who'd accompanied him on the trip up from Smoke's ranch in southern Colorado, stood nearby, their foreheads wrinkled as they tried to follow the conversation. During the two weeks it took them to drive the mares up into the mountains, Smoke had tried to teach them as much of the Nez Percé tongue as he could, but since they'd never heard it before, it'd been slow going for the two men, though they tried hard.

Cal, barely out of his teens and not much older than the young braves near the fire, leaned his head close to Pearlie, a grizzled veteran who was almost thirty, and asked, "What did that brave call the horse . . . Snowstorm?"

"Somethin' like that," Pearlie replied, being no more certain of what had been said than Cal was. "All I got was that he thinks the horse can run some."

"Let's see if he's right," Cal said, and he swung up into the saddle of his own Palouse stud, Dusty, while Pearlie climbed up onto his horse, Cold. Pearlie had named his horse Cold because he was cold-mouthed in the morning and would buck and snort and crow-hop for the first five minutes Pearlie was on his back.

Running Deer grabbed Storm's mane and swung up onto his back without bothering to put even a blanket on the mount. He kicked the horse's flanks and the stud reared up and raced across the corral, leaping up and over the lariat at the last moment.

As Cal and Pearlie spurred their broncs after the Indian, it was clear that Storm was indeed something special, for he left both Cal and Pearlie far behind as he raced at breakneck speed across the small plateau that contained the Indians' camp, weaving in and out of and through the many stands of small Ponderosa pine trees as if they weren't there.

Without even slowing down, Running Deer took Storm over the edge of the cliff and down the steep slope of the side of the plateau, and the stud never stumbled, but ran like he'd been born to do nothing else.

Cal and Pearlie, not wanting to break their necks, reined in at the edge of the cliff and watched in amazement as Running Deer and Storm made a wide sweep and raced back up the slope, just as fast as they'd gone down it. Man and horse were only slightly slower coming up the grade than they'd been going down it.

"Jimminy," Cal said, taking his hat off and sleeving sweat off his forehead with his arm. "That mount really *can* run like the wind."

"Wind, hell," Pearlie said, shaking his head, "more like a tornado!"

Cal waved his hat at the young brave as he raced by,

and was rewarded with a show—Running Deer swung his leg up and over the horse's neck and whirled around to ride backward without the mount ever breaking stride. He gave a couple of loud yips in greeting, and then he reversed himself and was suddenly riding facing front again.

After Running Deer had returned Storm to the corral and joined Smoke and the others near the fire, Smoke grinned and shook his hand. "If you ever want a job as a wrangler, Running Deer," he said sincerely, "come on down to the Sugarloaf and you'll have a job for life."

Running Deer glanced at the chief out of the corner of his eyes and replied, "Though it would be a great honor to work with the man my people call the Last Mountain Man, I could never leave these mountains or my people, for to do so would be to make my heart small."

Cal stepped over and clapped Running Deer on the shoulder, causing the young man to frown, as if such familiarity was unheard of among his people. "Golly, Running Deer," Cal said, his eyes wide, "I ain't never seen nobody ride like you do. It's like you was a part of that bronc."

Running Deer's expression softened somewhat at the compliment. "Thank you, Mr. Cal," he said formally. "We Nez Percé are taught to ride almost before we are taught to walk. It is something all of my brothers can do."

Pearlie nodded, his eyes twinkling. "Yeah, but I'll just bet you that they ain't none of them can do it near as good as you, Running Deer."

The young man ducked his head, unwilling to seem arrogant, but the chief chuckled. "You are right,

Pearlie. Running Deer is the best of the young braves on horseback. They all wish to be like him."

Smoke winked at the chief and put his hand on Running Deer's shoulder, leading him over to the small remuda of studs that Smoke had brought from the Sugarloaf. "Tell me what you think of these studs, Running Deer. I've brought them up here to trade with your people for some studs of a different bloodline so that my remuda back home doesn't get too inbred."

Running Deer nodded, his eyes on the horses. He ducked under the lariat corral and walked among them, running his hands on their necks, whispering in a low voice to them, checking a few horses' teeth or withers or hooves. After a few moments, he smiled slightly, about as much a seal of approval as he could make. "They are very fine, Mountain Man. Are they too of the Nez Percé?"

Smoke nodded. "Not these directly, Running Deer, but their fathers and mothers were all acquired from some of your brother tribes a few years back."

"I thought so, for I can tell they are of the true Palouse blood, undiluted by your American quarter horses or thoroughbreds."

He looked at the chief and gave a slight nod. "These will make very fine breeders for our mares, Chief Gray Wolf."

Gray Wolf returned the nod and turned to Smoke, holding out his hand. "It is, as you white-eyes say, a deal, Mountain Man."

After they shook hands, Gray Wolf clapped his hands together and yelled, "Now, it is time for a feast with our new friends! Have the squaws get the venison ready."

Smoke put his hand on the chief's shoulder and leaned down to whisper, "I've got a side of beef on one of those pack animals I've brought all the way up here from my ranch for you, if you'd like to have it instead of deer meat, Chief."

The chief's eyes lit up and he smiled broadly, revealing tobacco-stained teeth that were worn almost down to the gums. "It has been a long time since I've eaten beef, Mountain Man." He paused and then grinned wickedly again. "At least, beef that was freely given to us instead of that which wandered into our camp and accidentally fell upon a spear."

Smoke and Cal and Pearlie all laughed, for they had all heard many ranchers complain of the mountain Indians coming down and raiding their herds for beef to eat. Smoke sympathized with the Indians, for he remembered from his days in these same mountains how tiring a diet of only venison and moose and bear could become after several months.

Smoke nodded at Pearlie, who said, "Cal, grab that beef off the packhorse and let's eat. I'm so hungry my stomach thinks my throat's been cut!"

While the beefsteaks sizzled and spit on frying pans over the open fire, Running Deer and the other braves began to show Cal and Pearlie some of the games they played. They rode past a thick tree and threw spears while at full gallop; they shot arrows from horseback at bushes; they threw tomahawks end over end and tried to make them stick in the bark of the pine trees that surrounded the Nez Percé camp.

"It is good that your braves know how to be friends with white men," Smoke said as he and the chief smoked another cigar while the squaws got the meat and vegetables cooked.

Chief Gray Wolf nodded gravely, his eyes sad. "Yes, my friend, but not all white men are friends to us as you are. We must still be careful not to approach white men on the mountain unless we are invited, for some will still shoot to kill us on sight."

"It is still that bad?" Smoke asked, having hoped that things would have gotten better in the last few years.

"It has never changed," Gray Wolf said with a sigh.

CHAPTER 2

When the squaws signaled the chief the food was ready, Cal and Pearlie and the braves all gathered around the fire to eat large slabs of beefsteak and vegetables. There were no women present, as they typically ate whatever was left over later while the men all napped after their meal. After the men and Smoke and the boys had finished most of the side of beef he'd brought, Cal and Pearlie and Running Deer and some of the younger braves went back to playing the Indian games the meal had interrupted. Pearlie, of course, said now that his mind was off of food for a while, he'd be able to do a lot better in the highly competitive games.

Smoke and Chief Gray Wolf sat in the shelter of a lean-to and smoked, the chief his pipe and Smoke his cigar. Smoke had given the chief a pound of real ground coffee, and the chief had directed one of the squaws near his tent to make them a pot of it.

When he took his first sip, the chief's lips curled in a wide smile. "Much better than piñon bean coffee," he said. He smacked his lips and added, "This is much too good for the braves. I believe I'll save this for my use alone."

Smoke nodded, having tasted the bitter brew made from piñon beans in the past. "Even the white man has some good things to offer your people, Chief."

The chief slowly inclined his head in agreement. "That is true, Mountain Man, but even though my people live way up here in the High Lonesome, we have not escaped the corrupting ways of the white-eyes."

"Oh?" Smoke asked, trailing a stream of blue smoke from his nostrils.

"Yes. The yellow metal we take from the streams and mountain caves to make jewelry for our squaws is much sought after by the white-eyes from nearby towns. Some of my more . . . rebellious braves have learned that they can trade the yellow metal for firewater." He shook his head sadly. "It is a terrible thing what it does to these young men. They begin to act like a horse that has eaten . . ." and he gave the Nez Percé name for the bush white men called locoweed.

"I have seen the trouble that our whiskey can cause your people," Smoke agreed. "And there are some among us who think that men who trade liquor to you should be punished severely."

The chief's eyes were hard and as cold as the granite peaks of the mountains that surrounded them as he replied, "If I find out who has been doing this thing, you can be sure they will be punished"—he paused and turned his hard gaze on Smoke—"and punished to the death."

Smoke decided to change the subject before the chief became any more upset. He inclined his head toward the braves who were still playing their games off in the distant fields. "It appears that you have many fine young men in your tribe who still follow the old ways, Chief Gray Wolf."

For the first time in a while, the chief smiled. "Yes. My people are quite lucky that way. Some of the other tribes are having quite a problem keeping their young people in the mountains." He looked over at the remains of the beef they'd eaten earlier and held up his coffee cup. "Once they get a taste of the white man's food and drink, it is hard for them to live in the old manner." He grinned. "Dog just doesn't taste near as good as beef."

Smoke laughed. "You are not alone in that, my friend. Even in the land of the white man, we are having much the same problems. Our young people too are leaving the farms and ranches and heading into the big cities, tired of having to work hard from dawn to dusk and not having a whole lot to show for it at the end of the day." He shook his head. "I don't have a wrangler on my spread who is under the age of twenty-five, except for Cal. All of the boys in their teens want to go to Denver or even bigger towns to make their way in the new world."

The chief chuckled and held up his coffee cup in a toast. "To all the young ones who are not afraid to stay with the old ways, Mountain Man."

Smoke grinned and returned the toast. "I'll drink to that," he said.

Suddenly, from the distant field, Smoke heard a shout, and looked up to see Cal waving his hands in the air. It looked to Smoke like he was standing over a fallen body. "Damn!" Smoke exclaimed when he recognized the form of Pearlie lying still at Cal's feet.

When Cal pulled his pistol and fired three times in the air, Smoke knew Pearlie was in serious trouble. He jumped to his feet and bounded across the meadow, and was in his saddle and spurring his mount forward within seconds.

He jumped off his horse and ran to where Cal was bending over Pearlie, whose face was pale and waxen-looking. The young man was clearly unconscious.

Smoke knelt next to him and looked at Cal. "What happened?"

"We was playing fox and rabbit with the braves an'

Pearlie was the rabbit an' we was chasing him acrost the field when his horse stumbled in a prairie dog hole. Pearlie was thrown over there against that there log," Cal said, breathless, as he pointed a few feet away.

Smoke glanced over and saw a dead Rocky Mountain rattlesnake lying next to the log, Pearlie's knife pinning its head to the ground.

"Shit!" he said, knowing exactly what had happened. Pearlie had fallen against the log, moving it and disturbing the rattlesnake that was curled up underneath it. The frightened reptile must have struck him before he even saw it.

Smoke leaned over and began to examine Pearlie's body for the telltale twin punctures. "Where'd it get him?" he asked, his face knotted with worry. Mountain rattlers could be deadly if the bite was in a dangerous place.

"Before he passed out, Pearlie said it got him twice, once't in the leg an' once't in the neck," Cal said, pointing at the red marks on Pearlie's neck just over the blood vessel there.

"Damn," Smoke exclaimed, knowing there was little he could do about the neck wound. To cut it deep enough to get the poison out would also cut the big vessel in the neck and Pearlie would likely bleed to death.

He turned his attention to Pearlie's legs, quickly finding the bite mark there. He drew his big bowie knife from the scabbard on his belt and made crisscrossing cuts over the two puncture wounds. He lowered his head and began to suck the blood and poison out of the wound, turning his head to the side to spit the noxious liquid out between sucks.

After a few minutes, he stopped, sleeving blood off his mouth with his arm while Cal took his bandanna off and made a tight bandage over the wound, stopping the flow of blood.

"You think he's gonna make it, Smoke?" Cal asked, unshed tears in his eyes as he stared at his friend lying deathlike on the cold ground.

Smoke shook his head, knowing the chances weren't good. "I don't know, Cal. He's strong and he's a fighter, so he's got a better chance than most, and he's lucky that the snake struck him in the leg first. Most of its venom probably went into the leg and not into his neck."

Just then, Chief Gray Wolf came riding up on a Palouse pony. He dismounted and squatted next to Pearlie, his eyes narrow with concern.

"Mountain rattler," Smoke said, pointing to the twin bites on Pearlie's neck.

The chief's eyes widened for a moment, and then he shook his head slowly. "Such a bite always means trouble, and one in the neck is almost always deadly." He took a deep breath, not wanting to give his friend bad news. "I've only once seen a brave survive such a bite, and never a squaw or young one."

Smoke felt as if his heart was going to break. Aside from Cal, Pearlie was his best friend in the world. "Are there any towns near here that might have a doctor in them?" he asked, staring up into the old chief's eyes.

The chief looked at him, and Smoke could tell the old man didn't think it made much difference. He was sure Pearlie was going to die no matter what was done for him. He hesitated, figuring it wouldn't hurt to try to get the young white man to one of their doctors.

After a moment, the chief nodded. "There is such a town less than a day's ride from here. The white men call it Payday. It is full of men searching the mountains for the yellow and silver metals." He hesitated, and then he added, "It is a very tough town,

Mountain Man, but I believe there is a medical man living there."

"Can you have your men make me a travois to carry Pearlie on while you tell me how to get there?" Smoke asked.

The chief barked an order in his native tongue to several young men standing nearby, and Running Deer nodded and beckoned them to follow him as he jumped on his pony and rode like the wind toward a strand of nearby pine trees.

"I will do better than that," Gray Wolf said. "I will have Running Deer lead you to the town, and I will have some of my braves accompany you as far as the town to keep you safe."

Smoke frowned. "Keep me safe?"

The old man shrugged. "There are many bad men in the area who would rather steal the yellow metal than work to dig it out of the ground. If they think you have money, they might attack you, which would slow you getting help for young Pearlie."

Smoke smiled and put his hand on the chief's shoulder. Even though his lips were smiling, his eyes were dark and dangerous. "God help any man who gets in the way of Pearlie's getting to a doctor," he said.

CHAPTER 3

After Pearlie was placed on the travois and covered with blankets and furs against the cold, Chief Gray Wolf leaned down and placed a small leather pouch under the covers over Pearlie's heart. He looked up. "It is my medicine bag. It will help keep his heart strong and brave during his fight against the poison of the snake."

Smoke nodded his appreciation and shook the chief's hand, and then he and Cal began the long ride to the town called Payday. They had to go slow since the rarely used trail was so faint as to barely be visible, and it was bumpy with rocks and tufts of mountain grass.

As they rode, Running Deer looked at Smoke and saw his worried expression. He glanced back at the travois. "This man, Pearlie, he is like a brother to the Mountain Man?" he asked.

Smoke looked up, and then he too glanced back at Pearlie's pale, still body on the travois, watching it roll back and forth each time the travois hit a bump. "More like a son," he said slowly, realizing once again how much Pearlie and Cal meant to him and Sally.

He was thinking how devastated Sally would be if Pearlie didn't make it, when Running Deer spoke again. "He has been with you a long time?"

Smoke smiled, remembering how Pearlie came to work at the Sugarloaf. Pearlie had come into his and

Sally's lives in a very roundabout way. He was hiring his gun out a few years back to a man named Tilden Franklin in a town named Fontana near Smoke's ranch when Franklin went crazy and tried to take over the Sugarloaf, Smoke and Sally's spread. After Franklin's men raped and killed a young girl in the fracas just to get Smoke's attention, Pearlie decided he'd had enough of Franklin and his lawless ways, and he sided with Smoke and the aging gunfighters he had called in to help put an end to Franklin's reign of terror.*

Smoke smiled, thinking of the night he'd braced the young gunman known only as Pearlie and asked him if he was happy working for a man like Franklin. When Pearlie had stared at him for a moment before answering, "Not 'specially," Smoke had told him there was always room on his payroll for a good worker. Pearlie had packed his war bag and quit Franklin the next day.

Smoke pulled a cigar from his buckskin coat pocket and struck a lucifer on his pants leg, sucking the harsh smoke deep into his lungs as he thought about what had happened next.

Franklin had been so pissed off at Pearlie that he'd sent a group of the men riding for his brand after Pearlie. They'd chased him down and shot him in the back, then tied him to his saddle and dragged him to hell and gone through miles of cactus and rocks until he was so bloody and battered he was hardly recognizable. They'd left him for dead out on the plains, not reckoning on the strength of his character.

Pearlie had walked almost ten miles with two bullets in his back and hardly any skin left on his carcass to get to Smoke's ranch. He'd stayed conscious long

*_Trail of the Mountain Man_

enough to knock on Smoke's door, and then he'd collapsed into unconsciousness so deep Smoke had feared he was dead when he answered the door and found Pearlie lying so still on the porch.

Smoke had had Doc Spalding take the lead peas out of Pearlie's back and fix him up as best he could considering the damage that'd been done to the young man. When the doc had told Smoke it would be a miracle if Pearlie lived through the night, Smoke had just smiled and shaken his head. "This young'un's got too much sand to let post-suckers like Franklin's men kill him," Smoke had replied, though truth be told, he hadn't been all that sure that even a man as brave as Pearlie could survive the terrible damage that'd been done to him that night.

Pearlie was now honorary foreman of Smoke's ranch, and was in the midst of a fight every bit as tough as the one he'd been through when first he met Smoke.

"Yeah," Smoke said, answering Running Deer's question. "Pearlie's been with me for a spell, and I reckon no desert rattler's gonna succeed in putting him in the ground when a lot of hard men have failed."

Since they were moving so slowly, Smoke was able to push the horses closer and closer to Payday through the night. He stopped and made camp only after one of the young braves traveling with them fell asleep on the back of his horse and fell to the ground.

While Cal and Smoke made a campfire and pulled the travois with Pearlie on it close to the heat, Running Deer and his friends pulled salted, dried venison from their pouches and began to chew on the hard, jerky-type meat.

Smoke had the braves help him hobble the Palouse

studs they had with them, while Cal started a large pot of coffee to brewing and began to heat some pinto beans with large chunks of fatback in it. While the coffee and beans were heating, Cal cut up some onions and peppers and fried them in a large cast-iron skillet with steaks cut off a side of beef on the packhorse.

By the time the studs were hobbled near some mountain meadow grass, Cal had supper ready.

Running Deer raised his eyebrows in question when Cal handed him a plate with a still-steaming steak and a pile of beans on it. "You'll like this a whole lot better'n that there jerky you been chewin' on," Cal said, bending and pouring Running Deer a cup of coffee in a tin cup.

"Now tell yore friends to dig in an' help themselves to the beans in the pot and the meat in the skillet. I ain't no waitress, you know."

Running Deer yelled something in his Nez Percé tongue, and his friends came over to the fire and began to fix themselves plates. Running Deer sliced a bite of steak with his skinning knife and shoved it into his mouth along with a generous portion of beans.

As he chewed, he rolled his eyes and grinned at Cal. "You are right, Cal," he said, bean juice running out of the corner of his mouth. "This much better than pemmican." He almost added that even a squaw from their village couldn't have done better, but he held his tongue, knowing white men had strange notions about the roles of men and women in life. A brave would rather starve than stoop so low as to cook a meal—that was woman's work. But this white man, who was as manly as any of the braves in Running Deer's tribe, had not hesitated to cook for all of them and then to joke about it. Running Deer shook his head as he stuffed the beef and beans into his mouth and drank the delicious coffee. He figured he'd just never understand white men.

Cal just nodded, but Smoke could tell Running Deer's compliment pleased him by the way a scarlet flush crept up from his collar to cover his entire face.

Smoke bent his head to keep the young man from seeing his smile, and as he shoveled food into his mouth using his big bowie knife as both knife and spoon, he thought about the day Sally had brought Cal home to the Sugarloaf to work for him just a few months after Pearlie. . . .

Calvin Woods had been just about fourteen when Smoke and Sally had taken him in as a hired hand. It was during the spring branding that year, and Sally was on her way back from Big Rock to the Sugarloaf. Her buckboard was piled high with supplies, because branding hundreds of calves made for hungry punchers who could just about eat their weight in grub at the end of the day.

As Sally slowed the team to take a bend in the trail, a rail-thin young man stepped from the bushes at the side of the road with a pistol in his hand.

"Hold it right there, miss."

Applying the brake with her right foot, Sally slipped her hand under a pile of gingham cloth on the seat. She grasped the handle of her short-barreled Colt .44 and eared back the hammer, letting the sound of the horse's hooves and the squealing of the brake pads on the wheels mask the sound.

"What can I do for you, young man?" she asked, her voice firm and without fear. She knew she could draw and drill the young highwayman before he could raise his pistol to fire if it came right down to it.

"Well, uh, you can throw some of those beans and a cut of that fatback over here, and maybe a portion of that Arbuckle's coffee too," the young ambusher said, his voice weak and quavering as if he hadn't eaten for some time.

Sally's eyebrows rose. "Don't you want my money?"

The boy frowned and shook his head, as if the question made no sense. "Why, no, ma'am. I ain't no thief, I'm just hungry."

"And if I don't give you my food, are you going to shoot me with that big Navy Colt?" Sally asked, trying to keep the humor from her voice.

He hesitated a moment, then grinned ruefully. "No, ma'am, I guess not."

He twirled the pistol around his finger and slipped it into his belt, turned, and began to walk down the road toward Big Rock.

Sally watched the youngster amble off, noting his tattered shirt, dirty pants with holes in the knees and torn pockets, and boots that looked as if they had been salvaged from a garbage dump. "Young man," she called, "come back here, please."

He turned, a smirk on his face, spreading his hands, "Look, lady, you don't have to worry. I don't even have any bullets." With a lightning-fast move he drew the gun from his pants, aimed away from Sally, and pulled the trigger. There was a click but no explosion as the hammer fell on an empty cylinder.

Sally smiled. "Oh, I'm not worried." In a movement every bit as fast as his, she whipped her .44 out and fired, clipping a pine cone from a branch above him, causing it to fall and bounce off his head.

The boy's knees buckled and he ducked, saying, "Jiminy Christmas!"

Mimicking him, Sally twirled her Colt and stuck it in the waistband of her britches. "What's your name, boy?" she asked, a frown creasing her forehead.

The boy blushed and looked down at his feet, "Calvin, ma'am, Calvin Woods."

She leaned forward, elbows on knees, and stared into the boy's eyes. "Calvin, no one has to go hungry in this country, not if they're willing to work."

He looked up at her through narrowed eyes, as if he found life a little different than she described it. "I done tried that, ma'am," he said, a disgusted look on his face. "All the ranchers hereabouts said I'm too young to hire on to their spreads." He grimaced. "One said he'd have to have the cook fix me up a sugar tit to get me through a day of brandin'."

"If you're willing to put in an honest day's work, I'll see that you get an honest day's pay, and all the food you can eat," Sally said, trying to hide her smile. "After all, a man old enough to try and rob someone with that old gun you're carrying is old enough to earn his way on a ranch."

Calvin stood a little straighter, shoulders back and head held high. "Ma'am, I've got to be straight with you. I ain't no experienced cowhand. I come from a hard-scrabble farm and we only had us one milk cow and a couple of goats and chickens, and lots of dirt that weren't worth nothing for growin' things. My ma and pa and me never had nothin', but we never begged and we never stooped to takin' handouts."

Sally thought, *I like this boy. Proud, and not willing to take charity if he can help it.* "Calvin, if you're willing to work, and don't mind getting your hands dirty and your muscles sore, I've got some hands that'll have you punching beeves like you were born to it in no time at all." She hesitated, and then she added earnestly, "This is no handout, boy. If you come to work for my husband and me, you'll earn every dime we pay you, and then some."

A smile lit up his face, making him seem even younger than his years. "Even if I don't have no saddle, nor a horse to put it on?"

She laughed out loud. "Yes. We've got plenty of ponies and saddles." She glanced down at his raggedy boots. "We can probably even round up some boots and spurs that'll fit you."

He walked over and jumped in the back of the buckboard. "Ma'am, I don't know who you are, but you just hired you the hardest-workin' hand you've ever seen."

Back at the Sugarloaf, she sent him in to Cookie and told him to eat his fill. When Smoke and the other punchers rode into the cabin yard at the end of the day, she introduced Calvin around. As Cal was shaking hands with the men, Smoke looked over at her and winked. He knew she could never resist a stray dog or cat, and her heart was as large as the Big Lonesome itself.

Smoke walked up to Cal and cleared his throat, his eyes boring into Cal's. "Son, I hear you drew down on my wife today."

Cal gulped, "Yes, sir, Mr. Jensen. I did." He squared his shoulders and looked Smoke in the eye, not flinching though he was obviously frightened of the tall man with the incredibly wide shoulders standing before him.

Smoke smiled and clapped the boy on the back. He appreciated a man who'd own up to his mistakes, and be willing to take punishment for them without whining about it. "Just wanted you to know you stared death in the eye, boy. Not many galoots are still walking upright who ever pulled a gun on Sally. She's a better shot than any man I've ever seen except me, and sometimes I wonder about me."

The boy laughed with relief as Smoke turned and called out, "Pearlie, get your lazy butt over here."

A tall, lanky cowboy ambled over to Smoke and Cal, munching on a biscuit stuffed with roast beef. His face was lined with wrinkles and tanned a dark brown from hours under the sun, but his eyes were sky-blue and twinkled with good-natured humor as he stared at the boy with Smoke.

"Yes, sir, Boss," he mumbled around a mouthful of food, his gaze moving up and down Cal as if he were mentally fitting him for clothes.

Smoke put his hand on Pearlie's shoulder. "Cal, this here chowhound is Pearlie. He eats more'n any two hands, and he's never been known to do a lick of work he could get out of, but he knows beeves and horses as well as any puncher I have. I want you to follow him around and let him teach you what you need to know."

Cal nodded. "Yes, sir, Mr. Smoke."

"Now let me see that iron you have in your pants."

Cal pulled out the ancient Navy Colt and handed it to Smoke. When Smoke opened the loading gate, the rusted cylinder fell to the ground, causing Pearlie and Smoke to laugh and Cal's face to flame red. "This is the piece you pulled on Sally?"

The boy nodded, looking at the ground.

Pearlie shook his head. "Cal, you're one lucky pup. Hell, if'n you'd tried to fire that thing it'd of blown your hand clean off."

Cal laughed. "It don't matter none, Pearlie. I didn't have no bullets for it nohow."

Smoke laughed again, shaking his head at Cal's actions, and inclined his head toward the bunkhouse. "Pearlie, take Cal over to the tack house and get him fixed up with what he needs, including a gun belt and a Colt that won't fall apart the first time he pulls it. You might also help pick him out a shavetail to ride. I'll expect him to start earning his keep tomorrow morning at first light."

"Yes, sir, Smoke." Pearlie put his arm around Cal's

shoulders and led him off toward the bunkhouse. "Now the first thing you gotta learn, Cal, is how to get on Cookie's good side. A puncher rides on his belly, and it 'pears to me that you need some fattin' up 'fore you can begin think about punching cows."

Smoke glanced at Cal as he finished his meal, and he thought to himself that he truly couldn't love and care for a son any more than he did these two young men.

He took his last bite and started to get up as Cal walked over to him. "Give me that plate Smoke, an' I'll clean 'em up 'fore we put 'em away."

"Thanks, Cal," Smoke said, handing him the plate. He settled back and lighted up a cigar to have with the last few sips of his coffee.

He glanced over at Pearlie, lying as still as death on the travois, and wished he'd raise his head up and say, "Is that food I smell?"

Smoke grinned at the thought, knowing Pearlie was as sick as he could be to miss a meal and not complain about it.

CHAPTER 4

The next morning, Smoke woke to find a fine dusting of snow covering the camp. To his surprise, Cal was already awake and had a fire roaring and coffee boiling.

He chuckled to himself. Usually, Cal had to be forced out of bed with the toe of someone's boot, but he figured the fears about his good friend Pearlie had kept the boy from sleeping very well, and he was probably as anxious as Smoke to get Pearlie to a town and under a doctor's care as soon as possible.

Cal glanced over at Smoke and grinned. "Glad to see you finally decided to crawl outta them blankets, Smoke. We been burnin' daylight for more'n half an hour now. I thought for a minute there I was gonna have to light a fire under you to git your eyes open."

Smoke looked around the camp and noticed there was no sign of the Indians. "Where'd Running Deer and his friends go?" he asked, gratefully accepting the steaming cup of coffee Cal handed him.

"They lit outta here just after daylight," Cal replied. "Said the town's right on up this trail 'bout half a day's ride an' they figured even a couple of white-eyes like us couldn't manage not to find it."

"What about the horses?" Smoke asked, noticing there were none in sight.

"They're gonna drive them on over to the south side of the town and keep them there until we head back toward Big Rock. And Running Deer said not to worry or hurry, they'd stay with the studs as long as we needed them to an' make sure they had plenty of grass and water."

Smoke laughed. And he'd thought his being an old mountain man had impressed the young braves. Evidently not!

"You want me to scramble up a couple'a hens' eggs an' some fatback?" Cal asked.

Smoke glanced over at Pearlie, who lay still and pale as a corpse on his travois. "No," he answered, shaking his head and getting stiffly to his feet. "Since we're only a few hours from town, let's shag our mounts and see if we can get Pearlie there to see the doctor and worry about eating later."

"All right," Cal said, and he put his cup down and moved over to lay his palm on Pearlie's forehead. "He don't seem to have much fever. That's a good sign, ain't it?"

Smoke nodded, but he knew Pearlie was far from out of the woods yet. The only reason he was still alive at all was that the main portion of the snake's venom had gone into his leg and not into his neck. "Yeah, that's a good sign, Cal," he said, trying to keep the boy's spirits up. But it wasn't fever and infection Smoke was worried about. It was the effect the snake's venom was having on Pearlie's brain. It wouldn't do much good if the body survived but there was nobody home in the mind.

Cal sighed and moved to sit by the fire, taking a small canvas pouch out of his shirt pocket and beginning to build himself a cigarette.

Smoke noticed his hands were trembling so much that he could hardly keep the tobacco on the paper until he could lick it and seal it.

Cal looked up and saw Smoke watching him and grinned. "Kind'a cold this mornin', ain't it?"

Smoke nodded, knowing the trembling of Cal's hands was due more to his fear for his friend than to any cold in the air.

"Yeah, it is. So soon's you finish that cigarillo and your coffee, we'll get on our way."

Cal took a deep drag of the cigarette that was more paper than tobacco and then followed it with a deep draught of his coffee.

"Well, then, jingle them spurs, Smoke, 'cause I'm done," he said, jumping to his feet and stubbing out the worthless cigarette under his boot.

Smoke and Cal were about an hour down the trail when Smoke noticed two men ride out of the tree line on their right and begin to move toward them.

"Cal," he said in a low voice, nodding his head toward the men when Cal glanced at him. Both he and Cal let their hands drop to their thighs and they loosened the rawhide hammer thongs on their Colts. The men had made no threatening signs, but Smoke had survived a lot of years in the High Lonesome by being careful and not trusting anyone until they earned it. He smiled when he saw Cal's eyes as suspicious as his. Seems Cal was picking up his habits too.

As the men approached, Smoke saw that they were tough, hard-looking men and they wore their guns tied down low on their legs, as both he and Cal did.

"Howdy," the bigger of the two men called. Both were at least as wide as Smoke, though not as tall.

Smoke gave a half smile and inclined his head, his hand staying near the handle of his pistol.

"My name's Hog, an' this here is Bubba," Hog said, moving his horse around Smoke so he could get a closer look at Pearlie lying on the travois.

"Yore friend don't look so good," Hog said, taking

his hat off and sleeving sweat off his forehead with his arm.

Smoke noticed this and figured it was too cold for the man to have worked up a sweat riding, so he must be nervous about something. Perhaps what he was about to do?

"He got snakebit," Cal said, kneeing his horse around so he could keep an eye on Bubba, leaving Hog to Smoke without having to be told to.

"We're taking him to a town called Payday. You know it?" Cal added, still keeping his hand on his thigh next to his Colt.

"Yeah," Bubba growled, his eyes on Cal's hand. "It's on up the trail another couple'a hours."

Hog inclined his head toward Smoke's horse. "You men got any gold in them saddlebags?" he asked, trying, to sound like it was just a friendly question.

"Well, what we have or haven't got in our saddlebags is none of your business, mister," Smoke said in a cold but even voice. His eyes were flat and dangerous looking, and if the men were smart, they'd take notice that he wasn't a man to be fooled around with.

Hog's eyes flashed with anger and he spurred his horse right up next to Smoke's, trying to intimidate him with his massive size. Smoke noted the man was almost as wide as he was tall, and his hands were big as hams, with scarred knuckles indicating he had been in lots of fights.

As the man got closer, Smoke took a pair of black, padded gloves out of his belt and slid his hands into them one at a time, his eyes never leaving Hog's.

"That ain't a real friendly comment, mister," Hog said, glowering at Smoke from under scarred eyebrows as if he were trying to scare Smoke to death.

"Maybe that's because you aren't my friend, mister," Smoke replied evenly, moving his shoulders a little to loosen them up for what he knew was about to happen. He could read the signs in the man's little pig eyes that he was about to attack.

Sure enough, Hog scowled and swung a haymaker right fist at Smoke's head, hoping to catch him off guard and end the fight before it got started.

Smoke leaned back in the saddle just enough for the fist to connect with nothing but air, and then he twisted in his seat as he sent a straight right hand into Hog's chest. Two of Hog's ribs snapped with a sound like dry twigs breaking when Smoke's knuckles plowed into them.

Hog squealed like his namesake and let out a loud whoosh and flew backward out of his saddle to hit the frozen ground with a thud. He lay there, stunned and trying to get his breath, making high-pitched wheezing sounds as he gulped through an open mouth, his eyes wide open and full of tears of pain and rage.

Bubba, seeing this, reached for his pistol, but found himself staring down the barrel of Cal's Navy Colt before he could clear leather. He slowly raised his hands out away from his gun butt and tried to lick his lips, but his mouth was too dry. "Don't . . . don't shoot me, mister," he pleaded.

Cal grinned. "I won't, lessen you try to grab that hogleg on your hip."

Smoke eased down out of his saddle and walked over to take Hog's pistol out of his belt and throw it into a nearby snowbank.

Hog got unsteadily to his feet, both hands massaging his chest as he continued to gasp for air. "Damn you, you son of a bitch," he yelled. "I ought to beat you to death."

Smoke, who'd had about enough of this loudmouth, just shook his head and motioned for Hog to come on with his hands.

"Did you say talk me to death or beat me to death?" Smoke taunted, knowing getting the big man angry would give him the advantage in the fight.

Hog growled something unintelligible and rushed at Smoke, his hands stretched out in front of him as if he was going to tear Smoke's head off.

Smoke leaned to the side and threw a hard left hook into Hog's right kidney as he stumbled past, causing the big man to let out another yelp and to grab his side with both hands.

He bent over, breathing heavily, both hands now on his knees as he groaned low in his throat. He knew from the pain in his side that he'd be pissing blood for a week.

"If you've had enough, I'd like to get on my way," Smoke said, standing there with his hands hanging at his sides. "My friend needs to get to a doctor and you're holding us up."

"Sure, go on, mister," Hog gasped, still leaning over and looking at the ground, wondering if he could keep from puking until the man and his friend had left.

When Smoke turned to get back up on his horse, Hog pulled a long, thin-bladed knife from a scabbard on the back of his belt and rushed at Smoke, holding the knife out in front of him.

Smoke heard him and whirled around. As Hog rushed at him, Smoke stepped to the side and lashed out with his left foot, catching the side of Hog's left knee with his boot. Hog's leg gave way with a loud snap as the knee bent at an impossible angle and the big man screamed as he fell to the ground, both hands clutching at his knee.

Smoke bent over and picked up the man's knife, shaking his head. He put the blade on the ground, put his boot on it, and raised the handle, snapping the blade into two pieces.

He flipped the handle down onto Hog's lap and walked away. "I don't think your leg is broken," Smoke said as he climbed up onto his saddle, "but I wouldn't put any weight on it until you see a doctor if I were you."

"Take that pistol out of your holster and hand it over," Cal said, pointing at Bubba's holster with the barrel of his Colt.

"What . . . what're you gonna do?" Bubba asked, fear thickening his voice as he glanced at his partner lying injured and helpless on the ground.

Cal took the pistol and stuck it in his belt. "I'm gonna leave this in the middle of the trail up ahead. If you're smart, which you sure as hell don't look like, you'll get it and ride in the opposite direction."

Bubba's eyes narrowed. "And if we don't?"

Cal shrugged and used a line he'd often heard Smoke utter. "Why, then, I suppose I'll just have to kill you next time I see you."

Smoke laughed out loud and winked at Cal as they spurred their horses on up the trail toward Payday.

"You think they'll follow us and give us any more trouble?" Cal asked.

Smoke shook his head. "No. They've had enough for one day, and the big one I put down is gonna have trouble walking for at least a day or two, so I don't think they'll come after us."

Cal took Bubba's pistol out of his belt and pitched it onto the ground. "I almost wish they would," he said, glancing back at Pearlie. "I'm so mad I'd kind'a like to take it out on somebody."

Smoke nodded, knowing the feeling. "Yeah, but let's get Pearlie to the doc first, and we can worry about that other thing later."

CHAPTER 5

Smoke shook his head sadly as he and Cal passed a hand-lettered sign that read PAYDAY. The place could barely be called a town in his estimation. It consisted mainly of one long wide road with two smaller ones branching off it at right angles. There were very few buildings that were made entirely of wood and stone, most being large tents with a wooden front or perhaps at best a four-cornered open roof over the tent.

There were, however, some homes that were built in a more suitable manner, but they were few and far between.

It seemed every other tent along the main street was a saloon or gambling establishment, with only one general store and an assay office to break up the monotony of the bars. As he and Cal rode down the main street, they drew the stares of several of the townsfolk, who Smoke also considered unprepossessing. Most of the men in the town were hard-looking miner types wearing the canvas trousers made famous by Levi Strauss in recent years, and there were precious few females other than the occasional dance hall Gerties that walked up and down the street advertising their wares by wearing elaborately frilly, low-cut gowns and makeup caked so thick on their faces you could hardly tell their race, much less whether they were in fact pretty or not.

When Smoke passed the building that had a sign on it reading SHERIFF'S OFFICE and the one next to it that read BANK, he knew they wouldn't likely find much help for Pearlie here.

"Jiminy, Smoke," Cal said, glancing from side to side as they walked their horses through town, "I don't see no signs for doctor or anything like that."

"This place is hardly more than a glorified mining camp, Cal. I only hope Chief Gray Wolf was right about there being a medical person here."

Smoke reined his horse in front of the sheriff's office and got out of the saddle. He walked up to the door to see if the sheriff could direct him to a doctor, but found the door locked.

"Sheriff ain't here, mister," an older man with a full gray beard said from his seat on a rough-hewn bench on the small boardwalk in front of the office.

"You have any idea when he'll be back?" Smoke asked.

The man got up from his bench and ambled over to stand next to the travois with Pearlie on it. He leaned to the side and spit a stream of brown tobacco juice into the dirt, and then he sleeved off the part that had run down his chin with his arm.

"Nope, can't say as I do."

Smoke sighed, and the man asked, "What's wrong with your friend? He shot or somethin'?"

"No," Cal said, swinging his leg over his saddle and jumping to the ground. "He's been snakebit real bad. We came here lookin' for a doctor."

The man nodded. "Nearest real doctor's up in Pueblo, 'bout fifty miles from here."

"Damn," Smoke said, glancing at Pearlie and knowing he'd never survive a fifty-mile trip on the travois.

"But," the old man continued, scratching his unruly hair, "we do got us a dentist, an' he takes care of most of our doctorin' when we need it . . . an' when he's sober."

Smoke whirled around and had to restrain himself from choking the old man for taking so long to tell them that. "Well, where is the dentist?" he asked.

"You take that first cross street there an' go left. His office is 'bout a hundred yards down that road on the left. You can't hardly miss it since it's a regular two-story house an' he's got a big ol' barber pole in front painted red and white."

Smoke and Cal swung up into their saddles and started off toward the dentist's office. Even though it was just past noon, Smoke hoped the man was sober, for if he wasn't and it cost Pearlie his life, Smoke knew he'd make the man regret his thirst for alcohol.

Ten minutes later, Smoke was knocking on the office door. A man with red, bleary eyes and a two-day growth of beard answered the door. "Yeah, whatta you want?" he growled, his eyes squinting at the brightness of the sunlight.

"We have a man who's been badly snakebit," Smoke said, turning and pointing at Pearlie, who lay as still as death on the travois.

The dentist's eyes opened wider and he craned his neck to peer around Smoke at Pearlie. "You cut it and suck the poison out?" he asked.

"He had two bites," Smoke answered. "I cut and sucked the one on his leg, but the one on his neck was right over a blood vessel and I didn't dare cut into it."

"Neck bite, huh?" the man said, coming out into the street and pulling his braces up over his shoulders as he bent to take a closer look at Pearlie. "When did he get bit and which one did he get first?"

"Yesterday, about noon, and he got the leg first,"

Cal said, moving to squat next to Pearlie and wipe the sweat off his forehead with his bandanna.

The dentist nodded and straightened up, yawning. "Well, that's lucky," he said. "And it's a good sign he's managed to stay alive this long."

"Can you help him?" Smoke asked. His voice was level but his eyes were full of concern.

The dentist shrugged. "I don't rightly know, mister. I'll take him in and feed him plenty of beef broth and try to keep his wounds from festerin' up too bad, but that's about all I can do here."

He turned and opened the door all the way. "Bring him in here. I got a room where I keep patients who are recoverin' from one thing or another."

Smoke and Cal picked Pearlie up and carried him into the dentist's office, and on back into a room at the rear of the house that contained three double beds, each with a basin and towel on a nightstand next to it.

There weren't any other patients present, so Smoke picked the nearest bed and they laid Pearlie down on it gently. Smoke stripped Pearlie's pants and shirt off and pulled up the leg of his long underwear so the dentist could see the leg wound.

"My names Hezekiah Bentley," the dentist said as he bent down and gently probed around the red, angry-looking bite mark on Pearlie's leg with his fingers. The edges of the wound were dark blue and there seemed to be a small crater in between the twin punctures.

"I'm Smoke Jensen and this is Calvin Woods," Smoke said. "The patient's name is Pearlie."

Bentley twisted his head to stare up at Smoke. "You *the* Smoke Jensen?" he asked.

Smoke gave a half shrug. "I don't know of any others. Why? Does it make a difference?"

Bentley shook his head and turned his attention back to Pearlie, now examining the neck wound, which was also starting to shed a little puss and was as colorful as the leg bite.

"Nope. It's just that we don't get too many visitors around here, an' the ones we do get are miners, not famous gunfighters."

"I'm no gunfighter," Smoke said. "I gave that up years ago. I'm just a rancher now."

"Uh-huh," Bentley grunted, as if he didn't believe a word of it.

Smoke sighed. Why wouldn't people let him forget his past and get on with his new life with Sally?

"Well, Dr. Bentley, what do you suggest we do?" Smoke asked.

Bentley went over to a nearby basin and washed his hands. As he was drying them, he said, "Like I said, leave Pearlie here with me for a while. I'll keep his wounds clean and try to get some nourishment into him. If he wakes up and is in pain, I'll give him some laudanum, but that's about all I can do."

"You need one of us to stay here and help you take care of him?"

"Naw," Bentley said, shaking his head. "I've got me a housekeeper who helps me out when someone's staying here, an' I expect you and your young friend would only be in the way anyhow."

"Well, Cal and I have a string of Palouse studs outside of town that we need to take back to my ranch in Big Rock, so if you think you won't be needing us, we'll do that and then come right back here."

He dug in his pocket, pulled out a wad of greenback bills, and put them in the dentist's hand. "This ought to take care of his board and medical care till we get back."

Bentley's eyes widened at the amount of money Smoke had given him. "Hell, Mr. Jensen, this'll take care of him for a year."

Smoke leaned down close to the man, and his eyes were flat and hard. "I don't plan on him being here a year, Dr. Bentley, but he'd damn sure better get your full attention while he is here, and he'd better be a whole lot better when we get back. You understand me?"

Bentley's face was suddenly covered with a fine sheen of sweat and he nodded his head vigorously. "Yes, sir, Mr. Jensen. You can count on me to do my best for the young man."

Smoke took a piece of paper and the stub of a pencil out of his pocket and wrote something on the paper. "Here's my name and the name of my town. I can be contacted by telegraph in care of Sheriff Monte Carson at that location." He paused. "You do have a telegraph here, don't you?"

"Oh, yes, sir. We just got it put in this last spring."

"Good, then I'll expect you to keep me informed, and if the news is good, there'll be plenty more of those greenbacks for you when I come back."

"That really ain't necessary, Mr. Jensen. I took an oath when I became a dentist an' I always take good care of my patients, payin' or otherwise."

"I wasn't trying to insult you, Doctor, but I expect to pay people who work for me, and I've always found that the better the pay, the better the job done."

Bentley grinned. "Well, now, I didn't say I wasn't gonna take the money, Mr. Jensen. I just wanted you to know I'll do my dead-level best to keep your friend alive."

Smoke returned Bentley's grin. "I know you will, Dr. Bentley, and I'll expect nothing less."

Smoke turned to go, and then he hesitated and turned back around. "Oh, one more thing, Doc," Smoke said, and his grin was gone and his face was dead serious.

"Yes, Mr. Jensen?"

"I've heard tell that you have a large thirst and you tend to slake it at the nearest saloon."

Bentley's face colored and he started to protest, "Why, that's outrageous. . . ."

Smoke held up his hand. "Now, Doc, I don't care what you do when you don't have a patient under your care, but as long as my friend is here, you will stay sober . . . or you will be dead. Do I make myself clear?"

"But . . . uh . . ." Bentley began, and Smoke stopped him with a shake of his finger. "Those are really your only two choices, Dr. Bentley," Smoke said firmly. "Sober and alive, drunk and dead—do you understand?"

"Yes . . . yes, sir," Bentley said, his eyes dropping and unable to meet Smoke's stare.

"Good. Then we'll see you when we get back, and Doc, we'd better see both you *and* Pearlie."

"But, Mr. Jensen," Bentley protested, "I've already told you, your friend is powerful sick. He could die at any time, whether I'm drunk or sober!"

"Well, if he does die, you'd better be damned sure you're sober when it happens and you'd better stay that way until I get back here or there will be hell to pay," Smoke admonished, and he turned and walked out of the room.

The doctor took a handkerchief out of his pocket, wiped the fear-sweat off his forehead, and then bent over Pearlie and began to check his vital signs. He'd never been more concerned about a patient's welfare in his entire professional career.

One good thing, he thought. He wasn't a bit thirsty!

CHAPTER 6

Smoke and Cal got on their horses and rode out of town to the south to meet up with Running Deer and the braves holding their studs for them. Cal, who was leading Pearlie's horse on a dally rope, slowed his horse when they came abreast of a large wooden barn with a sign on it that read LIVERY STABLE and called to Smoke, "Hold on, Smoke. I'm gonna leave Pearlie's hoss here just in case he gets well and wants to go for a ride 'fore we get back."

Smoke smiled and nodded, though he thought it would be a miracle if Pearlie got well that fast. "Sure thing, Cal. Heck, he may even beat us home since we're gonna be herding those broncs."

Cal tied his horse to a hitching rail out front and walked Pearlie's mount into the large barn. He was out ten minutes later and was smiling. "I told the boy to let the doc know he was holdin' Pearlie's hoss just in case," he said as he climbed up into the saddle. "I also told the boy to exercise him every day and to make sure he gets plenty of grain."

Smoke grinned. "You tell that boy how Cold got his name?" Smoke asked, thinking if he hadn't, the livery boy was going to get the ride of his life the first time he climbed up on Pearlie's horse in the morning.

Cal nodded, returning the grin. "Yep, only I maybe

didn't tell him just how little Cold likes to be ridden in the morning. I figure he'll find out soon enough."

As they rode out of town, Smoke had an idea. "Say, Cal, it's less than half as far to Pueblo as it is back to Big Rock, isn't it?"

Cal pursed his lips, thinking on it for a moment, and then he nodded. "Yep, I reckon that's about right. Why?"

"Well," Smoke said, "it'd take us a couple of weeks or more to drive those ponies all the way to Big Rock and then get back here to see how Pearlie's doing."

"Uh-huh," Cal said. "And that's if we don't take a day or two to let our butts recover from all that time in the saddle."

"Why don't we take them on up to Pueblo instead? We can put them on a railroad car and have them taken to Big Rock. I can wire Monte Carson to have Louis or someone else meet the train and take the horses out to the ranch." He grinned. "That'd save us a passel of time and we wouldn't be so worn out from the long trip."

"Yeah, an' we'd be able to get back here twice as fast to watch over Pearlie too."

"Good, then that's what we'll do."

"Hey, Smoke," Cal said, looking back over his shoulder at the town. "I seen some train tracks outside of town here an' a small station platform. Why don't we just load the hosses here? That'd save us the ride to Pueblo."

Smoke shook his head. "I considered that, Cal, but this is just a quick stop on the train's way. They won't allow loading of livestock at such a place, just people."

As they spurred their horses forward, Cal said, "Whew, Smoke. I'm sure glad you thought of that. I really wasn't lookin' forward to spending the next three or four weeks living in this here saddle."

Smoke laughed. "Me neither, Cal, me neither. These old bones just won't take that kind of punishment anymore."

Cal laughed, though he knew that even though Smoke had over twenty years on him, he could ride Cal into the dirt any time he wanted to.

When they met up with Running Deer, the young brave's first question was how was Pearlie doing. Smoke shook his head and shrugged. "The doctor thinks it is a good sign that he lived this long after the bite. He's hopeful Pearlie will wake up soon, but he really doesn't know what's going to happen over the next few days."

As Running Deer handed the dally ropes to Cal and Smoke, he grew serious. "I will have our tribe do a healing dance around the campfires every night until the Great Spirit tells us that our new friend is well."

"Thank you, Running Deer. I'm sure that the Great Spirit will hear and listen to your people, for the Nez Percé are much favored by the Great Spirit."

Running Deer gave a half smile. "That is true, Mountain Man." He glanced around at the mountain peaks on all sides of them. "For look at the wonderful home He has given us to live in."

"And tell Chief Gray Wolf that when this is over, before we head back home, I will see that another side of beef is delivered to your village in thanks for all that you have done to help us."

Running Deer's smile widened. "I would like to say there is no need, Mountain Man, but my belly will not let me deny it the chance to once again feast on something other than venison or bear or dog."

Smoke gave the young brave a salute and turned his horse's head around to the northwest to head for Pueblo and the railroad yards.

As they rode away, Cal looked at Smoke and grimaced. "Did he say they ate bear and dog?"

Smoke nodded.

"I remember last year when you took Pearlie and me up into the High Lonesome to teach us something about living out in the wild and you fixed us bear one night."

"Uh-huh," Smoke said.

"I never ate anything that tasted worse in my entire born days," Cal said, shuddering as he remembered the pungent, wild taste of the bear meat. "However, I'd have to say I'd rather have two helpings of bear than one helping of dog."

"Oh, bear isn't so bad if all you got to compare it to is venison," Smoke said, his eyes far away as he remembered his days in the mountains with Preacher. He even remembered a couple of times during extended winter storms when he would've given all he owned to even have dog to eat.

"That's the problem," Cal said. "I ain't never been hungry enough to eat bear and I hope to never let myself get that hard up."

Smoke laughed. "Hell, Cal, when I was a little younger than you and I was traipsing around these mountains with Preacher, he made me eat things that would make a billy goat puke."

"Why'd you put up with that?" Cal asked.

Smoke's face sobered as he thought back to just how difficult things could get in the mountains in the dead of winter. "Sometimes we'd have blizzards that would last for ten days to two weeks and that would leave the snow so deep a horse couldn't walk in it. We'd put on our snowshoes and go and look for food. If we were lucky, we'd find a rabbit or two, but usually all we'd be able to dig outta the snow would be field mice or maybe muskrats if we got really lucky."

"You ate muskrats and mice?" Cal asked, a look of horror on his face.

Smoke smiled grimly, remembering. "I said if we were *lucky* that's what we'd find. If we weren't lucky, many times we survived by chewing on bark and leaves, and one really bad winter we ended up eating one of our pack mules."

Cal swallowed and turned pale. "I wish you hadn't told me that, Smoke."

"Hey, Cal, mule isn't all that bad. In fact, Indians consider mule meat a delicacy. It's sweeter than beef and not nearly as tough as horse."

"That's enough!" Cal called, "I don't want to hear any more about it."

"Sure, after all," Smoke said with a smile, "I wouldn't want to spoil your appetite."

"Speaking of that, isn't it about time we stopped for lunch?"

Smoke reached into his saddlebag and pulled out a paper sack with grease stains on it. He pulled out a long, stringy piece of meat and tossed it to Cal.

"I think we should just stop once a day, for supper, so we can make better time. For our nooning, we'll have to get by on this jerky I got from the Indians."

Cal took a bite of the meat and began to chew, a sour look on his face. "If there's anything that tastes worse than beef jerky, it's venison jerky," he moaned.

"I know, it doesn't go down very well, but not stopping for lunch will save us a day and a half and get us back to Pearlie that much sooner."

"In that case, I guess I'll just have to make the best of it," Cal said.

"I'll tell you what, Cal. Since you're being so brave about all this, tonight I'll cook up some extra biscuits and a little more beef than we need for supper. We can put the beef between two halves of the biscuits and have that for lunch tomorrow."

Cal grinned around the lump of jerky in his cheek. "How about breakfast? Are we gonna do without that too?"

"Naw, we'll just get up a little earlier, that's all. After all, the horses can't go all day without stopping to graze and water themselves."

"Then when we fix breakfast, maybe we can cook a couple of extra pieces of fatback too. That'd go mighty good with biscuits later in the day."

"You get up early and get the fire going, and I'll take care of fixing us something to last until supper," Smoke said, all the talk of food making his stomach growl.

"That's a deal," Cal said, and then he winced and grabbed his jaw. "Ow, I think I almost broke a tooth on this here jerky."

"Want me to see if I can find us some field mice or nice juicy muskrats to chew on instead?" Smoke asked, a glint in his eye.

"No . . . no, that's all right," Cal said hastily. "I'll just chew this jerky a little more carefully from now on."

CHAPTER 7

Sheriff Buck Tolliver rode down the main street of Payday slowly, so everyone could see he was leading two horses behind him, each with a man folded face-down across the saddle.

He wanted the townspeople to see just how tough he was so they'd never even think of going against him, no matter what the provocation. As he rode, he nodded solemnly to the citizens who stared at the bodies riding silently behind him. One nice thing about being sheriff, even if it was in a little shitty town like Payday, he thought, was that few men had the temerity to question you about anything you did—even if it involved killing two men.

He planned to tell anyone who asked that the two men were claim-jumpers and that he'd had to kill them to protect the men whose claim they were trying to steal, but that was just a lie he'd cooked up on the way back to town.

In truth, the men were two miners he'd come upon who were dancing around a campfire just outside of their mine. Tolliver had ridden up and dismounted, a wide smile on his face. When they heard him, the men stopped dancing and pulled pistols and pointed them at Tolliver, until he opened his coat and showed them the star on his chest. The two relaxed and even kidded each other about being so scared about somebody finding out about their good fortune. Tolliver continued to smile and nod as the men offered him a drink from their bottle of whiskey, which was already almost half empty.

He accepted the bottle and took a deep swig, sleeving off his mouth as he asked, "What's the big occasion, gents?"

"We done struck the biggest vein of gold you ever seen, Sheriff," one of the men said, slapping Tolliver on the shoulder.

"We're gonna be the richest doggone miners in this here territory," the other one added, doing a little jig and turning in a circle while trying to drink from his bottle, but spilling more than he swallowed.

"Is that so?" Tolliver asked.

"Damn right!" the first man said.

Tolliver smiled gently, shaking his head. "I sure hope you've already filed on this land with the territorial land office over in Pueblo," he said.

Both men suddenly stopped their dancing. "Whatta you mean by that, Sheriff?" one asked.

"Well, if you haven't filed a claim and you let some scoundrel know you've hit a big vein, someone else is liable to rush on over to Pueblo and file on your mine and take it away from you."

"Damn, Joe, he's right," the man said, suddenly as sober as a judge.

"Don't tell me you haven't filed on this land yet," Tolliver said, as if he couldn't believe it.

"Well, not exactly," Joe said. "We filed on some land all right, but it 'twas about a mile over to the east. When that place didn't produce nothin', we come on over here and started digging without botherin' to go to town and file."

"Yeah," the first man said, a worried look on his

face. "We figured if we struck somethin' worthwhile, we'd have plenty of time to file on it later."

"Well, now, you see, gentlemen, that was your first mistake," Tolliver said, handing the bottle back to the man standing next to him.

"Our *first* mistake?" Joe asked from over near the campfire.

"Yeah," Tolliver answered, drawing his pistol. "Your second mistake was telling me about your gold strike," he added, firing point-blank into one man's chest and then taking careful aim as Joe turned and began to run toward the mine.

He slowly squeezed off two more shots, grinning as Joe was flung forward to fall and skid in the gravel on his face.

Without bothering to check and see if they were still alive, Buck moved to his horse, took some stakes with his name carved in them, and walked around the mine, driving the stakes into all four corners of the property. Then he looked around and wrote down some distinguishing landmarks to add to his quick claim when he got back to town.

On the way around the property, he noticed that the bottle of whiskey had landed right side up in the snow next to where the first man he'd shot had fallen. Not one to waste good whiskey, or bad for that matter, Tolliver bent and picked up the bottle. He raised it and said, "To your very good luck, gentlemen." Then he took a deep swig and gasped. It was good whiskey and tasted just fine.

Once he was finished, he went into the men's cabin, searched for and found four small canvas bags of gold dust and flakes they'd mined from the mine and small stream nearby, and stuck them in his saddlebags.

With a sigh, he saddled their horses and tied them together with a dally rope. Once that was done, he heaved the two bodies up on the horses and started his long ride back to Payday, thinking what a profitable day it'd turned out to be.

And the best part of it was, this fortune he wouldn't have to share with his partners in crime. It was to be his and his alone. None of his partners would ever have to know about this mine and how he'd obtained it. It would be his little secret, his and his banker's, of course.

He tied his horse up in front of the tent housing the local undertaker and stuck his head inside, interrupting Jonas Slackmeyer as he was planing the edges of a coffin down smooth and round.

"Hey, Jonas," Tolliver called, to get the man's attention.

Slackmeyer straightened up and wiped sawdust from his forehead with a dirty rag in his back pocket. "Yes, Sheriff?" he answered.

"I got you two new customers out here on a pair of horses. Give 'em the cheapest coffin you got and bury 'em over in boot hill."

"And who will pay for their burial, Sheriff? The city?" Slackmeyer asked.

"Yeah," Tolliver said, flipping him a two-dollar gold piece. He figured it was the least he could do. "And when you're done, take the horses over to the livery and tell the boy to take 'em out to my spread and add 'em to my remuda."

"What about the saddles and such?"

Tolliver thought about it. The saddles were pretty much junk and not worth bothering with. Besides, he had plenty of saddles and tack already. Any more would just clutter up his barn. "You can sell 'em and keep whatever you get for your trouble," he said, figuring giving Slackmeyer a little bit extra would encourage him to keep his mouth shut about one of the men being shot in the back.

Slackmeyer grinned, dipping his head. "Why, thank you, Sheriff. I'll get right on it."

"And Jonas," he added, his face stern.

"Yes, Sheriff?"

"This is city business, so there's no need speaking about it to any of the townspeople. Understand?"

Slackmeyer grinned. "Of course, Sheriff, you can count on my discretion."

As Tolliver left, Slackmeyer took a deep breath. The man scared him half to death. If the townspeople knew half the shit about their sheriff that *he* did, they wouldn't sleep a wink at night.

Tolliver rode his horse to the livery to have the boy brush him down and give him some grain and to tell the boy Slackmeyer would be bringing a couple of horses for his remuda.

As he dismounted, he saw a strange horse in one of the stables. It was a striking animal—gray with a series of spots on its rump, and it was heavily muscled and sleek-looking as it stood munching on a bucket of oats in its stall.

Tolliver gave the boy his message, and then he nonchalantly asked who the new bronc belonged to.

"Oh, that hoss belongs to some man over at the doc's office," the boy said. "His friends left him here in case he got well enough to ride 'fore they get back."

"What do you mean before they get back?" Tolliver asked.

"They had a herd of hosses to take home, an' then they was gonna come back here to see how their friend was doin'," the boy answered as he unbuckled

Tolliver's saddle and pulled it off his horse with a grunt.

"What were these men's names?"

The boy shrugged. "I don't know. They told me the horse belongs to a man named Pearlie, but they didn't give me their names."

Tolliver nodded and started to walk off.

"I'll tell you one thing, though," the boy added as he grabbed a brush and began to brush Tolliver's horse.

Tolliver stopped and looked back over his shoulder. "What's that?"

"The man riding with the one who gave me the money to pay for the hoss's care is one of the biggest men I ever seen, an' he was dressed all in buckskins like some of those ol' mountain men who used to come through here."

Tolliver felt a chill go down his spine, and he turned and walked back to the livery boy.

"What did this hombre look like?" he asked, his voice low and hard.

The boy looked up, alarmed at the change in Tolliver's face from friendly to harsh. "Uh, I dunno."

Tolliver grabbed the boy by the front of his shirt. "Think, damnit!"

"Uh, he was 'bout six feet or a little more, wide shoulders, lots of muscles, and he had yeller-gray hair and no beard nor mustache."

Tolliver shuddered. "Anything else?" he croaked through a suddenly dry throat, letting go of the boy's shirt. "Was he heeled?"

The boy stepped back. "Yeah, now that you mention it. He carried two pistols. The one on his left hip was butt-first and the one on his right was tied down low on his thigh. He also had a big knife stuck in the back of his belt." The boy managed a halfhearted grin, still scared at the way Tolliver was acting. "He looked about as dangerous a man as I've ever seen, an' I sure as hell wouldn't want to do anything to make him mad at me."

"Damn it to hell," Tolliver muttered, whirling around and walking as fast as he could without actually running toward the doctor's office.

"It can't be," he said to himself, wiping at his brow to remove the sweat that suddenly broke out on his forehead. "It just can't be after all these years!"

His heart was beating so fast he thought it was going to jump out of his chest before he got to the doc's house.

Suddenly, he had a fearsome thought. He hadn't asked the livery boy how long ago the man had been there. Maybe he was still in town right now.

Tolliver slowed and let his hand drop to hang next to his pistol butt. *Hell, he might even have seen me ride up and be waiting for me this very instant.*

As he walked, Tolliver turned around and around, looking on all sides for the mysterious man dressed all in buckskins and carrying two pistols and a knife on his belt.

Jesus, he told himself, take ahold of yourself, Buck. It's been more'n twenty years since he's seen you. He couldn't possibly recognize you after all this time.

Still, he couldn't shake the bone-deep fear that coursed through his body at the very thought that Smoke Jensen might be in his town.

Because he knew if that was the case, one of them wasn't going to leave the town alive. . . .

CHAPTER 8

Buck Tolliver's heart had slowed down a little by the time he got to Doc Bentley's office without seeing Smoke Jensen anywhere around. He couldn't imagine what circumstances might have occurred that would bring the famous gunfighter to his little town out in the middle of nowhere, but if the man the boy in the livery was describing was Jensen, then Tolliver's prayers of more than twenty years had finally been answered.

Just thinking about what he was going to do to Jensen if he was in town caused his heart to hammer again and a fine sheen of sweat to break out on his forehead. He found himself clenching his teeth so hard his jaw actually creaked.

When he raised his hand to open the doc's door, he noticed his hand was shaking. This just won't do, he thought. Forcing himself to calm down, he paused and took a few deep breaths. It wouldn't do to let the doc see just how interested he was in the identity of the man in buckskins who'd visited while he was gone. No. That would mess up any plans Tolliver had for the man he hated more than anyone else in the world.

Finally, he was able to control himself enough to be able to talk to Bentley without arousing the man's suspicions, so he opened the door and strolled inside as if he didn't have a thing on his mind.

Bentley was straddling a chair in his main examining

room, his elbows out and his foot up on a footrest attached to the chair. A pair of trousers could be seen moving back and forth between the doc's legs, and Tolliver heard Bentley saying, "Just hold on a minute there, Clem. I've almost got the son of a bitch."

The patient addressed as Clem jumped and moaned loudly as Bentley's right arm flew back, and Tolliver could see his hand was holding a pair of dental forceps with a bloody tooth in them.

"There," Bentley said, climbing down off the poor patient, who was sweating profusely and whose face was pale and drawn-looking. He had a river of bloody drool running down his chin as if he'd been poked in the mouth.

Clem gently put his hand up to his swollen jaw and probed the tissues, a look of relief finally appearing on his face. "Damn, Doc, I thought you'd never get the bugger out. It's been painin' me for nigh on two weeks now."

Bentley held up the tooth and looked at it. "Yep, this is what was causing you all that pain, Clem. See how it's all black and rotted out inside." He shook his head. "You been eating too many of those peppermint sticks over at the general store and it's rotting all your teeth out. If you don't cut back, Clem, you're going to be seeing me again real soon to have some more work done."

Clem shook his head and climbed unsteadily out of the dental chair. "No, thanks, Doc. I'd just as soon not look if'n you don't mind, and I promise to give up peppermint for good. What do I owe you?"

Bentley pursed his lips as he dropped the tooth in a nearby wastebasket. "Oh, I suspect ten cents ought to about do it," he said, and he handed Clem a small piece of gauze and motioned for him to wipe the blood off his chin.

Clem took the cloth and wiped his mouth and threw the pad in the wastebasket without looking at the bloodstains on it. Then he dug in his pocket and pulled out a coin. "Here you go, Doc, an' much obliged."

Clem grabbed his hat off a peg and turned toward the door, seeing Tolliver for the first time. "Oh, howdy, Buck," he said, nodding as he passed on his way out the door.

"Howdy, Clem," Tolliver said, touching the brim of his hat in greeting. He could hardly restrain himself. He was busting at the gut to ask the doc about the man in buckskins and everybody wanted to jaw all morning.

"Good morning, Sheriff," Bentley said, moving to wash his hands in a basin on a small stand against the wall. As he turned around, still wiping them on a towel, he asked, "You having some tooth problems this morning, Buck?"

"No, thank the Lord," Tolliver said with a small shiver. He remembered the last time he'd had to have Bentley pull a tooth. The doc was lucky Tolliver had taken his gun off before climbing in his chair or Bentley would most probably have been shot during the extraction.

He looked more closely at the doc now, thinking something was different. The doc was clean-shaven for one thing, and his eyes were unnaturally clear for this time of day. Usually by now he would've had a few shots of whiskey and would be already slurring his words. As he stared at the man, Tolliver noticed his hands had a fine tremor, but not the heavy shaking too much alcohol caused.

"Something the matter, Doc?" Tolliver asked.

"Why . . . uh . . . no, Buck. It's just that I've decided to give up drinking for a while," he answered with a sickly grin. "I think the alcohol was impairing my treatment of my patients and so I'm trying to stay away from it." He shook his head and looked down at his trembling hands. "It is tough, but I reckon after a couple of days I won't even notice it."

Tolliver nodded as he wondered what in the world could make a drunk give up booze.

"That's mighty nice, Doc," Tolliver said. "I'm sure your patients will appreciate the fact that you're sober when you work on them, but why did you suddenly decide to give it up now?"

"Oh, I just thought it was about time. Now, you said you didn't have any tooth problems, Buck?" Bentley asked, wondering why the sheriff was here if he didn't have a medical problem.

"I was just over at the livery and the boy there said you had a new patient. Someone from out of town." Tolliver faked a yawn and covered his mouth with his hand as he added, "So I thought I'd just mosey on over and see what the story was." He smiled disarmingly. "You know how I like to keep up with any newcomers to town, especially if they suddenly come up in need of medical attention."

Bentley smiled back and threw the towel on a pile of similarly stained ones on the floor. "Oh, it's nothing for you to be concerned with, Buck. The man wasn't shot or stabbed nor nothing like that."

Tolliver didn't speak, just raised his eyebrows, knowing the doc wouldn't be able to resist telling him what was ailing his patient.

"Man got snakebit out in the foothills of the mountains. Hit him twice, once in the leg and once in the neck." Bentley shook his head as he walked over to a coffeepot steaming on a potbellied stove in the corner. "Wonder the poor man is still alive."

He picked up the pot and glanced at Tolliver. "You want a cup of coffee, Sheriff?"

Tolliver didn't, having had several cups already that morning, but he knew if he didn't take a cup he wouldn't have an excuse to stand around jawing with the dentist, so he nodded his head and took off his hat.

He hung his hat up on the peg by the door and accepted a cup of steaming coffee from Bentley. "So, how's the gent doing?" he asked.

Bentley took his own cup and sat down at the table in his dining room, motioning Tolliver to join him. "Can't rightly tell, Buck. He's been in a coma ever since he arrived. Hasn't stirred one little bit, 'cepting to moan in his sleep a couple of times."

"You got a name for this feller?"

Bentley smiled at Tolliver over the rim of his cup. "Why, Buck? You think he might be on one of them wanted posters you got hung up in your office?"

Tolliver shrugged. "Never can tell, Doc. Being on the run or planning on digging up some gold are about the only two reasons anybody'd want to come all the way up here in the mountains to Payday. Anyway, it's my job to check out any newcomers to the town."

"Well, you can rest easy," Bentley said, leaning back in his chair. "This man's a cowboy, up here herding some horses he and his friends bought from the Nez Percé."

Tolliver took a deep breath and had to restrain himself from reaching across the table and strangling the doc until he answered his questions and told him what he really came here to find out. "I didn't ask you what he did for a living, Doc," Tolliver snapped, a little more angrily than he meant to. Once again, he took a deep breath and tried to calm himself, knowing the doc would give him the information he needed sooner or later if he could just keep from aggravating the man. In a more gentle, conversational voice, he added, "I asked if you knew his name so I can wire it over to Pueblo an' see if he's wanted or anything like that."

Bentley's eyes narrowed, and Tolliver realized he had made him suspicious with his earlier outburst, so he forced himself to relax and lean back with a disinterested look on his face. "But it's all right if you don't know," he said, as if it didn't matter in the least to him.

"His name's Pearlie," Bentley said. "Don't know his last name."

"Did the men who brung him in give you their names?" Tolliver asked, still trying to mask his excitement and make the question seem ordinary.

Bentley grinned. "Yeah, an' you'll never guess who it was, Buck. First time I know of anyone famous ever set foot in Payday, leastways since I've been here anyway."

Tolliver sighed heavily, trying to keep his temper under control. "I didn't come here to play guessing games, Doc," he said as evenly as he could.

"Fellow who brought Pearlie in was named Jensen," Bentley said, his eyebrows raised to see if Tolliver would make the connection.

"Would that be Smoke Jensen?" Tolliver asked, hoping the doc couldn't hear his thudding heart.

Bentley slapped his hand on his thigh and grinned. "Yes, it was Smoke Jensen. Can you believe it, Buck? One of the most famous gunfighters in history, right up there with Wyatt Earp and Bat Masterson, right here in my little office bringing his friend in to see me for treatment."

"I know of him," Tolliver said, keeping his voice flat. "You don't have to tell me how famous he is. Fact is, Doc, he *was* a famous gunfighter a few years back, but that was a long time ago, and I haven't heard much about him in the last four or five years."

Bentley's eyes widened. "Buck, you don't think he's wanted by the law anywhere, do you?" he asked. "I didn't think of that when he told me who he was or I would've let you know he was here."

Tolliver shrugged. "Not to my knowledge, but I might just wire Pueblo or Denver an' see if there's any warrants out on him just to be sure. I do know that in his day it was said he killed over two hundred men in various gunfights."

Bentley nodded slowly, his eyes far away as he thought back to the day his patient had arrived. "You know something funny, Buck? I remember the day Jensen and another man brought his friend in to see me. Both Jensen and the young man with him had their guns tied down low on their thighs in the manner of gunslicks. I didn't think anything of it at the time, but it isn't the usual way cowboys around here wear their irons." He gave a short laugh. "Hell, it wasn't till he told me his name I even thought much about it."

Tolliver drained his cup and stood up. "Mind if I take a look at this patient of yours, Doc? Just in case I got a picture of him over at the office."

"No, you go right ahead, Buck," Bentley said, also getting to his feet.

Tolliver went into the room where Bentley kept his bedridden patients and stood next to the bed with Pearlie in it. He stared down at him as he slept and realized he didn't recognize him. The man who'd been with Jensen the last time Tolliver had seen him had been elderly twenty years ago and was most likely dead by now. This man was much too young to have ridden with Jensen when he was up in the mountains, or even later when he was on the owl hoot trail.

"All right, Doc," Tolliver said, putting his hat on and walking toward the door. "I'll let you know if I find out anything about Jensen or his traveling companions."

"You do that, Sheriff, an' I'll be sure and call you if I hear back from them or if this Pearlie fellow wakes up." He paused and looked worried. "At least I hope he's gonna wake up. I sure as hell don't want to lose a friend of a man like Jensen if he's as dangerous as you say he is."

"Oh, I suspect he's still dangerous, Doc, even though he's getting up in age for a gunfighter."

Tolliver stopped and suddenly realized why the doc had quit the drinking. He narrowed his eyes and stared at him. "That man in there being Jensen's friend wouldn't have anything to do with why you stopped drinking, would it, Doc?"

Bentley's eyes dropped and he hung his head. "Well, Jensen may have mentioned it'd be better if I stayed sober until Pearlie got well, but I was planning on doing it sooner or later anyway, Buck."

"Did he threaten you, Doc?" Tolliver asked, hoping the man would swear out a complaint against Jensen. It would give him an excuse to draw down on him and if he killed him, no one could ever say he wasn't just doing his duty.

"Uh, why, no, Buck. Jensen didn't threaten me. He just reminded me it'd be better for me not to drink while taking care of a patient."

"All right, Doc," Tolliver said, disappointed, "but if that boy in there comes awake, you give me a holler, 'cause I may just have a few questions to ask Mr. Pearlie."

CHAPTER 9

Tolliver was so engrossed in his thoughts when he left Doctor Bentley's office that he stepped out into the street right in front of an ore wagon.

The driver jerked the reins to the right and kicked his foot down on the wagon wheel brake, yelling at Tolliver to watch out as he did so.

The screeching of the metal brake pad got Tolliver's attention and saved his life. He glanced up and dove back, hitting the ground and rolling to the side so that the wheels of the wagon and the hooves of the big draft horses missed him by mere inches.

Bentley, standing at the window of his office, shook his head and scratched his chin. He'd known there was something strange about the way the sheriff had been so interested in his patient and in Smoke Jensen. Tolliver'd never before come asking about newcomers the doc had treated. He spent a moment wondering why before turning and walking toward the room where Pearlie lay.

Maybe when the young man woke up, if he woke up, he could shed some light on why Buck was so interested in him and his friends.

Bentley stood over Pearlie's bed for a moment looking down at the wan, pale face. One thing was for sure—this young man was no hardened criminal. The doc could tell that just by looking at his hands. They were callused and hardened the way only hard cowboy work could make them, and his fingernails had dirt under them. Bentley had seen his share of gunnies and hard cases in his younger days when he practiced in Denver, and not one of them had hands like these.

He shook his head and took a washrag out of the basin next to the bed, wrung it out, and gently wiped the sweat off Pearlie's forehead. Nope. Whatever the sheriff wanted with this boy and his friends, it sure as hell wasn't due to his job—it was personal.

Of course, if there was one thing Bentley had learned in his years of practicing medicine out West, it was that personal business was just that—personal. And it was always better to stay the hell out of other people's personal business, lest you be caught up in it more than you'd like. Yep, he thought, he'd just keep his mouth shut, treat his patient, and stay away from the booze. If he did all that, he might just come out of this with his skin intact.

That is, if Pearlie survived. Everything depended on that fact first and foremost.

Tolliver got up and dusted himself off, glaring at the wagon driver, who was staring back at him like he was crazy. The driver didn't dare say anything, though, for everyone in town knew all about Buck Tolliver's hair-trigger temper. After a few more moments staring, the drover just shook his head, leaned to the side and spit a stream of brown tobacco juice into the street, and slapped his reins against the horses' rumps. As the heavy wagon rumbled off down the street, the driver glanced back over his shoulder and shook his head again, showing Tolliver just what he thought of idiots who walked out in front of an ore wagon that weighed several tons.

Tolliver looked both ways this time before he crossed Main Street and headed back to his office. He needed to think about what he was going to do when Jensen came back to town. Even if Jensen was twenty years older than he had been the last time Tolliver had seen him, that didn't mean the man wasn't as dangerous as a grizzly bear in heat. Even old gunfighters could still manage a quick draw once in a while, and Tolliver didn't want to make the mistake of underestimating Jensen, not when his life depended on it.

He hung his hat on the door peg and sat at his desk, putting his feet up on the corner and leaning back in his chair, his hands crossed behind his neck.

He closed his eyes, but instead of making plans for Jensen's return, he thought about the last time he'd seen the man. . . .

Buck had been just over twelve years old that day back in his hometown of Homestead, Colorado Territory. It was the first time his older brother had let him ride into town with him and the other hands on his daddy's ranch.

After he'd helped them load up the buckboard with wire and nails and lumber, Jack Tolliver had given Buck a nickel and told him to buy him some peppermint candy sticks or maybe some licorice while he and the men stopped by the saloon for a couple of drinks.

Buck waited for nearly an hour, moving around the general store and looking at all the fine merchandise the owner had brought in by big freight wagons from Denver and Pueblo. Finally, he started getting antsy, wondering why his brother and the other men were taking so long. He'd spent all of his money and the candy was just about all gone, and the owner of the store was looking at him funny, wondering why the skinny kid was hanging around so long and not buying anything else.

He stuck his last peppermint stick in his mouth and walked out of the general store toward the saloon. Jack would box his ears for interrupting his drinking, but Buck knew his daddy had already had to warn Jack several times about his drinking and he didn't want Jack to get in trouble. He worshiped his brother and if he could help keep him out of trouble, then some sore ears was a small price to pay.

He looked ahead and saw two men dressed all in buckskins come out of the saloon and climb up on what looked like Indian ponies, the ones with the spotted rumps. Buck smiled. They were about the dirtiest men he'd ever seen in town. He figured they must be mountain men, 'cause his daddy had told him about them once. He'd said they were misfits who couldn't hold down regular jobs so they lived up in the mountains, eating berries and wild animals like the Indians did.

In fact, Buck thought, these men looked like wild animals themselves, with their dirty clothes, wild disarranged hair and heavy beards, and Indian moccasins on their feet instead of leather boots.

As the two men jerked their horses' heads around, the saloon batwings flew open and Jack and a few of the men from the ranch came bursting out. Buck started to yell hello, until he saw that Jack and the others were so drunk they were almost staggering as they pushed their way out onto the boardwalk, elbowing other citizens aside.

Buck stopped, his eyes opened wide when he saw that Jack and the other men had their guns in their hands and were pointing them at the backs of the two mountain men who were riding slowly down the street.

Jack fired first, snapping off several shots that evidently went wild since neither of the men on horseback were hit.

Quicker than a rattlesnake striking, the younger man with the sandy yellow-colored hair twisted in his saddle as he filled his hand with iron and fired back.

His first shot took Jack in the chest, knocking him back with outspread hands. Buck screamed at the sight of his brother being blown off his feet to land spread-eagled on his back on the boardwalk.

Buck raced forward, ignoring the smoke and loud explosions of gunfire up ahead of him. He raced to kneel next to his brother and took his face in his hands.

"Jack . . . Jack . . . !" he screamed at the open, staring eyes.

Finally, there was silence, and Buck glanced around to see Joe and Sam and Larry all lying on the ground with blood pumping from bullet holes in their bodies. None of the men from the ranch were left alive.

Buck screamed again and grabbed the pistol from Jack's lifeless hand. He stood up and whirled around, holding the big Walker Colt in both hands and prying the hammer back with his right thumb. He had no idea how many bullets were left in the chamber, but he didn't care. He just wanted to kill the men who'd shot his brother down.

The man with the yellow hair aimed his pistol at Buck, but pulled it up when he saw he was just a boy—a boy who still had a peppermint stick in the corner of his mouth.

Buck took aim, blinking away his tears, and fired, grinning fiercely when he saw blood spurt from the man's left shoulder as the force of the slug turned him half around in his saddle.

The older man, a man with a face full of gray whiskers and a stink on him Buck could smell from ten feet away, leveled a long, Sharps fifty-caliber buffalo gun at Buck.

To Buck, the hole in the barrel of that rifle looked to be big enough to put his fist in. He didn't care; let the son of a bitch shoot. He lowered his pistol between his knees and again used both hands to pry the hammer back, hoping to get one more shot off before the old man killed him.

He glanced up and saw the man with yellow hair hold up his hand and yell *no!* at the old man.

The old man just shook his head as he lowered his rifle barrel. Good, Buck thought, and he again raised his pistol and aimed it at the man with yellow hair.

The old man spurred his horse forward between Buck and the man who'd shot his brother, and he swung his rifle like he was swinging an ax.

The barrel hit Buck on the temple and put his lights out. It was the last thing he remembered until he woke up a day later out at the ranch with his daddy leaning over him.

Tolliver came back to the present and unconsciously fingered the scar on his left temple that still remained as a souvenir of that day. His father had told him the man who'd killed his brother was named Smoke Jensen, and that the sheriff had cleared the two men of all charges, since Jack and the other men from the ranch had fired first and had fired at the other men's backs without giving them any warning.

He explained to Buck that Jack and the others had gotten stinking drunk and had begun to make fun of the two mountain men and the way they looked and the way they smelled. When the old man had grabbed

Jack by the front of his shirt and slapped him back and forth with his open hand and then thrown him to the ground like a child, it had started a full-scale fight between the two strangers and the men from the ranch.

In spite of being outnumbered two to one, the two mountain men had kicked the ranchers' butts, leaving them bruised and bleeding on the floor when they walked out of the saloon. But, his daddy said, shaking his head, Jack wouldn't let it go. He had a snootful of whiskey and it made him liquor-brave, as his daddy put it.

He and the others had tried to back-shoot the two mountain men, and had paid for their foolishness with their lives. Buck's daddy added he didn't ever want Buck to mention Jack's name to him again, and he hadn't. But Buck had never forgotten the vacant stare in his brother's eyes on that fateful day. He'd vowed then to someday make things right and to make that Jensen fellow pay for shooting his brother down like a stray dog in the street.

It didn't matter to Buck Tolliver how much time had passed. For the past twenty years he'd prayed that someday he would come face-to-face with the bastard that killed his brother, and now his prayers were about to be answered.

Of course, he wasn't going to make the same mistake his brother did and go up against Jensen while he was drunk. No, sir. He would make careful plans and make sure that when he faced Jensen down and killed him, he would have the edge and not the gunfighter.

As he thought on it, he realized that Jensen had one weakness he probably hadn't considered. The man he'd dropped off at the doctor's was obviously a good friend. Maybe Tolliver could use that fact against the mountain man. It certainly deserved some serious consideration.

CHAPTER 10

Cal was just finishing his breakfast in the dining room of the Palace Hotel in Pueblo when Smoke Jensen walked into the room.

Cal wiped syrup off his lips and raised his hand to signal his position to Smoke. When Smoke started toward him, Cal got the waitress's attention and made a drinking motion with his hand so she would bring some fresh coffee for the mountain man. From the somber look on his face, Smoke was going to need it, Cal thought. He looked skyward and gave a silent prayer that Smoke hadn't gotten any bad news about Pearlie's condition. Cal didn't know what he'd do if Pearlie didn't make it through all of this. The man was like an older brother to him and his life just wouldn't be the same without Pearlie in it.

By the time Smoke threaded his way through the crowded room and took his seat, their waitress was pouring steaming coffee into a tall mug in front of him.

"You have any luck?" Cal asked, dreading the answer. Smoke had left him almost two hours earlier to go to the telegraph office so he could wire Big Rock and have Sheriff Monte Carson be on the lookout for the horses they were going to ship by rail car later in the day, and also to wire the town of Payday and see if there had been any change in Pearlie's condition.

Smoke picked up the coffee mug, took a deep swallow, and shook his head. "Not much. I got an answer back from Big Rock. Monte said he'd take care of the horses and wished us luck with Pearlie. Said the entire town would be praying for his recovery."

Cal nodded slowly. "I suspect they will. Pearlie's a right popular feller in Big Rock. He don't have an enemy in the world far as I know."

For the first time that morning, Smoke smiled, though it was a small smile. "You're right there, Cal. I've never heard anyone speak a word against Pearlie in all the time I've known him, and that's something to say about a man who's lived here as long as Pearlie has."

"Did you manage to get a message to the dentist and did you hear back from him 'bout Pearlie's condition?" Cal asked, hoping the news would be good, or at least not bad.

The smile faded from Smoke's face. "Yeah. The doc sent a wire saying Pearlie was no better, but the good news is he isn't any worse either. He said about all we could hope for was that every day Pearlie lives makes him a little stronger and gives him a better chance to survive the bites."

The waitress moved to stand next to Smoke with a pad and pencil in her hand. "You gonna want something to eat this mornin', sweetie?" she asked in a gravelly voice.

Smoke smiled. He hadn't been called sweetie since he was a little shaver. When Smoke hesitated, Cal said, "You might as well eat something, Smoke. We can't head back to Payday till this afternoon 'cause we still got to get those hosses loaded and on their way."

Smoke sighed. "You're right, Cal. It's just that worrying about Pearlie has about ruined my appetite."

The waitress, who'd overheard part of their earlier conversation, laid a meaty hand on Smoke's shoulder. In a kind voice, she said, "I know you're worried 'bout your sick friend, mister, but some of our flapjacks and scrambled hens' eggs will make you feel better. I guarantee you can face whatever comes your way better with a full stomach, no matter what it is."

Smoke looked up at her, touched by her concern. He smiled. "Might as well fry me up a side of bacon to go with 'em," he said. "And a touch more coffee would go down nicely too."

She smiled and winked as she put her pencil behind her ear. "I'll be right back with that coffee."

That evening, just before dusk, Sheriff Buck Tolliver was sitting in his office staring out of his window as he had been for most of the day. He kept turning things over in his mind, trying to figure out the best way to cause Smoke Jensen the same pain and suffering he'd gone through all these years whenever he thought of his dead brother and the terrible way he'd died—choking on his own blood in the dirt of the street of his hometown.

He knew that he could shoot the man when he came back to see about his sick friend, catching him unaware, but that somehow seemed too easy. The bastard wouldn't suffer near enough, no matter how long it took him to die. No, Tolliver would have to figure something else out for the gunman, something that would make him have the same sort of nightmares Buck had been living with for almost twenty years. If only he could do something that would hurt the gunman to the soul as his brother's death had *him,* Tolliver thought he'd be satisfied.

When Tolliver saw Hezekiah Bentley leave his office and make his way toward the Dog Hole Saloon to have his dinner, he had an idea. He knew how he could make Jensen suffer as he had, and even better, he'd do it so he could be there to taunt him with it and the man wouldn't be able to do anything about it no matter how much he suspected Tolliver might be behind it.

Tolliver grabbed his hat and followed Bentley into the saloon. He wondered if the doc was going to go back to his drinking, but noticed he shook his head when one of the girls approached his table and offered him a drink. I'll be damned, Tolliver thought, a wry smile on his lips, the doc is ordering water with his food.

Tolliver looked around the saloon, hunting for the reason he'd come into the place. Sure enough, Tolliver's cousin, Blackie Johnson, was at his usual place at the bar. Tolliver caught his eye and motioned him to come outside and talk. As he waited outside the batwings for Johnson, Tolliver gave a silent prayer that the man wouldn't be too drunk to do what he was going to ask him to do.

The sheriff uttered a low curse when Blackie stumbled through the batwings. Blackie grinned stupidly at Tolliver and held up his hand in greeting. "Yo, Buck, was-s-s goin' on?" he slurred.

Damn, Tolliver thought angrily, almost reaching out and slapping the shit out of his cousin. He was drunk as a skunk. Well, Tolliver figured, thinking rapidly, even a drunk man ought to be able to handle a man as sick as Jensen's friend was.

"Come over here, Blackie, we need to talk. I got a job for you to do."

"Aw, Buck, it's the middle of the night an' I'm busy with some friends in the saloon."

"First off, it's not the middle of the night, you fool, it's barely dusk; an' second of all, you ain't got no friends in the saloon nor nowhere else unless you're the one doin' the buyin'."

Johnson's face screwed up in anger, which turned to fear when Tolliver grabbed the front of his shirt and jerked him into the darkness of the alleyway next to the saloon. "Now here's what I want you to do," he said. "There's a gent over at Doc Bentley's who's sleepin' in one of his patient rooms."

Johnson gave a half grin. "Oh, you mean the man who got hisself snakebit?"

"Yeah. I want you to go over there and sneak in and put his lights out for good."

"You mean, kill him?" Johnson asked, his eyebrows raised. "Why? He ain't never done nothin' to me."

Tolliver took a deep breath. Blackie had always been as dumb as a post, and when he'd been drinking, he was even dumber. "You remember my brother Jack?" he asked, hating that he had to explain himself to Blackie, after all he done for him over the years. Hell, he thought, if he hadn't been sheriff, Blackie would've been sent to jail a dozen times at least.

Startled and somewhat confused at the change of subject, Johnson hung his mouth open for a moment before he answered. "Uh, sure, Buck. He was always nice to us when we was young'uns. He hardly ever beat up on us . . . at least not in no serious way."

Tolliver grabbed the front of Johnson's shirt again and pointed at Bentley's house. "That man lyin' in there is a close friend of the bastard who shot my brother down like a dog, Blackie. An' I want you to go in there and kill him to send that man a message for me."

Blackie cut his eyes toward Bentley's house, following Tolliver's pointing finger. "Well, sure, Buck, since you put it that way. Don't make no never mind to me." He hitched up his pants and took a step toward Bentley's before he turned back around, a puzzled look on his face. "But Buck, why don't you do it yourself since it was your brother he kilt?"

Tolliver took a deep breath to keep from slamming his fist into Blackie's dumb-ass face. "'Cause I'm gonna be in the saloon having a drink with Doc Bentley so no one will suspect I had anything to do with it, Blackie. Now, you gonna do what I ask or you gonna stand out here jawin' the night away?"

Blackie nodded and turned and took another step, stopped, and turned back around.

"Now what?" Tolliver asked hurriedly, worried that Bentley was going to finish his meal before Blackie ever got around to killing the man in his office. Since Bentley wasn't drinking anymore, there wouldn't be any reason for the doc to stick around the saloon after he'd finished his dinner.

"How do you want me to do it?" Blackie asked. "Gun, knife, or just strangle him?"

Tolliver sighed again. The man was a complete idiot. "I need you to shoot him, Blackie, so everyone can hear when it happens, and they'll know I was in the saloon and couldn't have been involved."

When Blackie raised his eyebrows and nodded in comprehension, Tolliver added, "So just go over there and put a gun between the man's eyes, blow his head off, and then hightail it out of the house and down the back alley until you're a couple of streets away from the doc's."

Blackie turned, and Tolliver stopped him with a hand on his arm. "And Blackie, make sure you don't get his brains an' blood splattered all over you, all right? Put a pillow over his head or something 'fore you shoot him."

"All right, Buck, but I ain't no idiot. You didn't have to tell me that."

"And just head on home when you're done, an' I'll check in with you tomorrow."

Blackie nodded and stumbled as he turned to walk toward the doc's house. Tolliver just shook his head and hurried through the batwings, his eyes searching for Bentley so he could join him for a drink or two until they heard the gunshot. He'd have the perfect alibi for the killing. He'd make sure to give Jensen enough hints that he'd be able to figure out who did it and why, but he wouldn't be able to do anything about it. At least not legally.

And if the old gunman made the mistake of drawing down on an officer of the law, it wouldn't matter who won the gunfight. If he manages to kill me, Tolliver thought, then he'll be back on the run for the rest of his life. But if he's lost some of his speed after all these years, then I get the pleasure of not only killing his friend, but of planting him forked-end-up in boot hill.

All in all, not a bad plan if I do say so myself, Tolliver told himself as he spied Bentley and raised his hand in greeting as he moved over toward his table.

CHAPTER 11

Blackie looked back over his shoulder to make sure Buck was gone and wasn't looking, and then he pulled a small pint bottle of whiskey from his hip pocket. It wasn't that he was afraid of his cousin . . . not exactly. There was just no need to stir up Buck's temper unnecessarily, that's all. He pulled the cork and upended the bottle, drinking until it was completely empty.

He sleeved his mouth off and chucked the bottle into an alley as he walked toward the doc's house. He only weaved a little as he moved back and forth from side to side of the small street. Damn that Buck, he thought. Just when I was gittin' a good snort on he has to come and tell me to go to work killin' a feller, even though he don't mean nothin' to me.

He chuckled and looked again to see if Buck was still gone, as if the man could read his mind. Hell, he thought, I don't care if'n the gent kilt his brother Jack or not. Jack wasn't all that good to me anyhow—always tellin' me an' Buck what to do as if he was our pappy 'stead of Buck's brother. Served the asshole right to git hisself all shot up 'cause he couldn't mind his own business an' went an' picked on a man tougher he was. Buck should'a realized that, 'cause his daddy shore did.

Course, Buck has been pretty nice to me, all considered, Blackie thought, even if he is bein' inconsiderate makin' me go to work in the middle of the night like this. Might as well do as he asks or there'll be hell to pay next time he has to stop somebody from pressin' charges on me or somethin'.

Well, Blackie figured as he walked up the stoop to Doc Bentley's back door, time to get this over with. Ol' Buck'll never let me forget it if'n I don't kill this stump-sucker for him, and what's worse, he won't give me no more of that gold money he's been takin' from the miners round here.

Blackie stumbled on the top step and fell against the back door, banging his head and making quite a bit of noise when the bell the doc'd hung there commenced to ringing.

"Sh-h-h!" he said to himself, holding a finger up against his lips as he used the other hand to stop the swinging of the bell. "Mustn't make so much noise, Blackie, or you'll wake the dead," he mumbled, chuckling at his own joke. "Oops, I forgot, he's not dead yet."

He reached down and opened the door, thanking the doc silently for never locking his doors. The door screeched on its hinges as he opened it and again he shushed himself, laughing softly as he tiptoed into the doc's kitchen, which was just off the back door.

Now, he thought, slipping his six-gun from its holster. Just which way is that bedroom?

He fumbled around in the semidarkness, banging into a table and knocking a lamp over on its side. Luckily, the bell holding the kerosene didn't break, so he just righted it and went on searching.

Up ahead, in the bedroom, Pearlie stirred, the noise bringing him almost awake. He moaned softly and tried to open his eyes, but the lids were stuck shut with dried tears.

He sighed, figuring he'd wait a few more minutes before climbing out of his bedroll and helping Cal and Smoke to get breakfast ready.

Blackie finally found the door to the bedroom and pulled the door open, holding his six-shooter out in front of him. As a cloud passed from in front of the moon, soft light filtered in the window and he could see a man sleeping soundly on the bed in front of him.

That must be the galoot Buck was talkin' about, he told himself. He laughed again softly to himself when he saw there was no one else in the room. *That's good,* he told himself, chuckling again. *Wouldn't want to kill the wrong galoot, now would we, Blackie ol' man?*

He tiptoed over to stand next to the bed and eared the hammer back on his Colt. Then, he hesitated as the moonlight struck a pocket watch and some silver and a wallet on the bedside table off to the side, along with a holster and rig with a knife in a scabbard.

Hey, looky there, he thought. *The gent may have some real money in that wallet, an' that watch has got to be worth four or five dollars over in Pueblo. I'd better get it 'fore I shoot him 'cause afterwards I won't have time.*

He turned, letting his gun point away from Pearlie, and took a step toward the bedside table, reaching out with his left hand to grab the money and watch.

Pearlie's eyes finally opened at the metallic sound of a pistol being cocked, and in the moonlight he could see a tall, lanky man standing over him with a gun in his hand.

"Son of a bitch!" Pearlie croaked, but his throat was dry and he barely made a sound.

When the man heard him and whirled around,

Pearlie reached up and grabbed the pistol with both his hands, surprised at just how weak he felt.

Blackie jerked at his gun, trying to free it from the sick man's grasp, but as he did so he stumbled over his own feet and fell backward against the side table, dragging the half-awake Pearlie with him.

As they tumbled to the floor, Pearlie's holster and rig fell off the table and banged him in the head, causing stars to blossom and shine behind his eyelids. "Jesus," he grunted hoarsely, shaking his head to try and clear it, but only making himself more dizzy.

Blackie grunted, and Pearlie could feel the barrel of the Colt turning toward him and he was too weak to stop it. He knew with a sudden crystal clarity that he was going to be dead in a very few seconds if he didn't do something about it.

His eyes fell on the knife in his scabbard, lying next to him on the floor. As quick as a wink, Pearlie let go of the pistol with one hand and grabbed the hilt of the knife, jerking it out of its scabbard.

As Blackie grinned, his teeth glinted in the moonlight and the barrel turned the last few inches toward Pearlie's face. Pearlie could see in the man's eyes he intended to pull the trigger and put his lights out.

In a last spasm of what little strength he had left, Pearlie jabbed out and upward with the knife, gasping when it hit Blackie under the chin and cut his carotid artery.

A great spout of blood spurted out as Blackie grunted and his eyes opened wide in surprise. Then he moaned and gurgled as he choked on his own blood, dropping his gun and trying to staunch the pulsating flow with both hands to his neck. His eyes found Pearlie's and looked surprised and helpless as he fell over backward, dead as a stone.

Pearlie sleeved the blood out of his eyes and struggled to his feet. Suddenly, his head felt light and his vision darkened and he fell into a dark pool at his feet, unconscious again.

When an hour passed and Tolliver didn't hear a gunshot, he began to get worried. Hell, with my luck, he thought, Blackie's passed out next to the bed with the sick man in it. He shook his head, and was startled when a very alert Doc Bentley asked, "Something wrong, Buck? You look like you swallowed a frog or something."

Tolliver forced a smile and shook his head. He wasn't used to Doc being this observant in the evenings. By now he was usually well on his way to passing out for the night.

"Naw, I just gotta get to making my rounds 'fore it gets too late," he said, wondering what in the hell was keeping Blackie from finishing the pilgrim off like he told him to.

Doc Bentley covered a wide yawn with the back of his hand and he pulled out a pocket watch. "I guess you're right, Buck. Hell, it's getting late and I got a couple of teeth to pull in the morning."

Bentley and Tolliver got to their feet. "Uh, I'll just walk along with you to make sure you get home all right," Tolliver said, ignoring the look Bentley shot at him.

"All right, but I really don't need a chaperon, Buck," Bentley said irritably. "Since I ain't drunk any whiskey at all and only one beer all night, I think I can make it the two blocks to my house by myself."

Tolliver shrugged. "Well, I got to go that way anyhow, so I might as well walk along with you as by myself."

Bentley nodded. "So long as you don't think I need it," he said, irritated that he still craved a drink of whiskey and even more irritated that he was too cowardly to get one.

The street the saloon was on went right by Bentley's back door, and when the doc and Tolliver got there, Tolliver noticed the back door was ajar.

"Uh-oh," he said, putting out his arm to hold Bentley back as he drew his pistol. "Someone's left your back door open, Doc."

Bentley snorted. "Naw, the wind just probably blew it open. Nobody'd try and rob me. Hell, everyone knows I don't have a pot to piss in, Buck."

"Nevertheless," Tolliver said, earring back the hammer of his pistol. "Let me take a look around before you come in."

"Oh, all right," Bentley said irritably. He sat down on the rear steps and leaned back against the wall of the house. "Just don't take all night. I'm tired and I want to get in my bed."

Tolliver eased the back door open and slipped inside. He moved through the house, keeping his gun pointed out in front of him. When he was near the bedroom door, he called softly, "Blackie, you there?"

When he heard no response, he moved slowly into the bedroom, and gasped when he saw the two men lying on the floor in a spreading pool of blood.

"Jesus," he whispered to himself. He holstered his pistol and knelt next to Blackie, making sure to keep his boots out of the blood.

Blackie's eyes stared sightlessly up at Buck in silent accusation with Pearlie's knife still embedded in his throat, and Tolliver knew he was dead as yesterday's news. Damn, he thought, now he had two deaths of family members he could blame on Smoke Jensen.

"You dumb son of a bitch," he whispered, shaking

his head. "You couldn't even kill a man who was already half dead."

Tolliver looked over at Pearlie, and could see his chest moving slowly up and down as he breathed.

He stood up, trying to think of a way out of this mess. After a few moments, he grinned sourly. There was only one thing he could do to salvage this.

He moved quickly to the bureau by a sidewall and took out Pearlie's trousers. He pulled Pearlie up into the bed and slipped his pants on, pulling them up under the nightshirt and fastening the belt, making sure not to get any of the already clotted blood that covered the sleeping man on him.

Looking around to make sure he hadn't forgotten anything, he walked out into the kitchen and called for the doc to come on in.

"You find anybody hiding under the beds?" Bentley asked, grinning sleepily.

"You'd better take a look at this," Tolliver said, keeping his hand with his pistol in it by his side and leading the doc back into the bedroom.

When Bentley saw Blackie's body on the floor lying in a pool of blood, and Pearlie lying on the bed with his pants on and his nightshirt smeared with blood, he gasped, "What the hell is going on here?"

Tolliver slowly raised his pistol. "I'm sorry about this, Doc, but you just got in the wrong place at the wrong time."

"What do you mean?" Bentley asked, his eyes wide. "Why are you doing this?"

"To repay an old debt, Doc." Tolliver shrugged. "It's really nothing personal."

He slammed the pistol down on top of Bentley's head, watching as the man folded and fell to the floor as if he'd been poleaxed.

He quickly holstered his pistol and bent down and

pulled the doc's watch and money and wallet out of his pockets and stuffed them into Pearlie's pockets, along with his belongings from the bedside table. Then he picked up Pearlie's gun belt and holster and strapped them around Pearlie's waist, rolling the unconscious man back and forth to do it.

He grunted as he picked Pearlie up and slung him over his shoulder. Moving as quickly as he could, he took Pearlie out the back door and went about fifty yards down the alley, dumping him in a strand of high weeds in a vacant lot.

Hurrying back into Bentley's house, he pulled his pistol out and aimed it at Bentley's chest. Taking a deep breath and feeling really bad about what he had to do, he squeezed the trigger.

The gun exploded and blew a fist-sized hole in the doctor's chest, killing him immediately where he lay.

Tolliver holstered his gun and sprinted out the back door and down the alley toward where he had laid Pearlie in the weeds.

As he ran out of the door, he never noticed the elderly lady at the top of the stairs in Bentley's house, or the horrified expression on her face as she watched what he'd done.

Tolliver squatted down next to Pearlie in the weeds, and waited until a sizable crowd had gathered around the doc's house, and then he stood up and yelled, "Stop! You, there, stop!" He waited a moment and then he slapped Pearlie on the head with the barrel of his pistol, laying his scalp open and snapping his head back.

He stood up and yelled, "Help me! I've caught the thief over here!"

Moments later, when some townsmen came up to them, Tolliver was bending over with his hands on his knees breathing heavily.

"I got the son of a bitch who shot the doc," he said breathlessly.

"What happened?" one of the men asked as they stared down at Pearlie lying unconscious with his head leaking blood all down his face to pool in the sandy soil under him.

"Me an' my deputy, Blackie Johnson, heard the gunshot in the doc's house. When we ran inside to check it out, we found this hombre standing over the doc's body. 'Fore we could react, he knifed Blackie and ran out the back door."

"Why'd he shoot the doc?" the man asked.

Tolliver shrugged. "I dunno. I think the doc caught him trying to steal his money and they must've had a fight an' the doc lost." He reached down and pulled the bills and the doc's watch that he'd stashed there earlier out of Pearlie's pockets, and held them up for the men to see.

Tolliver glanced down at Pearlie. "Now, pick this rotten bastard up and carry him over to the jail, before I shoot him down like the mangy dog he is."

"What about Blackie, Buck?" one of the men asked, looking toward the doc's house.

Tolliver shook his head. "He ain't gonna make it, Sam. The knife cut his throat almost clean through and he was bleeding like a stuck pig and already dead on his feet when I went out the door after this son of a bitch."

While Tolliver and the townspeople were all out back, watching Pearlie being carried to the jail, Doc Bentley's aunt, Janet Rule, gathered her bags together and snuck out of his house by the front door and walked to the hotel. She'd come to visit her only nephew the week before, but Tolliver hadn't known about it because he was out of town hunting down prospectors to rob.

Janet rang the bell on the desk until a sleepy-eyed desk clerk came out and let her book a room. He was too sleepy to ask what a respectable woman like her was doing booking a room in the middle of the night.

He just handed her a key and turned and went back to his room to get some sleep. He didn't even look at the name she signed on the hotel register.

CHAPTER 12

The next morning, Sheriff Tolliver stepped out of his jail to find an angry crowd of citizens milling around in the street and on the boardwalk.

Trying to hide his grin at how things were playing out just as he'd planned, he held up his hands and tried to look authoritative and stern as he addressed the mob in a loud voice. "What's going on here?" he asked, though he knew full well what was happening.

George Orwell, the president of the bank and one of Payday's leading citizens, held up his right hand with a coiled rope in it. "We're here to see justice is done, Buck. That son of a bitch in there killed our doctor and one of your deputies. For that, he's going to hang!"

Tolliver puffed out his chest and hooked his thumbs in his belt. "Now, George. You know I can't let you do that, leastways not till there's been a trial."

Bubba Barkley, who was standing in the rear of the crowd, shouted out just as Tolliver had told him to the night before. "Hey, Buck, why don't you just go on over to the saloon and get yourself some breakfast. Me an' the good citizens here will watch your jail for you." He glanced at his friend, Hog Hogarth, who was standing next to him all bent over to one side, most of his weight still on his right foot from the injuries Smoke had inflicted on him the previous week.

When Tolliver and the others had asked how he

came to get hurt, Hog had told them a rattlesnake spooked his horse and he got thrown into some boulders. He was too ashamed to admit a man had kicked the shit out of him, and he'd sworn Bubba to silence with threats of a severe beating if he told anyone the truth. Thus, Bubba and Hog had no idea the very man their boss was going after was the one who'd beaten the crap out of Hog.

Tolliver grinned as several of the men in the crowd shouted their agreement with Bubba's plan for him to make himself scarce so they could get on with the hanging. He shook his head, trying to look regretful. "Sorry, boys. I know you'd be sure an' do a real good job of lookin' after my prisoner, but I done told you, he ain't gonna be hanged till we've had us a real trial."

"But Buck," Mayor Sam Hemmings said, "it'll take at least two or three weeks to get a circuit judge up here, and that's only if there's one in the county. Hell, it might even take longer if he's over on the other side of the mountains."

Tolliver nodded slowly, as if he was thinking about what could be done, though that too was in his plans all along. "That's true, Sam, but as mayor, you could call a special trial an' appoint some . . . uh . . . impartial citizens to be on the jury an' we could go on and get on with it right away."

"But who'd serve as judge?" Hemmings asked.

Tolliver scratched his jaw, and then he smiled broadly. "Say, didn't that feller, Joshua Banks, that just came into town a few weeks back from Denver to try his hand at prospecting on Culver Creek say he was a lawyer 'fore he decided to come out here?"

Orwell nodded rapidly. "That's right, Buck. He told me that when he took out a loan on his prospecting equipment."

Bubba snorted and said, "Couldn't have been too good a lawyer if'n he had to take out a loan to buy some picks and shovels."

This remark caused the crowd to break out in laughter, all except Tolliver, who scowled at his friend. "There's no need for that kind'a talk, Bubba," he said. "Especially when we're talkin' 'bout the town's new judge."

The crowd laughed again, until Sam Hemmings asked, "All right, Buck, now we got our judge. What about the defense attorney and the prosecutor?"

"Well, of course I'll do the prosecutin', since it's my job to keep law and order here in Payday, an' I suppose since you're 'bout the most fair-minded man I know, you can defend the murderin' scum, Mayor."

Hemmings frowned. "I don't know as that'd be right, Buck, since I don't exactly believe in this man's innocence. I don't know how good a job I'd be able to do."

Tolliver shrugged. "Makes no never mind to me, Mayor. If you don't want to do it, I guess we can wait two weeks or maybe a few months to get the circuit judge here an' do it all up nice and proper."

When Hemmings heard the crowd of citizens behind him, men who he'd be counting on for their votes in the next election, set up a roar of disapproval, he knew he had no choice. Not if he wanted to keep his job—which he did.

He turned to the crowd and held up his hands. "All right, friends," he said in his best campaign voice, "I'll do it. I'll take the job."

"Don't worry, Mayor," Bubba shouted from the rear of the crowd, trying to redeem himself with Tolliver. "It'll be a short trial and a quick hangin'."

Hemmings, who really was a fair-minded man, held up his hands again. "Now, folks, I really must protest this sort of talk. We got to remember the man hasn't been found guilty yet, so let's try to keep neutral until we've heard all the evidence. At least, that's the way things are going to be if you want me to be a part of this trial. Otherwise, like Buck said, we can wait for a few weeks or months for a circuit judge to come up here."

George Orwell held up his hands and addressed the crowd. "Now, folks, simmer down. You all know Sam is right, and I for one wouldn't want him to have to do anything that went against his grain, even if it did mean his getting reelected."

This last comment sent up a roar of laughter from the crowd and caused Hemmings's face to burn a bright red.

"How about setting the trial for tomorrow, Mayor, assuming we can send somebody out to Banks' claim and get him back here in time to preside?" Tolliver asked, trying to sound reasonable and yet ignoring the fact that this gave Hemmings almost no time to mount a credible defense.

Hemmings thought for a moment, and then he nodded reluctantly. "That should be enough time for me to confer with the accused, though it won't give me much time to—"

"So be it then," Tolliver said, interrupting Hemmings before he could plead for more time. He grinned, unable, now that he'd gotten what he wanted, to keep the smug look of satisfaction off his face. "We'll have the trial in the saloon tomorrow morning at eight o'clock."

As the crowd cheered, he held up a warning finger. "But there'll be no liquor nor beer served until after the guilty verdict is in."

When the crowd moaned in disappointment, Hemmings started to protest at the sheriff's choice of words, but he was drowned out by Tolliver adding, "And then we'll have time for a couple of quick rounds on the town before we all have to get back to work."

This earned another cheer from the crowd, causing Tolliver to marvel not for the first time at how easily men could be manipulated—and it seemed the more of them there were in a group, the easier the manipulation. In a mob, it was usually the man with the loudest voice who swayed them rather than the man with the best argument.

As the crowd began to disperse, Tolliver noticed Robert Jacobson, the man who ran the general store and also minded the town's telegraph office, standing on the periphery.

"Hey, Bobby," Tolliver called, raising his hand to get the man's attention, "hold up a minute."

"Looks like the town's gonna have a hanging before too long," Jacobson said after Tolliver made his way through the milling crowd to stand next to him. "Course, it's a real shame 'bout Doc gettin' killed and all."

Tolliver's grin faded when Jacobson failed to mention his cousin Blackie Johnson's death. "Yeah, shame about Blackie too, Bobby."

Jacobson's face flushed and he nodded when he realized his mistake. "Course it was, Buck. I didn't mean no disrespect. It's just that Blackie was. . . ." He hesitated, trying to figure out something to say that wouldn't set the sheriff off. People out West were sometimes peculiar about their relatives, no matter how dumb or no-account they were.

Tolliver rescued him by putting his hand on Jacobson's shoulder. "I know, Bobby. Blackie wasn't exactly the town's most respectable citizen." He sighed as Jacobson nodded. "Still and all, he was my cousin and he didn't deserve to have some asshole stranger put a knife in his gizzard."

"No, no of course not!" Jacobson hastily agreed, shuddering at the mental picture Tolliver's words evoked.

Tolliver walked alongside Jacobson as he moved toward the store. "You hear anything on your telegraph from those friends of his, Bobby?"

Jacobson's brow knit as he thought about it. "Yeah, but it was yesterday. Got a wire from Pueblo to the doc about how the man was doing. I ran it over to his office and he had me wire back the man was still unconscious."

"Did they wire back an answer?"

Jacobson scratched his head. "Seems I recollect the party in Pueblo wired back he'd be here within the week to see how his friend was doing, Sheriff."

Tolliver nodded. He was going to have to work fast if he wanted to have the trial over and done with by the time Jensen returned from Pueblo. Of course, he reasoned as he thanked Jacobson and ambled over toward his office, he didn't want things to move too fast. He certainly didn't want the man called Pearlie to have already been hanged when Jensen got here. No, sir. That would make things too easy on the gunman. Nope. Tolliver wanted Jensen to have to face his friend and tell him there was nothing he could do to prevent his being hanged—and to make it worse, Jensen would almost certainly believe Pearlie when he told him he didn't kill the doc.

Tolliver rubbed his hands together and grinned as he thought about how frustrated and anguished Jensen was going to be when faced with the imminent death of his good friend. Tolliver would, of course, have to make certain the hanging was scheduled soon enough that Jensen wouldn't have time to get to any U.S. marshals or the governor or anyone else who might put off the hanging long enough for a real trial. That was going to be the tricky part, but Tolliver was certain he was up to it.

He stopped grinning and stood in the middle of the street, unmindful of the wagons and horses having to change course and go around him, when he realized the only course of action open to Jensen would be to use his guns. What if the man went crazy and started shooting up the town? Maybe I'd better take some precautions in that matter, he thought.

He changed course and walked over to the mayor's office.

"Howdy, Buck," Mayor Sam Hemmings said when he entered the office. "What can I do for you?"

Tolliver hitched his hip on the corner of Hemmings's desk and crossed his arms. "I been thinking, Mayor," he began. "This here Pearlie feller was brought into town a few days back by some pretty tough-looking hombres. The boy at the livery even said they looked like him to be gunfighters or some such thing." He didn't tell the mayor that the doc had told him it was Smoke Jensen who was Pearlie's friend. The fewer people who knew that, the better it would be all around. Couldn't have anyone on the jury afraid to render a guilty verdict knowing that the famous gunfighter Smoke Jensen might resent their vote.

Hemmings leaned back in his chair and looked worried. "Are you saying this Pearlie man might also be a gunfighter, Buck?"

Tolliver nodded. "Yeah, but that's not what's got me worried, Sam. I'm more concerned about what's going to happen if his friends on the owl hoot trail hear he's about to be hung in some small town out in the middle of nowhere." Tolliver paused to let the mayor think about that for a moment.

"Just what do you suppose they might do, Sam?" he asked.

Hemmings took a deep breath and turned in his chair to look out his window. "You think they might try and tree the town?" he asked, worrying about what would happen to all of his friends in the town if a bunch of gunmen rode in with their six-shooters blazing.

Tolliver shrugged. "It's a thought."

Hemmings turned his chair back around to face the sheriff. "What do you think we ought to do about it?"

"How about if you give me permission to hire me a couple of deputies, men who are good with guns."

"What do you think that'll cost the town, Buck?" Hemmings asked.

"A whole lot less than burying half the town if a bunch of gunslicks come in here with murder and mayhem on their minds and try and break their friend out of jail."

Hemmings nodded, his face suddenly pale. "All right, Buck. I'll have to clear it with the other members of the town council, of course, but I'm sure they'll see it the same way we do. Who do you have in mind to hire?"

"Well, I haven't really thought about it yet," Tolliver lied, "But, I figure Jerry Hogarth and Bubba Barkley would be good choices, an' maybe even Jimmy Akins and Jeb Hardy."

"You really think you'll need four more men?"

"Sam, we got to guard that jail twenty-four hours a day. Just how many men do you think that'll take?" Tolliver sighed. "I could work double shifts, but if I'm gonna maybe be in a gunfight, I'd hate to be too tired to think or shoot straight if it came to it."

Hemmings nodded, his lips tight, thinking about what this was going to cost the town. "All right, Buck, but you make it clear to them that the job is just until the trial is over."

Tolliver grinned. "You mean until the trial and the hanging is over."

Hemmings held up his hand. "Now, Buck, I warned you about that. Since I'm gonna be defending this man, I want the trial to be on the up and up, and I'm not going to be planning any hanging until the verdict is in."

"All right, Sam," Tolliver said, laughing good-naturedly. "I won't start building a scaffold until the jury has spoken."

"By the way," Hemmings said, "When would be a good time for me to interview Pearlie? I need to get his side of the story if I'm going to be able to do a good job of defending him."

Tolliver pursed his lips. "Oh, any time is all right with me, Mayor. But remember, the man is a killer so it's probably pretty safe to assume he's a liar as well."

"Nevertheless, he deserves to get the chance to give his account of what happened that night," the mayor said, inwardly cursing the fate that had put him on the side of the most hated man in Payday.

CHAPTER 13

When Tolliver opened the jail door and let Hemmings into Pearlie's cell, the mayor sucked in a deep breath and turned with angry eyes on the sheriff.

"Why haven't you seen to this man's injuries, Buck?"

Tolliver glanced at Pearlie, who was lying half propped up against the wall in his cot with dried, crusted blood covering the right side of his head and face. His skin was pale and his eyes were unfocused, as if he didn't quite know where he was or how he'd gotten here.

"I ain't no doc, Mayor, an' in case you forgot, this bastard killed the only doctor we had in town. What'd you want me to do, drag Bentley's corpse over here and ask him if he'd clean the son of a bitch up?"

Hemmings shook his head; Tolliver was impossible. The mayor went to sit on the edge of Pearlie's bunk. He gently shook Pearlie's shoulder. "How are you feeling, young man?" he asked, his voice kind, but his eyes were probing deep within Pearlie's as if he could somehow tell if the man were a murderer or simply a cowboy who'd been in the wrong place and at the wrong time.

Pearlie's eyes focused and he seemed to come out of a trance. He looked at Hemmings and then at the sheriff. "What am I doing in jail?" he asked, his voice a hoarse croak. He winced when his movement caused one of the scabs on the side of his face to break open and fresh blood began to ooze out of the wound and run down his cheek. "And what happened to my head? It feels like I been hit with an ax handle."

Hemmings glanced over his shoulder at Tolliver. "Buck, bring us a pail of water and a dipper, and then I want you to go on over to the saloon and see if Hattie Monroe is up yet."

"What do you want Hattie for?" Tolliver asked, a leer on his face as if the mayor was going to provide prostitutes for the prisoner. "I really don't think the man is up to a roll in the hay this morning, Mayor."

Hemmings sighed, getting tired of Tolliver's smart mouth. "Hattie worked as a nurse at an army hospital back in the Civil War, Buck. I want her to take a look at this man's injuries and see if she can help him."

"How'd you know that about Hattie, Sam?" Tolliver asked. "You two good friends?"

Hemmings blushed a bright red. "We talked about it, Buck. Now, go and do what I asked, please."

Tolliver scowled and backed out of the cell. "All right, but I'm gonna have to lock you in while I'm gone, Sam. Wouldn't want the prisoner to try and escape."

Hemmings looked at Tolliver like he was crazy. "Escape? Why, the man can barely talk, let alone overpower me and run off into the mountains on foot and escape. Don't be a fool, Buck."

Tolliver blushed and scowled deeper and slammed the cell door anyway, locking it with a loud metallic click.

Hattie took one look at Pearlie and went into the sheriff's office and put some water on the Franklin stove to boil. "I'm gonna need some clean cloths, some alcohol—the rubbing kind not the drinkin' kind—and a needle and thread," she told Hemmings and Tolliver.

"What do you think is wrong with him?" Hemmings asked.

"For one thing," she said, looking at Tolliver with anger in her eyes, "he got hit pretty good by the sheriff here, and that was on top of just recovering from what I've been told was a couple of pretty nasty snakebites. And if that's not enough for you," she said, looking back at Hemmings now, "he's got a gash in his scalp that's gonna need to be sewn up, and I can only guess if his brains is scrambled or not."

When she'd finished, she began to dig in a small black valise like doctors carry. When Tolliver had gone to her at the saloon and told her they needed some nursing done, she'd brought her bag with her—the same one she'd carried in the Civil War when she'd treated hundreds of men in the field.

"Is he gonna be able to stand trial?" Tolliver asked, worried that any delay might put a crimp in his plans for vengeance on Smoke Jensen.

"He will be if you two get outta here an' get me what I asked for an' let me get to work fixin' him up," she said with hands on her ample hips.

Half an hour later, after she'd shooed the mayor and sheriff out of the cell and had cleansed the dried blood and dirt out of his head wound, Hattie bent over Pearlie with needle and thread in hand.

"I'm sorry, mister, but I can't give you no alcohol to numb the pain, not with a head injury like you got."

"Pearlie," he croaked up at her from where he lay on the cot.

"What?" she asked, leaning back with eyebrows raised.

"Pearlie. My name's Pearlie, miss."

She clucked. "My, aren't you the polite one, tryin' to be a gentleman after all you've been through."

Pearlie gave her a lopsided grin, wincing again when the movement caused his wound to open. "My mother always told me being polite didn't depend on the circumstances, it was just something you did or you didn't do, and she preferred me to do it all the time." He paused, and added, "An' I think I still got the back-strap bruises on my hide from when I forgot what she told me."

"Well," Hattie said, pleased but trying hard not to show it, "this ain't no social date, Pearlie, so you just lie back and grit your teeth, 'cause this is gonna smart a mite."

"Just a minute, miss," Pearlie said. He rolled on his side and reached down and unbuckled his belt, causing Hattie to raise her eyebrows. Pearlie just smiled wanly as he pulled his belt out and folded it over. "This is something Smoke Jensen taught me once when he had to remove a bullet from my carcass." And then he stuck the leather between his teeth and clamped down on it. His eyes closed as he laid his head back and nodded, signaling he was ready for her to begin.

"Well, I swan," she muttered under her breath, wondering how a man as brave and resourceful as this one could have done the awful things they were accusing him of. I guess one never knows, she thought as she leaned forward and began to sew Pearlie's wound shut. Of course, him knowing Smoke Jensen well enough to speak of him might just explain it. Hattie had been working in a saloon in a small town on the southern border of Colorado Territory some years back when Jensen had walked in and stood in the doorway, his hands at his side, his eyes roving back and forth around the room like he was searching for someone.

After a minute, he'd called out, "I'm looking for the three men who just rode into town about five minutes ago. Their horses are outside and I know they came in here."

When no one spoke up, Hattie saw him turn his eyes to her. She was standing off to one side of the room, next to a table with one of her regulars sitting at it. When she saw his eyes on her, she involuntarily looked at the three men standing at the bar who'd just burst in through the batwings like their tails were on fire.

Jensen smiled, and it changed his whole face. Suddenly he wasn't a fearsome gunfighter, but one of the most handsome and masculine men she'd ever seen.

His smile faded when he turned his body slightly to face the men at the bar and called out, "What kind of low-life, mother-grubbing bastards attack a woman living alone outside of town and shoot her and her two kids just to rob a few dollars she had hidden in her kitchen?"

One of the men blushed a bright scarlet and blurted out, "She didn't need no money livin' out there with her kids like that an' we did. If she would've given it to us nice-like, we wouldn't have had to shoot her kids to get her to tell us where it was."

Smoke's face turned as hard as granite, and Hattie had never seen anyone look so mean and dangerous.

"You'd better fill your hands, gents, or I'm going to come over there and beat you to death with my bare hands!" he growled.

All three men put their drinks down, turned to face Smoke, and went for their pistols.

In a shorter time than it takes to tell it, both

Smoke's hands were filled with iron and he was blazing away before any of the men even cleared leather.

The smoke and cordite billowing through the room made Hattie's eyes burn and water, but a few minutes later, she saw the three men sprawled out on the wooden floor, covered with blood and dead as stones.

Smoke holstered his pistols and addressed the crowd in the saloon. "There's a lady in a cabin about five miles south of town who's been wounded pretty badly. Her two children are dead, but she may make it if someone will go out there and tend to her wounds." He paused and looked down at the dead men. "When I found her, she told me these men did it after she was kind enough to offer them water for their horses and a fresh-cooked meal." He shrugged. "It's your town, do what you want."

After he'd left, Hattie had taken this same medical kit she was using now on one of Smoke Jensen's friends and gone out to tend to the Widow McKay. After that, whenever she saw something in a newspaper or magazine about Smoke Jensen, she'd taken the trouble to read it. She'd found he'd killed a lot of men, but she'd never read once that anyone he'd killed hadn't provoked it or deserved it.

Later, after she'd finished sewing up Pearlie's head and done the best she could with his other wounds, she stuck her head into Tolliver's office and called out, "I'm done in here, Mayor Hemmings." She pointedly didn't speak to Tolliver or acknowledge his presence. There was something about the man she just couldn't stand—even before she'd seen how he treated his prisoners, she'd always felt there was something wrong about him, something evil.

Hemmings got up from his chair in front of Tolliver's desk and walked back into the room holding Pearlie's cell. As he paused to thank Hattie, she whispered, "I hear you're going to be defending him in court." She paused and blushed a mite as she added, "He sure don't seem like a man capable of cold-blooded murder, Mayor."

Hemmings's eyes narrowed. "What do you mean, Hattie?" he asked.

Her blush deepened and spread all the way down to her bosom, and she dropped her gaze. "Over the past few years, working in saloons like I have been doing, Mayor, I've gotten so I can read men pretty good." She looked up at him to see if he understood what she was saying. "You have to learn that in my profession or you can get pretty badly hurt."

Hemmings nodded. He knew what she meant. Though most men out West treated women with respect and kindness, men full of liquor in the presence of a prostitute often acted like swine, or worse.

"Anyway," Hattie went on, "that man in there has a gentle soul, and he is a gentleman. I think he could kill, if he thought the person he was up against deserved it or he was pushed into it, but I don't for a minute believe he'd kill someone like Dr. Bentley, who'd helped him out, for a few dollars and a gold watch."

"But Hattie," Hemmings said, glancing over his shoulder to make sure Tolliver wasn't nearby, "the sheriff said he saw him do it."

Hattie sneered, following Hemmings's glance toward the door to Tolliver's office. "Oh, and you think Buck Tolliver is so high-and-mighty he ain't never lied?" she asked.

When Hemmings didn't answer, she leaned close and whispered in his ear, "You come see me, Sam, where we can talk private-like, an' I'll tell you some things about Buck that'll curl your toes."

She jerked back, her eyes wide with fright, when Tolliver strolled through the door and eyed her suspiciously. "You 'bout done in her, Hattie?" he asked, moving a toothpick around in his thick lips. "'Cause if you are, I'm sure they have need of you over to the saloon."

Without looking at Hemmings again, Hattie ducked her head and moved past Tolliver, shrugging to the side as she passed him in the doorway so their bodies wouldn't touch.

After she'd left, Tolliver snorted. "Whores," he said derisively. "If it wasn't for what they carry between their legs, there'd be a hunting season on 'em."

Disgusted by Tolliver's crudity, Hemmings walked down the hall to Pearlie's cell. When he opened the door, he looked over his shoulder at Tolliver. "I need to talk to this man alone, Sheriff."

Tolliver looked dubious. "I don't know, Mayor. He might be dangerous now that Hattie's fixed him up and he's feeling better."

Hemmings sneered, "I think I can handle a man who's had his head half-caved in and can barely sit up in bed, Buck."

"All right, Sam, don't get your dander up," Tolliver said defensively.

"And you might see about rustling up some grub and water for the prisoner, Buck, 'less you're planning on starving him to death before the trial."

Tolliver just shook his head as he turned and walked down the corridor toward his office, thinking they'd be wanting him to get lace curtains for the bastard's cell next.

* * *

Hemmings looked around the cell, and since there

was no other place to sit, he eased down on the edge of Pearlie's bunk bed down by his feet.

"Now, Pearlie," he began, "there are some things you need to know. Dr. Bentley and another man named Blackie Johnson were killed the other night at the doc's house. The sheriff says he saw you standing over the doctor's dead body and when he and Blackie walked in, you stabbed Blackie and hightailed it out and back down the alley until the sheriff ran you down and knocked you out." Hemmings hesitated, noticing the blank look on Pearlie's face, as if he were hearing this for the first time. "I need you to tell me what you say happened that night."

Pearlie winced at the sudden pain as he turned his head to look up at Hemmings. "You mean when I caught that man going through my things?" he asked.

Hemmings's brow knit in surprise. "You mean Dr. Bentley was going through your things?"

Pearlie shrugged. "I don't know any Dr. Bentley. The last thing I remember 'fore waking up to find a tall man with booze on his breath riflin' my things was being bitten by a snake up in the mountains."

Hemmings realized that was the truth, that Pearlie would have no way of knowing the doc had been taking care of him since he'd been unconscious the entire time. Maybe he'd woken up like he said, found himself in a strange house, and decided to steal himself some money and a watch. When the doc woke up and caught him at it, he must've killed him without knowing who he was.

"So," Hemmings said after working this out in his mind, "your story is when you found this man in your room, you shot him to keep him from stealing your things?"

Pearlie shook his head, wincing again when the movement brought on a stabbing jolt of pain. "No,

I didn't shoot no one," he said, putting his hand up to the side of his head. "The hombre pointed his gun at me an' I grabbed it. We struggled and fell on the floor. I was able to get my knife outta my gun belt and stab the son of a bitch just 'fore he could shoot me in the head. Last I remember, he was lying next to my bed with blood everywhere, and then I must've passed out. When I come to, I was lying right here where you see me an' a nice lady was fixin' to sew my head back together."

"But that doesn't make any sense, young man," Hemmings protested. "The doc was shot and *then* Blackie Johnson was stabbed."

Pearlie frowned. "I done told you, mister, I didn't shoot nobody, an' I sure as hell didn't hear no gunshot before I woke up."

He closed his eyes and tried to remember all he could about that night. After a moment, he opened them and said, "The man I stabbed had the beginnings of a beard, like he hadn't shaved in a few days, an' he stunk of sweat like he hadn't bathed in a month, an' he smelled of alcohol like he'd been drinkin' a lot that night." Pearlie grinned. "Funny how 'bout all I remember 'bout him is the godawful stench on him." Pearlie paused and laid his head back, exhausted. "Now, that's all I can tell you, 'cept to say again, I didn't shoot nobody. I done the stabbin', but it 'twas in self-defense. I could see it in his eyes, Mr. Hemmings, that man meant to kill me as sure as I'm laying here in this here jail."

Hemmings told Pearlie to get some sleep and that the sheriff should be back in a while with some food.

Pearlie had grinned. "You know, Mr. Hemmings," he said looking around at the cell and the bars on the windows, "for 'bout the first time in my life I can honestly say I ain't a bit hungry."

Hemmings smiled and told him he had to eat to get his strength back so he could heal, and then the mayor went into Buck's office, sat at Buck's desk, and pulled his tobacco pouch out of his pocket and built himself a cigarette. After he lighted it, he sat there smoking and thinking about Pearlie's story. It didn't make any sense according to what Tolliver had said. He'd said that Pearlie shot the doc and then stabbed Blackie when they ran into the house.

He shook his head. It just didn't add up, unless maybe Pearlie had blacked out and shot the doc and not been able to remember it. Hemmings knew men who'd drunk until they passed out and then didn't remember a thing they'd done the night before.

But, he thought, if that were so, how come he could remember killing Blackie so clearly? Nope, it just didn't make sense. Someone was lying about what had happened that night. But if Pearlie was telling the truth, that meant it must have been the sheriff that killed the doc, and what possible reason could Tolliver have to kill Dr. Bentley, and why would Blackie have been going through Pearlie's belongings? Blackie was dumb as a stump, but he'd never been known to be a thief as far as Hemmings knew.

Damn, he thought, how did I ever get mixed up in this mess? He grinned ruefully to himself as he inhaled a lungful of acrid smoke. Maybe being mayor in Payday isn't worth all this grief after all. But then he smiled and shook his head. "Yep, I guess it is," he muttered, struck with that most powerful urge among politicians, the urge to stay in office as long as possible.

CHAPTER 14

Janet Rule eased down the stairs in the hotel, going slowly and making sure that she didn't see any sign of the sheriff looking for her.

Maybe she'd get lucky and be able to get out of town before he realized she'd been staying with her nephew. She knew she didn't have long before some busybody told him she'd been there, so she had to make tracks. She knew she didn't dare go back home to her house in Pueblo, because once Tolliver realized she'd been in the house that night and might have seen him, he'd either come for her or send someone to Pueblo to make sure she wasn't able to testify against him.

She didn't understand why someone would want to kill her nephew. He was such a kind man who only cared about helping people. Sure, he'd had his trouble with the bottle, but in the last couple of days of his life he'd seemed to be getting that under control. What a shame, to be cut down in the prime of life like that for no good reason that she could think of.

In her seventies, she knew she could never ride a horse all the way to some other town, and the thought of trying to drive a buckboard or surrey that far didn't appeal to her either. And, if she tried to buy a ticket on the next train, the stationmaster would be sure to remember her if Tolliver came asking, which he was sure to do once he found out she'd been Hezekiah's houseguest at the time he killed him.

At the foot of the stairs, she glanced around and, seeing no one who seemed overly interested in her movements, she slipped into the dining room. It was still very early and the place was almost deserted except for her and a young boy in his teens who was mopping the floors.

That's it, she thought. She sat at a table near where he was working and opened her purse, extracting a handful of bills. When she got a chance, she motioned him over to her.

"Yes, ma'am?" he asked. "The waitress is out back helping the cook with the mornin's biscuits. She'll be here in a few minutes."

"Young man," Janet said, "how would you like to make five dollars?"

The boy's eyes opened wide. Five dollars was more than he made in two weeks sweeping out the place. "Yes, ma'am!" he said, wondering just what it was he was going to have to do to earn so much money.

Janet handed him the bills and said, "Take this money on over to the train station and buy me a ticket on the next train out."

"Uh, where do you want to go?" the boy asked as he took the money and stuffed it in his jeans pocket.

"It doesn't matter," she said, lowering her voice, "just get me a seat on the very next train leaving, but you've got to do it without raising any suspicions or getting the attention of the stationmaster."

The boy looked around to make sure no one was near enough to hear him, and then he leaned down and whispered back at her, "Are you in trouble, ma'am?"

Janet thought furiously for a moment, and then she took out her hanky and wiped at her eyes as if she'd been crying. "Yes, son. There's a man who is threatening to hurt me because I owe him some money. If I don't get out of town fast and without anyone knowing where I've gone, I'm afraid he's going to beat me."

The boy looked horrified that anyone would pick on a nice old lady like this. Heck, she reminded him of his own granny. "You can count on me, ma'am. I'll run right over there and get your ticket for you."

"Thank you, sonny. Thank you so much," Janet said, patting his arm in a grandmotherly way.

After he'd left, Janet raised her hand to signal the waitress that she was ready to order. "I'll just have a cup of tea and perhaps a biscuit and a little gravy if you don't mind," she said.

After the waitress left, the table next to Janet filled with what appeared to be local businessmen.

Without meaning to, Janet overheard them talking excitedly about the upcoming trial of the man the sheriff said had killed Dr. Bentley and Blackie Johnson.

"That blackguard," she muttered to herself. "He's going to try and hang some poor innocent for what he did." She began to shake her head back and forth. "That just won't do—it won't do at all!"

"What did you say, dear?" the waitress asked, having heard the old lady muttering to herself.

"Oh, nothing," Janet said, picking up her biscuit and slathering gravy on it. "Nothing at all."

Smoke and Cal were just finishing loading up the last of the Palouse studs into a railroad stock car when Smoke heard a man laughing behind him.

He shut the loading gate, dusted his gloved hands off, and turned to see what was so funny. Four men were leaning on the stockyard fence, their arms crossed on the top rail as they watched Smoke and Cal work.

Smoke nodded and touched the brim of his hat. "Howdy, gents," he said amiably, thinking it was about time for some coffee.

One of the men, who had a face that had seen lots of wear and tear, sneered and inclined his head toward the stock car. "What you boys gonna do with them there Injun ponies? Try and join a tribe?" He threw back his head and laughed heartily at his own lame joke.

Before Smoke could answer, he snorted and added, "Maybe you two ought'a grind 'em up an' feed 'em to your dogs, 'cause that's all that Injun hosses are good for."

As he and his cronies laughed at this bit of wit, Smoke's lips got tight. He ambled over to stand in front of the men and said in a good-natured tone of voice, "You seem to have an awfully big mouth, mister." When the men all stopped laughing and stared at Smoke as if he were crazy to speak like that to the man, who was a little under six feet tall and weighed well over two hundred pounds, Smoke added, "Care to put your money where your big mouth is?"

The man bristled as one of his friends said, "You gonna let him talk to you like that, Axel?"

Axel's eyes narrowed. "Whatta you mean about my money, mister?"

Smoke glanced over at his and Cal's Palouse horses where they were tied up at a hitching rail near the entrance to the stockyard. He'd sent the horse he rode up onto the cattle car and was now riding the one called Storm. "My friend and I are both riding those 'Injun' ponies as you called them. I'm willing to bet any amount of money you want to wager that either one of our horses can beat any horse you bring in a race—short or long, it doesn't matter."

Axel glanced at the Palouse studs Smoke had indicated. Both were sleek and well muscled and both just stared back at the man.

"You say I can bring any hoss an' you'll bet on the race without even seein' him run?"

Smoke nodded. "That's right, Axel," Smoke said sarcastically, "unless you were just speaking out of your hat a while ago and want to admit to these friends of yours that you don't know shit about horses or that you're just too cowardly to bet on your judgment of horseflesh."

Smoke watched the big man's muscles bunch under the skintight shirt he wore as his mouth opened and closed twice without him being able to think of any suitable retort. "It's your call, Axel," Smoke continued, grinning widely. "Put up or shut up."

"How about I just kick your ass all around this here stockyard instead?" Axel asked, sticking out his chest as if he might frighten Smoke with his size.

Smoke shrugged. "You're even stupider than you look, Axel, and that's going a ways," Smoke said. "I was hoping to earn some money from you, but if you want to dance around a little and get those stubs you call teeth knocked out, it's fine with me."

Cal glanced at Smoke. He knew the mountain man didn't usually respond to ignorant people like Axel, but he guessed Smoke was in a foul mood because he was worried about Pearlie.

Cal shook his head and whispered in a loud manner to Axel's friends, "You better tell your friend there to just shut up and go on about his business while he can still eat solid food. Otherwise, in about ten minutes he's gonna be drinkin' his food for the next few weeks."

The man next to Axel laughed. "Your friend said he wanted to make some money . . . how about you, kid?"

Cal grinned. "Sure, I can always use some extra. What did you have in mind?"

The man pulled a crumpled-up wad of bills from his jeans pocket and counted them slowly. "I got eight dollars here says Axel cleans your friend's plow and doesn't even break a sweat doing it."

The other two men quickly reached into their pockets and pulled out money also. After conferring among themselves for a moment, the first man held up a handful of greenbacks. "All told we got thirty-three dollars here. You can bet it all or any part."

"Oh, I'll definitely take it all," Cal said. He reached into his pocket and brought out his wallet. After a minute, he blushed and glanced at Smoke, who grinned and handed Cal a wad of money so thick it made the other men's eyes widen in surprise.

Cal peeled off thirty-two one-dollar bills, added one of his own, and handed them to the man. "That'll cover your bet," he said, and climbed up on the fence railing to watch.

Axel pulled a soiled pair of gloves out of his rear pocket and slipped them on as he climbed up and over the fence, grinning at Smoke as if he were going to eat him for breakfast in the next few minutes.

Smoke pulled his own gloves tight and tilted his head as he looked at Axel's scarred eyebrows, cauliflower ears, and bent and misshapen nose. "I usually try not to mess up my opponent's faces when I fight, out of courtesy," Smoke said easily as he and Axel walked in small circles around each other, sizing each other up. "But I can see from yours that you like to fight, and that you usually lead with your nose, so I guess I don't have to worry overly much about what you're going to look like when we're done."

"All you got to worry about, stranger, is who's gonna pick up your pieces when I'm through with you," Axel growled, and he quickly stepped forward and swung a haymaker right cross at Smoke's jaw, obviously hoping to catch the mountain man unawares and end the fight quickly.

Smoke barely leaned his head back and let Axel's fist breeze by, missing his chin by inches.

While Axel was off balance and leaning forward, Smoke reached out and slapped him with an open palm, back and forth, snapping Axel's face to and fro but not hurting him, only his pride.

"This is going to be easier than I thought," Smoke said, grinning widely as Axel's face reddened with fury and embarrassment at the way Smoke had slapped him like a girl.

"You're not only dumber than a post, you can't fight either," Smoke said as he shifted slowly from one foot to the other, keeping his balance.

Axel yelled incoherently at the insults, lowered his head and spread his arms and rushed at Smoke, intending to get him in a bear hug and break his spine.

Smoke danced lightly to the side, stuck out his foot, and tripped the big man, tapping him smartly on the back of the head as he sprawled on his face.

Cal grinned at Axel's friends. "Any more bets, gentlemen?" Cal taunted. "I'm now giving two-to-one odds."

He was met with stunned silence, as Axel's friends watched a man who'd beaten up any and all challengers in Pueblo get his clock wound.

Axel screamed and jumped to his feet, whirling around with his fists up. Smoke danced forward and shot out three lightning-fast jabs with his left hand, smashing Axel's nose and snapping his head back.

When Axel's eyes clouded and went unfocused,

Smoke decided to take mercy on him and end it quickly. He twisted his shoulders to the right, and then swung his right hand with all of his might in a mighty uppercut that hit Axel just under the sternum, lifting him off his feet and sending him sprawling backward to land spread-eagled on the dirt, vomit erupting from his bloody mouth.

Smoke rolled him over with the toe of his boot so he wouldn't drown in his own vomit, and then he turned to the men still hanging on the fence. "I believe you're holding our bet money," he said, not even breathing heavily and definitely not sweating.

One of the men jumped down from the fence and grabbed at the six-gun hanging on his hip. Before he could clear leather, Cal drew and backhanded him in the face with his pistol, sending shattered teeth flying and splitting his lips and knocking the man out cold.

Smoke just shook his head. "When will men like you learn it's always easier to just pay your debts than to get stupid and maybe dead?" He cut his eyes at the other men and let his right hand rest on the butt of his pistol, an ominous warning that he would tolerate no further nonsense.

"Here, mister," the man holding the money said in a quavering voice, glancing at his friend's bloody and battered face and at Axel lying motionless on the ground, snoring softly through his ruined nose.

Smoke handed Cal the money and Cal casually stuck it in his pocket. "You ready to hit the trail, Smoke?" he asked.

Smoke smiled and held out his hand. "Sure, as soon as you give me back the money I gave you to cover your bet."

"Oh, yeah," Cal said, grinning as he counted off thirty-two bills and handed them to Smoke. "I almost forgot."

"Uh-huh," Smoke said, taking the money and walking off with his arm around Cal's shoulders. "I was born at night, Cal, but not last night," Smoke said, laughing, "and I didn't come into town on a turnip wagon neither."

CHAPTER 15

Robert Jacobson knocked twice and then walked into Sheriff Tolliver's office. "Hey, Buck," he said, stopping short when he saw that Tolliver was deep in conversation with some other men.

Tolliver looked up, annoyance written on his face. "Yeah, Bobby? What is it?"

Jacobson looked pointedly at the other men and cleared his throat. "Uh," he said hesitantly, holding up a yellow piece of paper, "I got another wire from that fellow we were talking about the other day."

Tolliver glanced at Hog Hogarth, Bubba Barkley, Kid Akins, and Jeb Hardy, who were all sitting around his desk. "Oh, don't worry about these men, Bobby. They know all about how I'm looking into that matter."

Relieved, Jacobson handed the sheriff the wire, even though it was addressed to Doc Bentley and wasn't supposed to be given to anyone else, according to the rules of the telegraph company. Jacobson told himself it was all right since the Doc was dead and the sheriff was in charge of prosecuting the man who killed him. "Here it is, Buck. Man said he was leaving Pueblo and headin' this way immediately and for Doc to do whatever he could to keep his friend alive until he got here."

Tolliver smiled sourly. Jensen sounded very concerned about the man named Pearlie. That was good. It meant Pearlie was more than just a casual friend or riding partner—it was almost as if he was family. Having Smoke care deeply about the man would suit Tolliver's plans nicely.

Tolliver looked up. "Did the wire say if the man who sent it was waiting for a reply?"

"Uh, yeah. Now that you mention it, he is."

"Good. Just send back that nothing has changed and the man is still unconscious . . . and sign the doc's name."

Jacobson's brow wrinkled and he began to sweat as he looked around at the other men present. Ordinarily, it wouldn't bother him overly much to go against the rules of the company, especially for a good cause, but there were far too many witnesses here for comfort. If any one of them talked and the company found out about it, Jackson knew he'd be fired immediately. "Well, now, Buck. I can't hardly do that. It's not only against the law, it's against the rules of the company I work for. I could get fired if they find out," he finished lamely, his voice rising in pitch until it was an irritating whine.

Buck got to his feet and reached into his pocket and pulled out a five-dollar bill. He folded it over into a small square and stuck it in Jacobson's shirt pocket. He patted his chest, none too lightly. "And you could get a lot worse than fired if you don't do what I tell you too, Bobby. You understand me?" Tolliver asked, his voice harsh and hard. "This here is a murder investigation, and I expect my orders to be carried out to the letter, and without question. Is there anything about that you do not understand?"

"Sure, Buck, sure. I didn't mean nothin' by it. I'll go and get that wire right off," Jackson said hurriedly, his eyes no longer on the men at the table but on Tolliver, as if he expected the man to reach out and slap him.

"Good, 'cause I wouldn't want Mr. Smoke Jensen to have to wait on word of what's going on with his dear friend," Tolliver said gruffly.

After Jacobson left, Tolliver went back to his desk and sat down, leaning back and putting his feet up on the corner and his hands behind his head. The trial was supposed to start the next day, and it was at least a three-day ride to Payday from Pueblo, if you pushed it.

Hog Hogarth's eyes opened wide and he coughed as if he were choking on something he ate that didn't go down right. "Uh, Buck. You say that galoot that brought that snakebit man into town is Smoke Jensen? Smoke Jensen the famous gunfighter that's killed over two hundred men?"

"That's right, Hog," Tolliver said, realizing this was the first time he'd told his men who they were going to be going up against. "Why? Does it matter to you one way or the other?"

Hog sat back in his seat, his left hand going unconsciously to the sore ribs and flank that still ached from where he'd been beaten. "Uh, not really, Buck."

Bubba shook his head. "The hell it doesn't," he exclaimed. He looked at Hog and said regretfully, "I got to tell him now, Hog, considering who it is we went up against."

"Tell me what?" Tolliver said irritably.

"You remember when Hog an' me came in from being out on the trail and Hog was all crippled up?" Bubba asked, leaning forward in his excitement.

"Yeah, you said he fell off his horse," Tolliver answered.

"Well, that weren't actually the entire truth of the matter," Bubba continued, ignoring the angry look Hog was giving him. "In point of fact, Hog and me braced the two men bringing that sick man into town. Words were said and Hog got into a fistfight with the big man wearing buckskins, the man you now tell us was Smoke Jensen."

Tolliver's eyebrows rose. "You mean to tell me Smoke Jensen beat the shit outta Hog and it was a fair fight? Jensen didn't cheat or anything?"

Bubba shook his head and Hog let his gaze drop to the table, ashamed of everyone finding out he'd been beaten in a fair fight. "Hell, no, Buck. That Jensen is one mean son of a bitch."

"But he's older than dirt," Tolliver said. "Hell, he must be pushing forty-five or fifty."

"I don't give a shit if he's a hundred and fifty, the man is built like an ox and fights like a grizzly bear," Bubba said, rolling his eyes around to make sure the others were listening. "And I for one don't have any intention of ever tangling with that man, leastways not in a fair fight."

Jeb Hardy took a cigar out of his jacket pocket, licked the length of it, and then he put it in his mouth and chewed on it without lighting it. His cold, hard eyes fixed on Tolliver. "How long you gonna let this Jensen thing distract you, Buck? Every day you sit around here messing around with this Pearlie character trying to get to Jensen, we're losing money."

Tolliver stared back. "I'm gonna do whatever it takes to first make Jensen's life a living hell, Jeb, an' then I'm gonna kill him." He paused, his face going flat. "And if you don't like it, there ain't nothing you can do about it."

Hardy's eyes flashed and he straightened in his chair. His right hand automatically pulling back the right edge of his jacket to expose his Peacemaker Colt hanging on his hip. "Oh, you don't think so?" he growled.

Tolliver felt a stab of fear course though his chest and he thought his heart skipped a beat. Hardy was the fastest man with a gun he'd ever seen, and he certainly wasn't afraid to use it, having killed at least fifteen men that Tolliver knew about, and no telling how many others he didn't know about.

He let his feet drop to the floor and he sat up straight, his hands out toward Hardy. "Now, Jeb, don't get your dander up," Tolliver said reasonably. "You know I've got a heavy score to settle with Jensen, and I've been waiting plumb near all my life to do it."

The rigidity went out of Hardy's shoulders and he seemed to relax. "That's so, Buck, but it don't give you call to talk to me like some hired hand neither."

"No offense meant, Jeb. We been friends too long to let something like this come between us."

"Hell with friendship," Hardy said, but his lips were grinning. "I'm talkin' about business and when we're gonna get back down to it."

Tolliver took a deep breath, relieved that the tension was over. "Well, the trial starts tomorrow and it shouldn't last more'n a day . . . two at the most. Jensen should get here about three days from now, about when I'm ready to hang his friend. I might let him stew for another day, and then I'm gonna hang his friend right in front of him and kill him right after that."

Kid Akins snorted. He'd seen Buck draw, and while he was faster than the average man, he was no match for him, or for Jeb Hardy for that matter. "You sure you gonna be able to take Jensen, Buck?" he asked, smiling to show Buck there was no malice nor disrespect in his question.

Tolliver pursed his lips. "Hell, I reckon I can. Jensen was full growed when he shot my brother, an' that was more'n twenty years ago. I'd guess he must be close to forty-five by now, and years piled up on a man who's lived as rough a life as Jensen will tend to make him a mite slower than he was when he was young and full of piss and vinegar."

Akins laughed again and inclined his head toward Hog. "From what I seen that old man do to Hog with his bare hands, Buck, I wouldn't be too sure about him slowing down a whole hell of a lot."

"I don't know either, Buck," Hardy said, shaking his head. "From what I hear when I talk to some of my friends from back when I used to hire my gun out, even though Jensen is retired, word is he is still pretty damn fast." He stared at Tolliver through his cigar smoke. "Hell, I heard tell he killed a whole passel of men up in Canada a year or so back, and that don't sound like the work of a slow, old man to me."

"Well," Tolliver said, his face dark and flushed from what he was hearing, "if Jensen kills me, I guess I'm just gonna have to depend on my friends here around this table to take him out for me."

Hardy glanced at the others and gave a half smile. "Now, why would we risk going up again a man as fast as Jensen just to avenge your death, Buck? It sure as hell wouldn't bring you back to life, now would it?"

Tolliver mulled this over for a minute, and then he took pen and paper out of his desk. He bent over and spent another couple of minutes writing, and then he held up the paper for all the men to see. "Here's a good reason, Jeb. I've just written out my will leaving all of my assets to the man who kills Smoke Jensen, and I guess you all know that I've managed to put away quite a nice bundle over the past few years we've been stealing claims."

Hog Hogarth's eyes narrowed. "Just how much we talkin' 'bout, Buck?" he asked. "Not that I think Jensen is gonna kill you nor nothin', but just in case I happen to go up against him again, I'd kind'a like to know what I'm gonna gain by killing the bastard."

"I'd guess what with the land and gold claims and all, it'd be close to a half-a-million dollars, Hog. And it'll all go to the man who plants Smoke Jensen in the ground."

"You know, of course, a will like that ain't exactly legal, Buck," Hardy said.

"Oh, I'll have my lawyer in Pueblo write it up all nice and legal-like, and since he'll be the executor of my will, he'll know exactly what I want him to do."

Hardy smiled slow and easy, but his eyes stayed as dark as a snake's eyes. "I could write that will up for you, Buck, seeing as how I've still got my license to practice law."

Tolliver grinned. "No offense, Jeb, but I'd just as soon not everyone know about what I got stashed away and where, leastways not while I'm still alive."

"Well, not to wish anyone bad luck, Buck, I will say that if Jensen does somehow get the best of you, I will take the son of a bitch down myself."

Kid Akins laughed. "You'll have to stand in line for that kind of money, Jeb ol' son."

"The hell with shooting him," Hog said, holding up two hands as big as hams. "I'll just wring the bastard's neck."

Akins laughed. "Yeah, just like you did last time you went up against him, huh, Hog?"

Hog stuck out his lower lip like a child pouting. "He tricked me, that's all. He tripped me when I wasn't looking."

Bubba didn't say anything, but just sat there staring at Tolliver. He didn't know exactly how much half-a-million dollars was, but he barely had two dimes to rub together, and he'd been in the game with Tolliver since the very start. He wondered how the sheriff had gotten so rich while *he'd* done all the dirty work and was as poor as a church mouse.

He sighed. He'd need to work it over in his mind, but he didn't intend for Buck to retire rich and him have to go back to mucking out stalls for a living. No, sir!

In the Pueblo telegraph office, Smoke took the wire from the telegraph operator and frowned as he read it.

"Bad news?" Cal asked, his face going pale, thinking that maybe the wire said Pearlie was already dead.

"Yeah, but not as bad as it could be," Smoke said, handing the wire to Cal. "Pearlie's not awake yet, and the doctor says there's been no change in his condition."

"So, at least he's not getting any worse," Cal said, trying to sound optimistic.

"That's right, Cal," Smoke said, smiling slightly. "Let's keep our hopes up as we ride, and remember, Pearlie's a fighter. He won't go down easily."

"Damn right," Cal said, hitching up his pants and taking long strides trying to keep up with Smoke as they strode toward their horses.

"How long you reckon it'll take us to get back to Payday without running a string of horses?" Cal asked.

"Three days by the trail, but we can cut a full day off that by cutting through a couple of mountain passes I remember from my days up in these parts with Preacher."

Cal glanced up at the surrounding peaks that were still covered with snow. "You think those passes will be open this early?" Cal asked.

Smoke grinned. "They will be after we go through them."

CHAPTER 16

Joshua Banks, wearing a dress suit for the first time in over two months since he gave up practicing law to run his claim and try to find his fortune in the hills around Payday, slapped his hand down flat on the desk behind which he sat looking out at just about everyone who lived within ten miles of the town. He winced as his hand stung and burned, wishing yet again he had a gavel like a real judge and vowing for the tenth time to bring a wooden hammer with him if the trial lasted more than one day—which he doubted it would since the evidence stacked against this Pearlie was so overwhelming.

The trial was being held in the Golden Nugget Saloon and Poker Emporium, the largest structure in the city. The oldest and best of the many saloons and bars in the area, it was made entirely of wood instead of being a wooden front with a tent in the rear like most of the buildings in Payday.

Banks glanced over the crowd, most of whom were staring at Pearlie with undisguised hatred or talking to their neighbors with fire in their eyes. These people had all at one time or another availed themselves of Dr. Bentley's services and all had an interest in seeing his killer hanged by the neck until dead.

Banks shook his head. He was sure that most of the good citizens of Payday thought this entire trial was a waste of time and that the murdering scum should just be hanged so they could go on about their business of pulling gold and silver out of the ground. He had no idea how in the world he would be able to convene a jury that was even remotely fair and impartial, but he was damn sure going to try. One of the reasons he'd elected to give up the practice of law was the corruptness of most of his fellow practitioners. Banks was a rarity among lawyers, and even among men; he was an idealist who felt the guilty should be punished and the innocent freed. Unfortunately, in the few years he'd actively practiced law, he'd found the opposite was often the case, with guilt or innocence more often being a function of the amount of money the accused had rather than his guilt or innocence.

He pointed at the first two rows of chairs that had been hastily arranged in front of his desk. "You men get up and go sit in those jury chairs over there," he said.

A couple of the men gave Pearlie, who was sitting in a chair across the room next to his defender, Sam Hemmings, a withering look that showed they'd be happy to be the ones who sentenced him to die.

Once the men had all taken their seats, Banks began to ask each of them a question. "Josh, I'll start with you," he said. "Have you formed any opinion as to the innocence or guilt of the accused?"

Josh Pringle grinned and looked around at the crowd. "Sure have, Joshua. He's guilty as sin!"

When the crowd erupted with laughter and a few catcalls, Banks banged his hand down on the desk with a resounding smack. "Josh, call me Your Honor whenever I'm in this chair, and you are excused from jury duty."

Pringle's mouth dropped open and he started to reply when Banks pointed a finger at him. "I fully intend to run this trial like it should be run, and anyone in this room who doesn't believe me is welcome to spend a few nights in our jail and a few dollars in fines. As long as you good people elected me to do the dirty work of being a judge on this case, I will be a judge and that means I can fine you, imprison you, or do both as I see fit! Do I make myself clear?" he asked, staring around at the suddenly quiet crowd.

When no one said anything in reply, he added, "The only thing that makes us a town instead of a lynch mob is this court and how we conduct ourselves. If you can't handle that, then you might as well get a rope and go find the nearest tree . . . but you'd better bring two ropes, 'cause you'll have to kill me first to do it!" His eyes flashed as he went on. "I don't intend to be a rubber stamp for a lynching. This will be a fair trial and we will abide by all the rules of jurisprudence."

As he continued with his questioning of the potential jurors, Banks found that they'd learned from his quick dismissal of earlier men how to answer his questions. Suddenly, it appeared that practically every potential juror was supremely fair-minded and impartial, and of course they didn't think Pearlie was guilty yet—they were all going to wait and judge him after all the evidence was in. In a pig's eye, Banks thought. They've just learned to say the right things to get on the jury and probably not one of them was telling the truth.

But, since he could find no real reason to throw them out of the jury pool, and since it was evident that he wasn't going to find twelve men who were really ready to listen, he finally shrugged and seated the twelve men he thought would at least give Hemmings a chance to argue his case, for whatever good it would do the poor bastard named Pearlie.

Banks looked out over the crowd and said, "Now, we're gonna start this here trial, and if anybody in here gets the notion he can disrupt these proceedings by opening his big mouth, then he'll find himself on the outside looking in, and his wallet will be lighter by twenty-five dollars. Is that clear to everyone?"

His question greeted by silence, Banks turned to Sheriff Buck Tolliver, who was sitting at a table on the opposite side of the room from Pearlie's.

"You may begin your prosecution, Sheriff."

Tolliver stood up and cleared his throat. "I'll begin by calling Jonas Slackmeyer to the stand."

The town's undertaker rose ponderously in his characteristic black coat and trousers and boiled white shirt and made his way to the front of the room, where he took a seat in the witness's chair next to Banks's desk.

"Now, Jonas," Tolliver began, "did you examine the bodies of Dr. Hezekiah Bentley and Blackie Johnson on the night of their deaths?"

"I did," Slackmeyer said in his deep, gravelly voice. His demeanor was solemn and grave, as befitted his profession and his duty as medical examiner.

"And what did you find?"

"Well," Slackmeyer said, rubbing his chin and looking upward as he recalled the night, "Blackie was stabbed once in the throat. Looked like the knife entered just below the chin and sliced through the Adam's apple and cut the main artery to the head. He bled out like a stuck pig," Slackmeyer added indelicately. "There wasn't a teaspoon of blood left in the man's entire body."

Tolliver winced at the crudity, and then he nodded and turned and picked up a large knife from his table. The blade was still stained with dried, crusted blood. "Was this the knife you found sticking out of poor Blackie's neck?" Tolliver asked.

"I object to the prosecutor calling Mr. Johnson 'poor

Blackie,' Your Honor," Hemmings said. "Blackie wasn't poor, he just elected not to work for a living."

This statement caused Banks and Tolliver to frown, but almost everyone else in the room broke into laughter, for they all knew Blackie had been pretty much of a deadbeat.

"We'll strike the word 'poor' from the question," Banks intoned, glancing down at one of the girls from the saloon who was taking notes of the proceedings.

Slackmeyer waited until the judge was finished and then he nodded and grunted, "Yeah."

Tolliver then picked up Pearlie's gun belt with its holster and pistol still in it and its empty knife scabbard on the rear of the belt. "And does this rig belong to the defendant, Pearlie, as far as you know?"

"Yes, I was told it was his by you, Sheriff," Slackmeyer answered, drawing another laugh from the crowd.

Tolliver held up the belt and holster and theatrically slid the knife into the scabbard on Pearlie's belt, showing it was a perfect fit.

When there was an angry murmur from the crowd, Banks banged his hand down on his desk again, glaring at the offenders with narrowed eyes until they quieted.

Tolliver dropped Pearlie's rig on his table and turned back to Slackmeyer. "Now, what about Dr. Bentley?"

"Doc was shot once in the chest. Appeared to be at close range as his shirt was all burned and stained with gunpowder."

"When you examined Doc's body, was he wearing a side arm?" Tolliver asked.

Slackmeyer shook his head. "Hell, no. Everybody knows Doc never went heeled." He grinned sadly as he looked out at the crowded courtroom. "He even told me once he didn't hold with guns. Said they was only good for two things—killing people and cracking walnuts, an' he wasn't partial to walnuts."

A few men in the room laughed quietly at this remembrance of a man they all liked, and almost everyone glared angrily at Pearlie once again.

"That's all," Tolliver said, and took his seat.

When Slackmeyer started to get up, Sam Hemmings called, "Just a minute, Jonas. I have a couple of questions for you."

Slackmeyer sat back down, a puzzled expression on his face as if he couldn't think of anything else he had to say.

Hemmings stood up and moved to stand in front of the witness stand. "Did you notice anything else about Blackie Johnson when you examined him?"

Slackmeyer thought for a moment, and then shook his head again. "Nope."

Pearlie had told Hemmings when he gave his rendition of the occurrences that night that the man he'd fought with and stabbed had smelled strongly of alcohol, as if he'd been drinking heavily.

"What I'm getting at, Jonas, is the smell. Did you smell anything unusual about Blackie?"

Slackmeyer grinned widely. "No, nothing unusual. Blackie smelled like he always did, like he hadn't bathed in a month of Sundays and like he'd drunk up half the liquor in the saloon that day."

As the crowd stirred, Banks silenced them with another glare.

Hemmings pursed his lips, thinking. So far, what Pearlie had told him checked out, and the newcomer would have no way of knowing Blackie was a habitual drunkard.

"So, you'd say Blackie was drunk at the time he was stabbed to death?"

Slackmeyer nodded, sobering a little. "Hell, Sam, you know Blackie was always drunk if he'd been awake more'n a hour, so I guess I'd have to say he was pretty well lit at the time of his death."

"All right," Hemmings said. "Now, how about the doc? Anything unusual there?"

"He didn't stink, if that's what you mean?" Slackmeyer said, his eyes turning a bit angry, as if Hemmings was trying to sully the doc's reputation.

"No, Jonas, that's not what I mean. Was there anything unusual about the body's position or anything else?" Hemmings asked, not really knowing what he was looking for, since Pearlie had told him he remembered nothing after his scuffle with the man who was trying to rob him.

"No . . ." Slackmeyer began, and then he hesitated, his eyes going unfocused for a moment as he thought back to that night. "Well, yes, there was one thing."

"Oh?"

"Yeah. The doc had a large bump and a gash on the top of his head, like he'd been pistol-whipped or something before he was shot."

Hemmings was suddenly interested. "You don't think his head injury could have come from falling down and hitting his head after he was shot?"

"Naw, couldn't have been that. There was blood in his hair from the cut, from where it'd bled. The doc had a hole in his chest right through his heart from the bullet. He died instantly, so if he'd hit his head while falling, the wound wouldn't have bled 'cause the heart would've already stopped pumping."

"Was the head wound serious enough to cause the doc to be knocked unconscious?" Hemmings asked.

Slackmeyer scratched his chin. "Yeah, I 'spect so, though it's awfully hard to tell with head wounds. They tend to bleed heavily, so even a small wound can look real bad if all you have to go by is the amount of blood."

"So whoever did this knocked the doc out and then stood over him and placed his pistol against his chest and shot him to death?"

"Oh, I wouldn't go that far, Sam, though it certainly could've happened that way," Slackmeyer said, but his eyes now had a flicker of doubt in them. He knew what the sheriff had told everyone the night of the killing, and it didn't jibe with what he'd just testified to. He took a deep breath. He was going to have to give this some thought.

"That's all I have," Hemmings said, and sat down next to Pearlie.

Tolliver stood up. "I guess I'll have to call myself as the next witness, since I'm the only other one who was there that night and really saw what happened," he said, giving Slackmeyer a withering glare for daring to say the doctor might not have died as he'd testified to.

Banks nodded. "All right, Buck. Just get up there in the witness chair and tell us what you saw."

Tolliver took his seat facing the room. "Well, I was out making my rounds, and Blackie Johnson joined up with me. Like Jonas said, he'd been drinking some over to the saloon and he said he wanted to take a walk to get some fresh air."

Some men in the room snickered at this, knowing that Blackie would never willingly leave a saloon once he'd started drinking until he was thrown out or the place closed for the night. Tolliver glared at them and then he continued. "When we walked down the alleyway behind the doc's house, we noticed the door was open but there weren't any lights burning."

He paused, as if he were trying to recall the exact events of the night. "Suddenly we heard a shot and we both pulled our pistols and ran into the house. When we ran into the parlor, we saw a figure in the dark standing over the doc. Quick as a wink, that man over there," he said, pointing at Pearlie, "stuck a knife in Blackie's throat and shoved his body against me, knocking my gun out of my hand as he ran out of the door. By the time I picked it up and chased him, he was a good ten feet ahead of me and running like hell. I finally caught him at the end of the street and slapped him in the head with my gun and knocked him out." He took a deep breath, and then he added, "When I caught my breath, I looked in his pockets and found the doc's watch and ring and some cash money in them. I figure he was robbing the doc's house when the doc came home and caught him. They must have struggled, and he must have hit the doc over the head with his pistol before he shot him."

He leaned back in his chair. "And that's about it," he said.

"Sam," Banks said, "you got any questions for the sheriff about his testimony?"

Hemmings got to his feet. He'd never particularly liked Buck Tolliver personally, but had always worked fairly well with him on town business. "Buck, that story doesn't make a whole lot of sense to me."

Tolliver's face turned red and he sat forward in his chair, his muscles bunching under his shirt. "What do you mean by that, Sam?" he asked ominously, as if he were ready to jump out of the chair and hit Hemmings in the mouth.

"Well, first off, why'd you let a man as drunk as Blackie was go into a house with you to investigate a gunshot? That's not typical of the way you patrol our streets after dark, is it? In the company of a drunk?"

Tolliver took a deep breath and leaned back, knowing he was going to have to keep his wits about him when he answered these questions or the people in the town might start wondering just what he'd been up to that night. "I didn't exactly *let* him go with me, Sam. You know Blackie. When he asked to walk along with me, I wasn't exactly expecting a double murder. Far as I knew, we were just taking a walk in the evening air. And then when we heard the shot, we just both drew our guns and ran into the house without thinking much about it. There wasn't a lot of time for discussion on the matter."

Hemmings nodded. "And secondly, if my client had just shot the doc and was standing over him with his gun in his hand, why did he take the time to draw his knife and stab Blackie instead of just shooting him and you?"

Tolliver panicked. He hadn't thought of that when he'd made up his story. "Uh . . . I'm damned if I know, Sam. Why don't you ask him?" he said, grinning at the crowd to mask his confusion.

Hemmings didn't return the smile. "I did, Buck. He says he didn't do it, so why don't you make a guess as to what would make a man pull a knife when he has a perfectly good gun in his hand?"

"I told you, Sam, it was dark in there. Maybe . . . maybe he had a gun in one hand and his knife in the other and he just struck out with the hand closest to Blackie."

"So, let me get this straight," Hemmings said. "Pearlie is robbing the doc's house, the doc comes home and catches him, and they have a fight. Pearlie pulls out his gun and his knife during this fight, hits the doc over the head and knocks him out, and then he stands over the body with his knife and gun in his hands and shoots the doc in the chest, making enough noise to wake the entire town instead of just reaching down and cutting his throat if he wanted to kill him. Is that what you think happened?"

Hemmings was getting excited. Suddenly, he believed Pearlie, or at least he knew that things hadn't happened like the sheriff said they did. He could see it in Tolliver's eyes, the way panic hit them when he questioned him. The man was lying through his teeth. He didn't know why Buck was lying, but he was certain he wasn't telling the entire truth.

Tolliver's jaws clenched and his face turned beet red. "How the hell do I know what happened 'fore we got there, Sam? All I know is we heard a shot and ran in to see what was going on. Blackie got stabbed and that son of a bitch over there ran out of the room and down the alley until I knocked him out and found a bunch of Doc's things in his pockets."

He took a deep breath and leaned back in his chair, forcing himself to calm down. "What went through his mind or why he shot the doc instead of knifing him, I don't know."

Hemmings gave him a flat look and said, "I have no further questions of this witness, Your Honor."

There was a murmur among the men in the crowded room, and more than a few sets of eyes were watching Tolliver, wondering just what was going on between him and Hemmings.

Banks pursed his lips. The tension in the room was thick enough to cut with a knife. He knew he'd better defuse the situation or Tolliver and Hemmings were going to come to blows. "I think we'll adjourn for lunch," he said, glancing at his pocket watch. It was a quarter to twelve—close enough. "Everyone back here at two o'clock, and I don't want anyone to talk to the jury during the break," he said, and he glanced over at the bartender standing behind the bar to his left. "And I don't want any liquor or beer served in this room until after the jury verdict is in."

CHAPTER 17

When the trial resumed after lunch, Banks noted the crowd seemed to be in a much better humor, making him surmise a lot of them had drunk their lunch rather than chewed it.

He started to smack his hand down on his desk to call the court to order, stopped, and looked at his red, raw palm. He looked over at the bar. "Curly, bring me that wooden hammer you use to open beer kegs, if you would please?" he asked.

Once he had the hammer, he banged it down a couple of times, smiling to himself, and said, "This court is now in order." He inclined his head toward Hemmings. "Are you ready to begin, Sam?"

Hemmings got to his feet, and Banks could see the resignation of defeat on his face. "Yes, Joshua . . . uh, I mean Your Honor," he replied. "The defense is ready."

Banks looked at Tolliver, who was sitting at his table with a smug, self-satisfied expression on his face that made Banks angry. It was all right to win a case, but you didn't have to look so all-fired happy about sending a man to his death, even a murderer. "Is the prosecution ready?" he asked archly.

Tolliver gave him a nod and a wink. Asshole, Banks thought. He looked at Hemmings and nodded for him to go ahead with whatever defense he could mount.

Hemmings turned to Pearlie. "Pearlie, would you take the stand, please?"

Pearlie got up and walked to the witness chair, his stride long and confident with no evidence of shame or embarrassment in his manner. He still had a thick cloth bandage on his head where Tolliver had hit him, and the wounds and bruises on his face were still colorful, but his expression was one of quiet confidence that he was in the right and nothing bad could happen to him.

Banks shook his head slightly, and wanted to call out to the young man to not be so sure. It wasn't important to know you were right. You had to prove it to twelve people who had absolutely no reason to believe a word you were saying.

"Now," Hemmings began, "would you tell us what happened in your own words?"

Pearlie nodded. "The last thing I remember before waking up the other night was being up in the mountains with my friends. We were buying some horses from the Nez Percé and I was out in a meadow when I fell off my horse and ended up getting snakebit in the leg and neck. After I killed the snake with my knife," he said, his eyes involuntarily going to the evidence table where his knife lay covered with a dead man's blood, "I must've passed out."

He looked directly into Hemmings's eyes. "I've been told by you, Mr. Hemmings, that after I passed out and became unconscious, my friends brought me here to see the doctor, but I was asleep during all that time. The next thing I remember is waking up the other night in the dark and finding a man standing over me with a gun in his hand. At the time, he was going through my things that were laid out on a nightstand next to my bed. Of course, I didn't know where I was and right then I didn't remember 'bout bein' snakebit—all I saw was that big six-killer the man was holding as the moon glinted off its barrel."

Pearlie paused and cleared his throat, which was becoming hoarse and raspy. Hemmings poured him a glass of water and waited patiently while he drank it down.

When Pearlie continued, he sounded better. "Well, sir, the man evidently heard me wake up and he turned and pointed his gun at me. I grabbed the barrel and we wrestled around a bit until he fell backward and pulled me out of bed onto him. When we hit the floor, my belt and holster fell off the bedside table and I saw the handle of my knife. I didn't know why, but I was weak as a newborn kitten, so knowing I couldn't hold the barrel of that Colt away from me forever, I grabbed the knife and jammed it in his throat." Pearlie paused, his face becoming pale when he remembered how much blood had spurted out of the man's neck. "I . . . uh . . . managed to hit him in the neck and he jerked back and fell down and died. When I tried to get up, everything went black, and the next thing I remember is waking up in jail with a real bad headache and a pretty woman fussing over a cut on my face and head."

Hemmings, who'd been watching the jury and the crowd out of the corner of his eyes noted, that the men were interested in what Pearlie was saying, but he also knew that that didn't mean they believed him.

"And that is all that you remember of the night the two men were killed?" he asked.

Pearlie nodded. "Yeah, like I say, I did kill the one man with my knife, but only 'cause he was aiming to kill me. I never even saw the doctor that was trying to help me, and I ain't the kind to steal from someone bent on doin' me a good turn." He hesitated and his face filled with color as he added, "Or steal from anyone, for that matter."

"So you have no idea who might have come in and killed Dr. Bentley?"

Pearlie hung his head. "Mr. Hemmings, I don't even know how I got my pants on. Last I remember, I was in some kind of nightshirt in a strange bedroom and lying in another man's blood."

"That's all I have, Pearlie," Hemmings said. He turned to the sheriff. "Buck, your witness."

Tolliver stood up at his table and fixed Pearlie with a hard, flat look. "I have no questions for this lying son of a bitch," he said.

He ignored Hemmings when he jumped up and hollered, "I object, You Honor!"

Tolliver didn't wait for the court's ruling but continued. "I know what I saw and I saw the bastard standing over the doc's dead body and I saw him stick his knife in Blackie's throat right in front of me."

"I won't have any name-calling in this court," Banks said, slapping his hammer down on his desk and glaring at Tolliver. "Now if you're through with this witness, and if Sam has no further witnesses," he said, looking at Hemmings, who shook his head, "then I'll give the case to the jury."

"Hey, Joshua," a voice called from the back of the room.

Banks looked up, irritation on his face. "What is it, Bob?" he asked.

Robert Jacobson, the owner of the general store, stood up. "Why ain't you all calling Miss Rule to testify? Maybe she could tell you what she saw that night."

"Miss who?" Banks asked, raising his eyebrows.

"Janet Rule," Jacobson answered. "She's the doc's aunt and she was staying with him for a few days 'fore he got kilt." He looked around the room. "I know 'cause the doc bought some special bathing salts for her when she got in the week 'fore he got killed."

Tolliver turned pale as all the blood ran from his face. Damn, he thought, I didn't see nobody else in the house that night. He had a sudden urge to run from the room, get on his horse, and ride like hell out of town.

Banks looked around the room. "Well, has anyone here seen or heard from this Miss Rule since the night of the murders?" he asked.

Joe Samuelson raised his hand and said, "I saw an older lady that night, Joshua. She woke me up and took a room in my hotel."

"Why would she go to a hotel the same night her nephew was killed?" Banks asked.

Samuelson shrugged. "I dunno. Maybe she didn't want to stay in a house with two dead men in it."

As the crowd gave a low laugh at this bit of humor, Banks frowned and asked, "Is she still there?"

Samuelson shook his head. "Nope. She paid her bill the next morning and took off. I ain't seen hide nor hair of her since."

"She happen to say where she was going?" Tolliver asked, trying to hide his excitement at this new development. Maybe if he found out where she was first, he could make sure she never gets to tell anyone her story, if she did in fact see him kill the doctor.

"Nope. She just walked out of the lobby and disappeared," Samuelson answered.

Tolliver turned back to Banks. "Joshua, I'll try and find this lady, but evidently she don't have nothing to add or she'd be here to tell it. Why don't you let the jury be thinking on what they want to do while I go look for her? If she has something to say about that night that'll be helpful, then I'll bring her in."

"I object, Your Honor," Hemmings said. "The defendant should have the benefit of this woman's testimony before the jury is released to deliberate."

"I agree, Sam," Banks said gravely, "but it's like Buck says. If she's in town, she's sure as hell heard about the trial, and if she's not here, then she evidently doesn't have anything to add. On the other hand, if she's left town, there isn't anything we can do about it since she could be just about anywhere by now. If Buck can find her before the jury comes in with a verdict, then I'll allow her to speak. Otherwise, we go with what we have."

"But—"

"I've spoken," Banks said, and then in a more kindly tone of voice he added to Hemmings, "My hands are tied, Sam. There's nothing else I can do." He looked up and addressed the crowd of spectators. "Court's adjourned while the jury deliberates." He glanced at the jury. "You men go on over to the livery and you can have your meeting there while you decide if this man is guilty and if he is, what sentence you'd like to impose."

"Uh, Joshua, it's almost dinnertime," one of the men on the jury said. "Can we go home an' eat an' then do our deliberatin'?"

Banks smiled. "No, George, you can't. I'll have something sent over from the hotel dining room to tide you over until you've made your decision."

Sheriff Buck Tolliver didn't waste any time hanging around the courtroom after Banks sent the case to the jury. He practically ran out of the saloon and over to his office. His cronies Jeb Hardy and Kid Akins followed him at a discreet distance. Bubba Barkley and Hog Hogarth headed instead for the nearest bar, Hog still limping badly on his injured leg, telling Hardy and Akins to let them know if Tolliver needed anything.

"Damn, damn, and double damn!" Tolliver ranted, pacing around his office like a wild man, kicking at the stove and throwing the empty coffeepot against a wall.

Hardy and Akins walked in just in time to see the coffeepot carom off the wall. "My, my," Hardy said, grinning at Akins, "the sheriff seems to have a burr under his saddle this afternoon."

Tolliver whirled around, panting, his hair askew, looking like he was in the midst of a fit of apoplexy. "Why the hell didn't you tell me the doc had some old-maid aunt visiting him?" he asked. "You knew I'd been out of town for over a week when she came."

Hardy shrugged. "You didn't ask, Buck," he said in an even tone, though his eyes were flat and hard at the way Tolliver was talking to him. "Besides, how were we to know you were going to hatch some hare-brained scheme to kill that fellow that was lying unconscious over at the doc's place?" He paused, and then he added, "You didn't exactly share your plans ahead of time with us, Buck ol' man, and after it was over and all hell broke loose, I plumb forgot about the old lady being there visiting."

Tolliver began to calm down, realizing Hardy was right. He hadn't told his friends what had really happened at the doc's until well after everything had gone horribly wrong and Blackie was dead.

He took a seat behind his desk, but was so agitated he couldn't sit still, and fidgeted in his seat like a schoolboy with a full bladder. "Well, we have to find her and make sure she didn't see anything that night."

Hardy leaned back in his chair and shifted the toothpick he was chewing on from one side of his mouth to the other as he stared speculatively at Tolliver. "What do you mean we, Buck? Far as I remember, the boys and me didn't have nothing to do with that little fuck-up you engineered at the doc's." He glanced at Kid Akins. "All we're being paid by the city to do is to guard the town in case some of the defendant's hardcase friends try to shoot it up."

Tolliver's face went flat and he tried without much success to hide the anger in his eyes. "No, you're not on the hook for that, Jeb, but we've been making a pretty good living with our little operation against the miners in the area." He too sat back and crossed his legs at the ankle as he put them up on the corner of his desk, trying to appear in control and unafraid, though it was difficult. "It would seem to me that if I get arrested for murder and hanged, it might just put a crimp in your plans to retire within the next year with enough money to live out the rest of your days without ever having to work again."

Hardy pursed his lips and glanced at Akins, who merely shrugged. They could see Tolliver had a point, and a good one. They'd all been living high on the hog the way things were, and Buck was right, losing him and the protection he offered them by being sheriff would be a major blow.

Before he could answer, Tolliver added, "And if that's not enough of a reason for you to help me, you might want to consider that if I'm in jail, then the extent of my holdings and bank accounts are sure to come out." He looked from Akins to Hardy, his eyes becoming dark. "And if people around here start to investigate just how I accumulated all that money and all those claims, they might just stumble upon some other men in the town who have a lot more than they should in the bank and whose names are on some of the same mining claims as mine."

Hardy's face flushed. "You're not threatening to

spill the beans on our little arrangement, are you, Buck?" he asked, his voice silky smooth with danger. "'Cause if you are, the simple way for the boys and me to protect ourselves from hanging would be to put a lead pill in your skull."

Buck's eyes widened and his hand moved to his thigh just above his pistol. "That might not be as easy as you think, Jeb; and it might keep you out of jail and your neck out of a noose, but it sure as hell wouldn't make you any money in the future."

Hardy sighed and sat back, relaxing as he realized Tolliver was correct. "You're right, Buck," he said in a more normal voice. "Why should we mess up a good thing, a scheme that's going to make us all rich?"

Tolliver let his feet flop to the floor and he leaned forward on his desk. "I'm glad you see it that way, Jeb. Now, what you and the boys can do for me is to ask around town about this Rule lady. She's either staying here hiding out with someone, or she's left town, an' the only way she could've left town is by train or by stagecoach."

Kid Akins leaned against the stove, which was cold and unlit since Tolliver had been in the saloon/court all morning. "Why do you need us to do the askin', Buck? After all, you're the sheriff around here."

"Oh, I'll do some light snooping, Kid, but I can't seem too anxious about it or it might seem suspicious." He grinned. "And if she did see me kill the doc and she finds out I'm asking around about her, she's sure to hightail it outta here first chance she gets."

Akins frowned, "Well, just what reason can I give for askin' 'bout some old lady's whereabouts?"

"Just tell them you owe the doc some money for a past treatment and you want to make sure his family gets what's coming to them," Tolliver said, exasperated that he had to do all the thinking for his band of thieves.

Hardy gave a lopsided grin. "Or you could just tell them you're looking for a date to the next Sunday picnic."

Tolliver and Hardy both laughed at that, for they all knew Akins had a reputation for jumping just about anything that walked on two legs and was female, and they weren't too sure about two legs.

CHAPTER 18

As the jurors pulled up square bales of hay to sit on in the livery, Danny Boyd, a miner from the foothills near town, groused, "I don't know why in the hell we're even bothering to sit down. It's a clear as the nose on your face that the son of a bitch is guilty."

Royce Peterson, a rancher from the lowlands south of town, cocked his head and disagreed. "I don't know, Danny. The boy don't look like no killer to me."

Jack Dunhill, a man who did odd jobs around town to earn drinking money, broke in. "Well, now, Royce, anybody can be a killer if the situation is right."

"Yeah," Peterson said. "Anyone can kill on the spur of the moment or if they're frightened enough, but to knock a man out and stand over him and shoot him while he's unconscious, and then to stab another man in the throat, takes someone who's a lot more cold-blooded than that Pearlie fellow appears to be." He looked around at the others. "Did you see the way he looked right in Sam's eyes while he was telling his story? Hell, I'd bet my last dollar that boy didn't have nothing to hide and he was telling the whole truth."

"Hang on here a minute," Boyd said heatedly. "The sheriff says he saw him standing over the doc's body and saw him stab Blackie Johnson in the neck. Now, either Pearlie killed the two men, or the sheriff is lying about what happened that night." He paused and glared around at the other eleven men in the livery stable. "And I can't for the life of me think of why the sheriff'd be doing that."

Willie Baker, a cook at the hotel dining room, agreed. "I think Danny hit the nail on the head. Either Pearlie killed 'em, or the sheriff did. Now, I don't think Buck Tolliver is above lying about some things, but I can't see him killing the doc for no reason at all, and Pearlie did admit he killed Blackie."

"But he said he did that in self-defense," Peterson argued back. "And I know Blackie Johnson was not above pilfering someone else's belongings if the occasion presented itself. Why, just last year, the Widow Paulson said she hired Blackie to do some odd jobs around her ranch and she said half her milk money was missing after he left."

Wally Broadman, a drover who drove the wagons loaded with gold and silver ore to Pueblo, spoke up. "I can see that we have some disagreement among the troops," he said good-naturedly. "And we haven't even talked about the doc's aunt and what she might have to say yet."

"Yeah, how about that?" Peterson said, sticking his chin out like he was ready for a good argument.

Wally held up his hand. "I have an idea that might just get us outta here 'fore the cows come home."

When everyone looked expectantly at him, he said, "Now it all boils down to this: Either the boy is lying and he done it, or the sheriff is lying and he done it. Since we don't have no evidence or even any reason the sheriff would do something like that unless Miss Rule can tell us different, we got to figure it's the boy that's lying. How about we vote guilty on the charges of murder and sentence the young man to hang, but add in our verdict that the hanging is not to be carried out for at least two weeks to give the sheriff time to track down Miss Rule and see just what she has to say, if anything. That way, if she clears the boy, he can be released, and if she don't, he gets to dance on the air."

After some more desultory discussion, the men all agreed to do as Wally suggested, and the verdict was delivered to Joshua Banks at the office in the bank he had been using during the trial.

When he read the verdict, Banks shook his head sadly. He knew it was the correct verdict considering the evidence, but damnit all, sometimes you just got a gut feeling something was wrong. That was the way it was for him in this case. Everything pointed at Pearlie as guilty, but Banks just couldn't bring himself to believe the boy was a stone-cold killer like he'd have to be to do what had been done.

Banks put on his coat and hat and sent a boy who worked in the bank to go and get the sheriff so he could give him the verdict personally. He knew the sheriff wasn't going to like the part about the hanging being delayed until Miss Rule could be found, but Banks agreed with the reasoning behind it. If there was another witness to the crime, it was only fair to the defendant for her to be found and questioned before he was hung by the neck until dead.

Sheriff Buck Tolliver tried to hide his anger at having his hands tied when Banks summoned him and gave him the news of the verdict and its prohibition against staging the hanging until after Miss Rule had been found and questioned.

He nodded, doing his best to keep his clenched jaws shut tight and not to rail against the stupidity of the jury for having the effrontery not to fully believe his testimony.

"All right, Joshua," he said stiffly. "I'll send a wire to

the sheriffs in Pueblo and Denver to be on the lookout for someone fitting Rule's description."

Banks sighed. He could sense Tolliver's anger. "Don't take this as an insult to your word, Buck. It's just that the jury didn't seem to feel Pearlie was the sort of violent man who could do such cold-blooded murders."

Tolliver snorted and slapped his hand against his thigh. "And what am I, Joshua? A man who'd lie about something as serious as the doc's murder?" He almost growled when he added, "A man I been friends with for several years?"

Banks shook his head. "Come on, Buck. You know you haven't exactly gone out of your way to be a friend to the people of this town. Hell, half of them cross the street when they see you coming down the boardwalk 'cause they know you got a bad temper and they're half-afraid you'll explode at them over some minor infraction."

"That's the trouble with people, Joshua," Tolliver spit. "They want someone tough enough to keep the peace and keep the desperados from overrunning their town, but then when they hire someone like that, they don't want him coming into their nice neat houses and stinking them up with the scent of his dangerousness."

"You're right, Buck," Banks said, shrugging. "It's not fair, but it *is* the way people are, and you were aware of that when you took the office—and the job."

"Yeah, well, after this is all over, the good citizens of Payday might just be looking for someone else to keep their fat out of the fire," Tolliver said, whirling on his heels and storming out of the office.

Banks took a deep breath and smiled slightly, muttering, "And perhaps that would be a good thing, Buck, a good thing for this town and everyone in it."

He got slowly to his feet, grabbed his hat, and prepared to reconvene court and read the verdict to the defendant and the rest of the townspeople. All in all, he figured it was a fair and just verdict, especially given that it required Miss Rule to corroborate the sheriff's story about what happened before the young man could be hung.

Two days later, a trail-weary Smoke Jensen and Cal Woods road their horses down the main street of Payday. They were about frozen clear through from their journey through the mountain passes between Pueblo and Payday, where they'd slogged through snow that was clear up to their horses' withers.

"You want to get something to eat first or head straight to the doctor's office?" Cal asked.

"Let's take a quick look in on Pearlie and make sure nothing's changed before we go to the hotel," Smoke suggested, though every weary muscle in his body cried out for rest and a hot bath.

When they reined up in front of the doctor's office, they found the door locked and a black wreath of dead flowers nailed to the door.

Smoke shook his head. "I don't like the looks of this, Cal."

"Me neither, Smoke, but Pearlie's just a patient of the doctor's. If he'd died, there wouldn't be no wreath on the door."

Smoke stood on the porch and looked around the town, wondering just what had happened in his absence. There was a sense of something going on, something that had changed the town and made its citizens seem more somber, less friendly. Finally, he crossed the street and stopped a man walking toward the general store.

"Say, mister," he said, "excuse me, but could you tell me why the doctor's office is locked up in the middle of the day and why there is a wreath on the door?"

The man glanced at Smoke and Cal's trail-soiled clothes and their lathered horses and said, "You just got into town, didn't you?"

Smoke and Cal nodded.

The man looked over their shoulder at the doctor's office and crossed himself. "Well, the doc was shot down and killed a week or so ago, along with a sheriff's deputy who was knifed to death when he came to investigate the shooting."

Smoke's heart began to race and he felt a cold sweat break out on his forehead. "What about the man who was staying with the doctor? The man who was unconscious from a snakebite?"

The townsman's eyes widened a bit and he looked over at the jail. "Why, that's the fellow that did the killing. He's in jail, convicted of two murders and scheduled to hang in the next week."

"That's a lie!" Cal almost shouted, taking a step toward the man as if it were all his doing.

Smoke stretched out an arm and held Cal back. "Take it easy, Cal. We'll get to the bottom of this later, after we've had a chance to talk to Pearlie."

He turned back to the man. "Sorry about my friend, mister, he's a mite excitable. Now, did you say the accused man is in the jail?"

The man slowly edged away from Smoke and Cal as if he were afraid they might attack him at any moment. "That's right, mister." And then he hurried away, glancing back over his shoulder a time or two to make sure the two crazy men weren't following him.

Cal turned and headed toward the jail, until Smoke again stopped him with a hand on his shoulder. "Hold on, Cal, don't go off half-cocked."

"But ain't we gonna go see about Pearlie?" Cal asked, almost jumping up and down in his anxiety to get to his friend and help him.

Smoke nodded. "Yeah, but not looking like saddle tramps. The man said he wasn't scheduled to hang until next week, so we've got time to kind'a scout out the situation before we go blundering into something without knowing exactly what we're facing." Smoke looked around again at the surrounding town. "I don't like the mood the town is in. It's as if they're all heated up about something. The whole town feels like a powder keg about to blow, and I don't want us to get caught in the explosion."

Cal took a deep breath. "You're right, Smoke. Something fishy is going on here 'cause Pearlie wouldn't shoot nobody, not unless they was gonna shoot him first."

Smoke walked back across the street to the rail in front of the doctor's office, grabbed his horse's reins, and swung up into the saddle. "Let's get our horses taken care of and then get rooms in the hotel and get cleaned up. After we've had a bite or two to eat and had time to ask some questions around town, we'll mosey on over to the sheriff's office and see what we can find out from Pearlie."

Cal brightened up marginally. "You think they might have a hot bath over there?" he asked.

"They'd better or I'm gonna shoot somebody myself," Smoke said, grinning.

CHAPTER 19

Smoke and Cal walked into the hotel and placed their saddlebags on the floor in front of the desk.

The desk clerk took one look at their road-weary look, dirty and dusty buckskins, and unshaven faces, and turned up his nose. "I'm afraid this is a quality hotel, gentlemen," he said in a snooty voice, "and very expensive. If you desire . . . uh . . . less luxurious accommodations, you might try Barstow's tent around the corner."

Smoke took a deep breath, and he curbed his anger, realizing he really couldn't blame the man because they did rather look like itinerant saddle tramps. Instead, he took a wad of greenbacks out of his pocket that was large enough to choke a horse, and held them in his hand ready to count out what he needed. "And just how much would two rooms, a hot bath, someone to do our laundry, and a visit from a good barber cost in this town, sir?" he asked amiably.

The clerk's Adam's apple bobbed up and down in his skinny neck as he swallowed twice. "Uh . . . that ought to cover it," he said, reaching out and taking a twenty-dollar bill off the top of Smoke's stack of money.

Smoke grinned. "I just want to rent a couple of rooms, not buy them," he said in a light voice.

The clerk gave a polite laugh, turned the register

around, and handed Smoke a pen. While Smoke signed the register, the clerk picked two keys out off the wall behind the desk and handed them to Cal.

"Now, about that bath and the barber," Smoke said.

"It'll take me at least an hour to heat up enough water for two baths, unless you want to share the water?"

"Not hardly," Smoke said grimly.

"All right then, I'll have a boy take your things up to your rooms if you want to get a bite to eat while you wait . . . Mr. . . . uh . . ." The clerk whirled the register around and read the name. "Smoke Jensen?" he asked, almost choking on his tongue.

"That's right," Smoke said easily.

"Is that *the* Smoke Jensen?" the clerk asked, turning pale when he realized how he'd talked to one of the most famous gunfighters and most dangerous men in the country just a few short moments before.

"I'm the only one with that name I've ever come across," Smoke said, having to bite his lip to keep from laughing at the terrified expression on the clerk's face.

"You hankering to eat?" Smoke asked Cal, who just shrugged. "Aw, the hell with it," Smoke said. "Let's go see Pearlie while they heat up our water."

He turned to the clerk. "Have those baths ready in an hour and have the barber standing by a half hour after that," he said, flipping a five-dollar gold piece on the counter. "That's for your trouble," Smoke said as the clerk magically made the gold piece disappear without seeming to look at it.

Smoke didn't bother to knock on the sheriff's office door, but just jerked it open and strode inside, almost giving Tolliver a heart attack when he looked up and saw his greatest enemy walk in.

Tolliver cleared his throat and reached down under the desk to unhook his rawhide hammer thong in case Jensen caused any trouble.

"Yeah?" Tolliver croaked through a dry mouth, and then he cleared his throat and tried again. "Can I help you gentlemen with something?"

"We hear you got a friend of ours locked up here," Smoke said quickly, his eyes narrowing as he saw something vaguely familiar about the sheriff's face.

"Would that be a man named Pearlie?" Tolliver asked, leaning back in his chair and starting to enjoy the look of discomfiture on Jensen's face.

"It would."

Tolliver got slowly to his feet, picking a ring of keys up off a nail in the wall behind his desk. "I'm gonna have to ask you to leave your weapons out here," he said, inclining his head at the several pistols and knives on Smoke's and Cal's belts.

Smoke just stared at him. "I don't think so," he said, his voice low and hard. "Nobody gets my guns while I'm still alive, Sheriff, and that includes you."

When Tolliver's face turned red and his cheeks puffed out, Cal said, "Look, Sheriff, if we wanted to start trouble we'd have come in here with our guns in our hands and you wouldn't have stood a chance. We just want to talk to our friend for a few minutes to find out his side of the story."

Tolliver cooled down at the reasonable tone of Cal's voice. He snorted. "The jury has already heard his side of the story an' they didn't believe a word of it, but I guess it won't hurt to let you have a few words with him."

When Smoke turned to enter the door into the cell block, the sheriff added, "But I'm gonna be watching from the door and I'm gonna have an express gun in my hands. You try to slip that boy a weapon, an' it'll be the last thing you ever do."

As Smoke walked through the door and the sheriff took a short-barreled Greener off the wall rack, Smoke muttered loud enough for Tolliver to hear, "And if you point that shotgun at me, it'll be the last thing *you* ever do."

Tolliver's face paled at the threat, but he opened the door and pointed them toward the last cell on the row. As they walked down the short corridor, Tolliver leaned back against the doorjamb, the express gun cradled in his arms, but he was careful not to point it in Smoke's direction.

When Pearlie heard the cell-block door open, he sat up on his bunk and blinked his eyes against the sudden light from the doorway. His cell had no window in it and it was almost as dark as night.

"Who is that?" he asked, his voice weak and thready from lack of water and disuse.

"It's me and Cal," Smoke said, making sure to keep a few steps back from the bars on Pearlie's cell door.

"Smoke . . . Cal . . ." Pearlie cried with relief. "I thought you'd forgotten all about me."

"Not a chance," Cal said. It almost broke his heart to see the way Pearlie looked. He appeared to have lost ten or fifteen pounds, his skin was pale and shrunken-looking, and his eyes were lackluster. It just wasn't the same old Pearlie he'd come to know. "It just took us a while to get the hosses on the way to Big Rock and to get back here to see you."

"Pearlie," Smoke said, "it's real good to see you awake and doing better, but what the hell happened to get you arrested for murder?"

Cal's eyes narrowed when he noticed the black-and-blue swelling and gash on Pearlie's head. "And what the hell happened to your head?" he asked.

Pearlie leaned up against the bars, his hands clinging to them as if he were drowning. He cut his eyes toward the sheriff down the corridor. "That was a gift from the sheriff, though I don't remember it much."

Smoke took out his fixings and built two cigarettes, using the routine to get his temper in check. He felt like running back down the corridor and beating the shit out of the sheriff for what he'd done to his friend. He handed one to Pearlie, who looked as if he needed it, and he lit it and then the one he screwed in the corner of his mouth.

"Why don't you tell us about it?" he asked, leaning back against the wall, crossing his feet at the ankles, and smoking slowly as he watched Pearlie.

Pearlie told them how he'd awakened to find a strange man with a gun in his hand going through his things and how they'd struggled and how he'd ended up stabbing the man to death.

"And was that the doctor?" Cal asked.

"No, evidently not," Pearlie said. "It was some man named Blackie Johnson, the sheriff's cousin and part-time deputy."

"What happened then?" Smoke asked.

Pearlie shrugged. "I don't rightly know, Smoke. I got up off the floor and things started to go kind'a crazy. I blacked out and when I woke up, I was in jail with this gash on my head and a pretty woman fixin' it up."

Cal grinned. "Leave it to Pearlie to fall into a bucket of shit and come out with a girl."

"And that's all you remember?" Smoke asked, trying to stay focused on his story.

Pearlie nodded, and then his knees buckled and he almost fell to the floor. He caught himself and stumbled back over to his cot and sat on it, leaning back against the wall and holding his head.

"What's the matter?" Cal asked, alarmed at how pale Pearlie looked all of a sudden.

"All I been getting to eat is bread and a little soup that's more water than meat," Pearlie said.

"The doctor said you needed lots of heavy beef stew to help you get over the snakebite," Smoke said.

Pearlie gave a half grin. "Well, since they claim I killed that doctor, they ain't exactly been trying to follow his advice about my welfare."

"We'll see about that," Smoke said grimly. "We'll sniff around town and see what we can come up with, Pearlie. You sit tight."

"Do I have a choice?" he asked, gamely trying to keep his spirits up.

Smoke smiled gently and handed him the bag of tobacco and some papers and matches. "You do like I said, Pearlie. Leave the worrying to us."

As Smoke and Cal walked down the corridor, Pearlie called out, "Say, Smoke."

"Yeah?" Smoke asked, stepping back to his cell door.

"There was something about the doc's aunt, a Miss Janet Rule, who was supposed to be in the house that night. She's disappeared, but she might know something about what really happened if you can find her."

Smoke nodded. "We'll see what we can do, pal."

When they got back into the sheriff's office and he'd relocked the door to the cell block, Smoke asked, "What's this I hear about there being a possible witness to the doctor's murder?"

Tolliver almost choked and his mouth went dry. "Uh, where'd you hear that?"

"Never mind. Is there?"

"Yeah, I guess so. The doctor's aunt was visiting and

she might've seen something, but I've got wires out to Denver and Pueblo and I'm sure we'll find her and she'll tell us your friend in there killed the two men."

"Well, I hope you don't mind if we do some looking for her too, Sheriff."

Tolliver felt sick at the thought of Jensen finding Rule before he did, but he forced a smile on his lips. "Of course not. The more the merrier."

"And just what is this I hear about the prisoner not getting anything but bread and water to eat?"

Tolliver shrugged and had to struggle not to grin. He loved seeing Jensen so worried about his friend, and his worrying was just starting. "The county don't have a lot of money to be spending on food for a man due to hang in a week," Tolliver answered smugly.

"Well, I'm going to pay to have the cook over at the hotel fix him three square meals a day and deliver them over here. Is that all right with you?"

Tolliver did grin this time. "Sure it is. Course I might have to sample them meals to make sure they're all right for the prisoner."

Smoke took a step toward the sheriff, who backed up and laid his hand on the butt of his pistol. Smoke grinned, his face only inches from Tolliver's. "I'd be very careful how you treat my friend, Sheriff. Very careful indeed, 'cause if he tells me you as much as touched him, or if I see any more evidence he's been pistol-whipped, then you'd better never cross my path again."

"Is that a threat, Jensen?" Tolliver asked, becoming angry when his voice quavered and broke a bit. "'Cause if it is, I could arrest you and put you in jail right now."

Smoke stepped back and regarded Tolliver with a speculative look. "I see you know my name, Sheriff. How is that?"

Tolliver could have kicked himself for making such

a blunder. He wasn't quite ready to let Jensen know they'd crossed paths before. "Uh . . . I've seen your face on some old wanted posters."

Smoke pursed his lips and stared into Tolliver's eyes. "My face hasn't been on a wanted poster in over ten years, Sheriff."

Tolliver smirked, trying to regain the high ground he'd lost. "I've got a long memory, Jensen."

Smoke reached out and poked Tolliver in the chest with a stiff finger. "Good, then you won't forget what I said about treating my friend right, will you?" When Tolliver failed to respond, Smoke added, "And I am going to have a talk with the mayor of this hole-in-the-wall and find out just why the town can't afford to feed its prisoners."

Tolliver didn't bother to answer as Smoke and Cal walked out of the door and moved down the street. He went to his window and watched them walk directly into the hotel.

Damn, he thought. This is getting out of hand. If Jensen finds Rule before I do and he talks to her, he might just be able to figure out what really happened.

He slammed his hand down on his desk. Damn that jury for tying his hands and setting the hanging date so far away. It would give Jensen far too much time to fool around trying to find out what really happened that night.

As he was thinking on how he might prevent that, he saw Bubba Barkley enter the saloon across the street. That was it. He'd send Barkley over to the hotel and see if the big man might be able to stop Jensen from finding the old lady. Hell, he'd offer the man a hundred dollars and Bubba would jump at the chance to prove himself tougher than the gunfighter, especially after the way the gunfighter had humiliated him and Hog in their first meeting.

It wouldn't be nearly as satisfying as killing Jensen himself, but he couldn't afford the luxury of that sort of vengeance now that the mountain man was looking for Miss Rule. Better to end it quick and get on with making money.

Besides, as long as Jensen got planted and it was him that caused it to happen, it didn't really matter who actually pulled the trigger, he reasoned.

CHAPTER 20

Tolliver locked up the jail and walked across and down the street to the saloon he'd seen Bubba enter. Sure enough, the big asshole was already sitting at a table with one of the ugliest saloon girls in town on his lap and a bottle of whiskey in his hand.

Bubba sure as hell wasn't no prize in the looks department, Tolliver thought, but as long as he was spending good money, he damn sure ought to make sure he got a better-looking woman to spend it on.

Tolliver shook his head as he saw Bubba not bothering with a glass as he tried to pour the whiskey down the woman's throat. She was laughing, but her eyes were cold and dead as he managed to get most of it on the front of her dress. She was obviously pretending to be having a good time, and Tolliver wondered why Bubba couldn't see that.

As ugly as she is, he'd do better pouring the rotgut down his own throat so he could manage to sleep with her without tying a feed bag to the nag's face, Tolliver mused as he made his way through the crowded room toward his friend.

Bubba glanced up through eyes that were either already red from a morning's drinking, or still red from the night before's drinking. Either way, the man was pretty well lit and Tolliver hesitated, not wanting to make the same mistake of sending a drunken man to do a delicate job of assassination as he had with Blackie.

Bubba looked up and noticed Tolliver approaching, and his little pig eyes cleared and stared with a surprising sharpness at the sheriff when he came up to the table. Maybe he's not as drunk as I thought, Tolliver figured.

"Hey, Buck ol' buddy," Bubba said, squeezing the whore's right breast with his right hand, which was draped over her shoulders, hard enough to make her wince. "Sit down an' have a little nip to take the chill off."

He moved his hand until his fingers were inside the top of her dress, and he moved them back and forth as he added, "I'm sure Molly won't mind an extra man at the table."

Tolliver frowned and jerked his head to the side. "Beat it, Molly. Bubba and I have some business to discuss and we need some privacy."

Molly made a pout and stuck out her lip, but when Tolliver raised his hand and stepped toward her, she jumped up off Bubba's lap and hurried away, looking back over her shoulder with a frightened expression.

Bubba looked after her and then up at Tolliver. "Well, now, Buck, you done run off my mornin's entertainment, so you might as well set and tell me what's on your mind."

Tolliver realized the slur had left Bubba's words and that the man wasn't nearly as drunk as he'd pretended to be. That thought made Tolliver wonder just how much of Bubba's apparent dumbness was put on and how much the man really knew about their business dealings together. It wasn't a comforting thought to start the day off with.

As Bubba raised the whiskey bottle to take another drink, Tolliver reached out and stopped him. "You might want to hold off on that stuff until you've heard what I have to say," he said, lowering his voice so the men at nearby tables couldn't hear him.

Now Bubba's eyes looked really interested. He sensed there might be some profit for him in Tolliver's strange actions. He set the bottle down, put his elbows on the table, and hunched forward so his face was close to Tolliver's over the table. "So, what's so damned important that you not only take away my slash, you mess with my drinkin' too?"

"I got a job for you, Bubba, and you can earn nice money if you can do it right now."

Bubba cocked his head to the side, and his eyes were sharp as tacks as they bored into Tolliver's. "Uh-huh, now that usually means you got some dirty work you want done but you want to keep your hands clean."

Tolliver sighed. He was right. Bubba was far from drunk, and probably not nearly as dumb as he let on most of the time. "Smoke Jensen and a friend of his just showed up over at the jail," he said.

Bubba nodded, remembering the way the man had humiliated him in their first encounter a while back. "Yeah, I heard. Nearly everybody in town knows that the famous gunfighter Smoke Jensen is in town, thanks to that little snot Samuelson from the hotel. But you was expectin' that, weren't you?"

"Yes, I was expecting him to show up, but Jensen's suddenly talking about looking for the Rule lady and finding out what she has to say about how the doc got killed."

Bubba's lips curled in a sly grin. "An' I'll bet you're afraid he'll find her 'fore you do an' she'll spill the beans 'bout how things really went down that night," Bubba said, his voice slightly mocking. Seemed his skin wasn't the only one that bastard Jensen was getting under, Bubba thought. Well, it was about time the high-and-mighty Sheriff Buck Tolliver got a taste of a little humility himself.

Tolliver frowned. This wasn't like Bubba. Something must've upset him to make his so ornery. "That's right, Bubba. Now he and his pal are staying over at the hotel. From the looks of them, they just came off a long trail ride, so I suspect they'll be cleaning up or taking a siesta for the next little while."

"So?" Bubba asked, raising his eyebrows and playing with Tolliver. He'd already figured out what Tolliver wanted him to do. Now he just had to make him say it and find out just how much it was going to be worth to him to get it done. "What's that got to do with me? He sure as hell didn't come to town to find out if I killed somebody and blamed it on a friend of his in order to get him hanged."

Tolliver glanced hurriedly around to make sure no one was watching or listening to Bubba shooting his mouth off. He figured he'd better get on with it before the whole town heard what Bubba was spouting off. "I'll pay you a hundred dollars to go over there, sneak up the back stairs, and put bullets in their heads."

Bubba broke out in laughter so loud it made everyone in the vicinity glance in their direction. "Shut up, you fool!" Tolliver hissed. "What's the matter with you this morning?"

Bubba's face sobered and he leaned forward. "You want me to sneak into the hotel and kill one of the most feared gunfighters in the country and another man for a measly hundred dollars? You, the man with half-a-million greenbacks in the bank, and me with not two dimes to rub together?" Bubba snorted, picked up the whiskey bottle, and took a large swig. "Uh-uh, I don't think so Mr. Sheriff."

So that was it, Tolliver thought. The idiot is pissed because I've made so much money in the past couple of years and he hasn't. Tolliver sighed and leaned back in his chair, knowing it was going to be a little more costly to get rid of Jensen than he'd figured. "All right, Bubba. Just what do you think the job is worth?"

Bubba pursed his lips, picked up the whiskey bottle again and took a small sip, and wiped his lips with the back of his hand before he answered. "A thousand dollars."

Tolliver snorted. "You must be joking! That's more'n most men make in two years."

Bubba shrugged. "I figure you can afford it, Buck, after all the money you made off my work the past year. An' if'n it's too much for you, then you can just mosey on over there an' do the job yourself." He smirked and leaned forward, whispering, "After all, it was your brother Jensen put in the ground, not mine."

"That's still a lot of money for a couple of minutes' work, Bubba."

Bubba grinned. "That's a lot of hombre you want kilt, Buck. And it ain't like it ain't been tried before, and nobody's managed to plant the man yet, so I think for a risk like that I ought to get paid big money."

When Buck didn't answer, Bubba shrugged again and looked across the room. "Molly," he yelled, motioning her back to him.

Tolliver reached out and pulled his hand down. "All right, you son of a bitch! A thousand dollars it is, but you'd better do a good job of it and not let anyone see you."

When Molly took two tentative steps toward them, Bubba shook his head at her and mouthed the word "later." Then he turned back to Tolliver. "I been sneakin' in an' outta that hotel for years, Buck ol' man. You just sit here and have a drink or two of my whiskey an' I'll be right back."

"No, that's too obvious," Tolliver said, worried that if Bubba screwed up the plan people would remember they'd been talking together. "I'll wait for you over at the jail."

"Whatever you say, Buck. Just have my money ready and waitin' for me."

"You do this right, Bubba, and I'll see that you get made a full partner in Hardy's and my dealings. That'll mean more money than you've ever seen in your entire life."

Bubba's eyes glittered with greed. "I'll hold you to that, Buck." As he got up, he thought to himself, "This is great. Not only do I get to pay that son of a bitch Jensen back what I owe him, I get to get rich doing it."

As Tolliver got up to head for the jail, he thought about the new way Bubba was acting, and he didn't like it. Not one bit of it. No, it was clear to him that once Bubba finished off Jensen, *he* would have to do the same thing to Bubba. He'd just have to make sure to get him out of town first, and then kill him and bury him where he'd never be found. Bubba was such a no-account type of person, people would just figure he'd gone on down the road to find another town to get drunk in.

Smoke and Cal walked into the hotel lobby, and Joe Samuelson immediately raised his hand. "Oh, Mr. Jensen, your baths are ready, and I've told the barber I will send for him the minute you're finished."

Smoke walked up to the desk. "What is your name?"

"Uh . . . Joe Samuelson," the clerk replied, afraid that he'd offended the gunfighter somehow.

Smoke smiled. "Well, Mr. Samuelson, you've done a good job, and I'll be sure and tell your boss how helpful you've been."

"Yes, sir, thank you, sir," Samuelson said. "The bathroom is on the second floor, just down at the end of the corridor. There are two bathtubs there and a stove with hot water in a bucket on it. I've instructed a boy to check in on you periodically to make sure there's nothing else you need."

Smoke nodded. "I'll tell you what, Joe," he said. "It's worth another five dollars to you if you'll get our horses taken down to the livery and rubbed down and fed plenty of grain for us while we take our baths."

Samuelson nodded and smiled. "Consider it done, sir."

Smoke smiled back, and he and Cal climbed the stairs toward the second floor. "Why were you so nice to that man?" Cal asked.

"Because he did a good job for us, Cal, and because hotel clerks tend to be gossips and he'll probably know as much about what goes on in this town as anyone. It won't hurt to be on his good side when we question him about this Rule lady and anything else he might know about Dr. Bentley's business."

Cal glanced at Smoke. "You think the real killer might be someone who had a grudge against the doctor?"

Smoke shrugged. "I don't know, but I'm betting that Samuelson will know if anyone in town had reason to want the doc dead." He looked at Cal. "There are only a few reasons a man is killed in cold blood, Cal: strong emotion like hate or love, for money or profit, or revenge for some past wrong done to the killer. We just have to figure out which one applies in this case and we'll be halfway to finding out who really killed the doctor."

When they entered the bathroom, they were pleased to find it full of steam from the heated water in their tubs. A young black man was busy heating more water on a large, potbellied stove in the corner, and he grinned at them when they entered. "Mr. Samuelson tol' me to git you men anything you need," he said.

Smoke looked around the room. There was a coffeepot on one of the burners of the stove, and a bottle of whiskey and two glasses on a chair in the corner right next to a box of cigars. He grinned. Samuelson had spared no effort to make them feel at home. He realized he might have to give the man a bigger tip since he was so good at his job.

Smoke and Cal shrugged out of their trail clothes, and they handed them to the young man. "Get these cleaned at the nearest laundry and have them sent back to our rooms at the hotel," Smoke said.

"Yes, suh," the young man said, gathering the pile of dirty buckskins and shirts in his arms.

"I think that'll be all," Smoke said, flipping the young man a fifty-cent piece, which he managed to catch without dropping any of the clothes.

"Thank you, suh," he said, and left with a wide grin on his face. Most customers of the hotel didn't bother to tip him, so he'd make sure the gentlemen's clothes were done just right.

Smoke tested the water with his hand, and then he grabbed the bathtub and eased it around until it faced the doorway. He slipped his Colt from its holster, laid it on the floor next to the tub, covered it with a small towel out of sight of the doorway, and eased into the water with a contented sigh.

Cal, without watching Smoke, did about the same thing, having learned from Smoke that safety is all about preparing for the unexpected. Once he had his tub also facing the door and his gun on the floor next to it, he poured them both cups of coffee, adding just a dollop of whiskey to each cup, and handed one to Smoke. Then, he took two cigars out of the box, lighted both of them, and handed one to Smoke before he climbed into his own tub.

"You know, Cal," Smoke said after he'd taken a drink of his coffee and a deep drag on the cigar, "one of the great pleasures in life is relaxing in a steaming-hot bathtub with a cup of good coffee and a fine cigar."

Cal laughed, exhaling a cloud of blue smoke and then taking a sip of his own coffee. "For you old fellas, maybe. As far as us young guns are concerned, most of the great pleasures in life involve a female with long hair and a pretty face and a trim figure to top it all off."

Smoke chuckled. "I may be 'old' as you say, Cal, but I'm not dead. And I do remember those days, believe it or not." He smiled, thinking to himself, "And that's just what I've got waiting for me back at the Sugarloaf."

Cal was about to reply when the door opened and a large, heavyset man with a cloth mask made out of an old flour sack over his face burst into the room. He had Colt pistols in each hand and his eyes were flashing with malevolence.

Smoke could see the man's teeth flash through the mouth-hole in the mask when he saw Smoke and Cal sitting defenseless in their tubs, drinking coffee and smoking cigars.

The man chuckled. "So this is how the great Smoke Jensen ends his days, huh? Soaking his sorry ass in a bathtub with a cup of coffee in one hand and a cigar in the other."

Smoke slowly raised his left hand with the coffee cup in it while he stuck the cigar in his mouth and laid his right hand over the edge of the tub. "You mind telling me who it is that's going to kill me and why?" he asked around the cigar, hoping to keep the man's attention off Cal, whose right hand had also moved over the edge of his tub.

"As for who, the name's Bubba Barkley, and as for why, it's 'cause you keep stickin' your nose in other people's business. You messed with me once before, Jensen, an' now I'm paying you back in spades!"

"What about me?" Cal asked, raising his eyebrows. "Why are you gonna kill me?"

When the man's eyes shifted toward Cal, both Smoke and Cal made their moves. Their pistols were up and fired in less time than it takes to tell it. Neither man bothered to aim, and Smoke's gun exploded only a scant fraction of a second before Cal's did.

Red blossoms of death bloomed on the man's chest as their slugs tore through his body and flung him backward against the wall.

Through the eyeholes in the mask, Smoke saw surprise flicker in the man's eyes just before they softened and took the long stare into eternity.

The head drooped and his body slithered down the wall, ending up sitting there with his legs splayed out and his arms hanging limp at his sides, streaks of his blood trailing down the wall to end behind his back.

Cal took a deep breath. He was still young enough that sudden death unnerved him a bit. "You think he's got friends outside?" he asked.

Smoke shook his head and laid his pistol back down on the floor. He leaned back in his tub and took a sip of his coffee, of which he hadn't spilled a drop, and then a drag on his cigar. "No, if there were more of them, they'd've come in here with him. They wouldn't've wanted to miss seeing us killed."

Cal glanced down at his now empty coffee cup and the sodden cigar he'd dropped into his bathwater in the excitement of the battle. He shook his head. "Damn, now I'm gonna have to get out of the tub an' get more coffee an' another cigar."

Smoke laughed. The boy was certainly growing up fast in the wilds of Colorado Territory.

"While you're up, son, I could use a warming myself," Smoke said, holding out his cup.

CHAPTER 21

Even above the chatter and the plunking of the piano in the corner, Tolliver thought he heard the sound of gunshots from the direction of the hotel. He decided to pretend not to hear them and to wait for someone to come and get him. That would give Bubba more time to get away and would solidify Tolliver's claim to not know anything about what was happening.

He smiled, thinking of how much he was going to enjoy seeing Jensen's bullet-riddled, dead body lying on the floor of the hotel. It would almost make all these years of waiting worthwhile. The only thing better would be if he could have watched Jensen's eyes when he first realized he was fixing to die.

Suddenly, Joe Samuelson burst through the batwings, his face white and pale. "Sheriff, Sheriff, there's been a shooting at the hotel!" he almost screamed, his voice going up a full octave in his excitement.

Tolliver tried to look surprised. "Anybody hurt?" he asked, getting to his feet and adjusting his gun belt, loosening the rawhide hammer thong as if he was afraid there might be more gunplay.

"Uh . . . I don't rightly know," Samuelson stammered. "I didn't go upstairs to look. I'd just gotten back from the livery taking Mr. Jensen's horses over there and I heard this godawful commotion upstairs with what seemed like dozens of gunshots all happening at once." He hesitated, and then he added in a whisper, "And then it got awful quiet, Sheriff, not nary a sound."

Tolliver made a show of bravado. "Well, come on then, Joe. I'll go have a look and see what's going on." As they left the saloon, he asked, "And you say the shots came from Smoke Jensen's room?"

"Oh, no, sir."

Tolliver felt a stab of fear. "The shots didn't come from Jensen's room? Then where did they come from?"

"Mr. Jensen and Mr. Woods weren't in their rooms. They were in the bathing room taking hot baths. It sounded like that's where the shots came from."

"Oh," Tolliver said, feeling relief wash over him like a flood. Bubba must've found them in the bathtubs and killed 'em right where they sat, soaking, he thought with satisfaction. Even better. He could just see it in his mind's eye. There they sat, all cozy and warm and feeling safe, when suddenly Bubba burst in and started blazing away with his six-killer. He hoped Bubba had waited a few minutes to give them both time to realize their days were over, that Jensen's luck had finally run out for good.

With Samuelson so close behind him he could smell the man's aftershave, Tolliver eased up the hotel stairs, his pistol in his hands for show. He really didn't expect to find a gunman there, knowing Bubba would be long gone by now.

The hallway was still full of gun smoke and the heavy, acrid smell of cordite when the sheriff and the desk clerk eased their way down the hall toward the bathroom.

"It must've come from in there," Samuelson said.

"Like I said, Mr. Jensen and Mr. Woods were in there bathing at the time."

"You think they could've shot each other in an argument or something?" Tolliver asked, already thinking that might be a good cover story for the killings.

"Oh, no, sir. They were very good friends," Samuelson answered. "And the boy that works in the bathing room said they'd already gotten in their tubs, so they wouldn't have had their guns close at hand if there'd been an argument or something like that."

"Where was the bath boy at the time of the shooting?" Tolliver asked, hoping the young black man hadn't been a witness to the shooting. That might complicate matters if he could recognize Bubba.

"Oh, he'd gone for more hot water," Samuelson said. "He was down in the lobby with me when the shooting started, and he took off like a scared rabbit." He shook his head. "I doubt he'll be back to work anytime soon."

"Well, you never know. . . ." Tolliver began as he stepped into the smoke- and steam-filled room.

"Howdy, Sheriff," Smoke Jensen said, holding up his coffee cup in a mock salute to the sheriff.

Tolliver's eyes opened wide when he saw Cal and Smoke sitting in their bathtubs as calm as you please, drinking coffee and smoking cigars as if nothing had happened.

"Uh . . . the clerk here says he heard gunshots," Tolliver began, and then he saw Bubba's body sprawled against the wall, blood still seeping from five or six holes in his chest, and holes in the wall where the bullets had gone through, with bloodstains trailing down the wall from the holes to his body.

"That would've been us, I suspect," Smoke said calmly. He indicated Bubba with a nod of his head.

"That gentleman burst in here with guns in his hands and said he was going to kill us." Smoke grinned. "Obviously, he was wrong."

Tolliver didn't know what to say. His chest felt like someone was sitting on it, and he could hardly catch his breath. "Uh . . . um . . . he say anything else?" he asked, hoping against hope Bubba hadn't had time to shoot his mouth off too much before he'd been killed.

Smoke glanced at Cal. "Did you hear him say anything else, Cal?"

Cal pursed his lips, and then he grinned. "I think I might've heard him say ouch when my first slug hit him in the chest."

Smoke laughed. "I don't think so. I got off the first shot."

Cal shook his head. "No, I think it was me, Smoke, shot him first."

Samuelson glanced at the two men in the tubs arguing over who'd drilled the man first, and then at the dead body lying in a pool of blood, and then he fainted dead away, his body hitting the floor with a thud.

Tolliver reached down and pulled the black cloth mask off Bubba's head. He sat back on his haunches and glanced at Smoke and Cal. "Either of you know this man?"

Smoke looked at Cal and nodded. "Yeah. The first time we were coming into town this man and a friend of his braced us and tried to steal our saddlebags."

Tolliver frowned. Damn that Bubba. It seemed the man just couldn't do anything right. "What happened?" Tolliver asked, though he knew the story full well.

Cal grinned. "Smoke beat the shit outta his friend, and then he and his friend decided they had better things to do than to mess with us."

"Sheriff," Smoke said, interrupting the talk.

"Yes?"

"Would you mind handing me that towel over there? Both my water and my coffee are getting cold."

Tolliver grunted and shook his head. He'd never seen anyone so cool in the face of an attempted murder. He hoped he hadn't underestimated the gunfighter.

He grabbed a pair of towels from a stack in the corner of the room and flipped one each to Cal and Smoke.

"By the way," he asked as Smoke and Cal stood up and began to towel off. "If he burst in here like you say with his guns out and you two were in the tubs, how is it you had time to get your guns from over there before he shot you?" He looked over at the chairs on the other side of the room, where Smoke and Cal's gun belts were lying.

"Our guns weren't over there, Sheriff," Smoke said easily. "Whenever I'm bathing, I always keep my Colt next to the tub on the floor, covered with a towel, just in case of events like this."

Tolliver arched an eyebrow. "You get attacked often while bathing, Mr. Jensen?"

Smoke shrugged, but Cal replied, "Why, I do believe this is at least the third time, isn't it, Smoke?"

Smoke grinned. "Third or fourth, I tend to lose count."

Tolliver couldn't believe the men weren't the least bit rattled by the attempt on their lives. As he stepped over the prone body of Samuelson on his way out of the room, he looked back over his shoulder. "Come see me in my office when you're done getting dressed," he said, "an' you can tell me more about what happened here."

* * *

Smoke and Cal took their time with the barber, and it was over an hour later when they appeared in Tolliver's office, cleanly shaven and with hair neatly trimmed and clothes that were neat and pressed.

Tolliver took a long look at the Regulator Clock on the wall and said sarcastically, "I'm glad you could finally make it."

Smoke's face went flat and his eyes bored into the sheriff's. "I wasn't aware there was a time limit, Sheriff. Besides, we told you all we know over at the hotel, and since you're so concerned, Mr. Samuelson is fine."

Tolliver blushed. He hadn't even slowed to make sure the clerk was all right after he'd fainted. He'd been too deep in his thoughts about how to handle this monumental fuck-up by Bubba. He knew Jensen was bound to find out Bubba and the sheriff were at least well acquainted, even if the fact that they were partners wasn't widely known.

He decided to be open about his association with Bubba and try to minimize the damage. "Have either of you seen or had any dealings with the murdered man since the fight earlier?" Tolliver asked, moving a sheet of paper and a pencil to the center of his desk in order to take notes.

Smoke's face colored slightly and his eyes flashed, turning dangerously dark. "The man wasn't murdered, as you say, Sheriff. He was killed while trying to commit a crime. That doesn't make it murder, which if I'm not mistaken is a crime itself."

Tolliver sighed. "All right then, have you seen the *dead* man since your first altercation with him?"

Both Smoke and Cal shook their heads. "We don't even know his name," Cal volunteered, "and we haven't seen hide nor hair of him or his friend since the fight."

Tolliver pursed his lips, as if considering whether to

give them that information or not. Finally, after a few moments, he said, "The man's name was Bubba Barkley, a well-known figure around Payday."

"Do you have any idea why he braced us?" Smoke asked as he pulled out his makings and began to build a cigarette. "It seems a rather extreme act just because his friend got his butt kicked a little and Cal took his gun away from him."

Tolliver shook his head. "No, none at all. The man had no known employment, living on odd jobs like mucking out stables at the livery and sweeping out the saloon to pay his bar bills." He hesitated. "In fact, I knew him fairly well, and to my knowledge he'd never before broken the law or robbed anyone that I'm aware of."

Smoke stared at Tolliver through the flame of a match as he lighted his cigarette. He tipped smoke out of his nostrils, and said, "Is that so? Were you close friends, Sheriff?"

A scarlet flush appeared on Tolliver's neck and moved steadily up his face to his forehead. "I didn't say we was friends, Jensen, I said I knew the man. That's an entirely different thing. However, I did just the other day offer him employment as a sheriff's deputy to help guard the town during your friend's trial."

When Jensen didn't reply but just sat there smoking and staring into Tolliver's eyes as if he could read his mind, Tolliver cleared his throat and broke his gaze. "So, Barkley didn't say anything about why he was trying to kill you two?" he asked, his voice sounding rough and coarse coming out of a dry throat.

"No, he didn't, Sheriff," Smoke answered, omitting to tell the lawman what Barkley had said about Smoke sticking his nose in other people's business, "but I'm sure we'll get some idea what was on his mind when we talk to people that knew him."

Tolliver's eyes opened wide and he leaned forward pointing his finger at Smoke like a gun. "Now you listen to me, Jensen. This is my town, and if there's any investigating to do about this, I'll be the one to do it."

Smoke got to his feet, dropped his butt on the floor and ground it out under his boot, and said, "Last time I looked, Sheriff, there isn't any law against talking to people, not even in a Podunk like this one. So now, if you're through asking us questions, we'd like to talk to our friend again."

Tolliver started to object, and then he saw the gunfighter's eyes go from pale to dark and dangerous, and figured it really wouldn't hurt anything to let them talk to the condemned man—hell, it might even make the mountain man suffer a little bit more, and that was fine with him.

"Sure, go right on in, the door's open," he said, smiling a little to show he was being generous by not making them take their guns off.

Smoke stared at him for a moment more, and then when they walked out of the room and closed the cellblock door behind them, Tolliver wiped sweat off his forehead. "Damn that Bubba," he muttered, "now the fat's really in the fire."

The only good thing out of all this is that now I won't have to kill the stupid son of a bitch, Tolliver thought.

When Pearlie saw Smoke and Cal, he jumped to his feet. He finally looked like the old Pearlie they knew, so both men were relieved to see he'd recovered from his earlier injuries.

"Hey, Pearlie, how you doin'?" Cal asked, sticking his hand through the bars to clasp Pearlie's.

Pearlie cocked his head to the side and gave Cal one of his old grins. "How the hell do you think I'm doin', young'un? They only serve three meals a day in this joint."

Smoke laughed. "Aside from that, how is the food?"

Pearlie looked at him and smiled. "Thanks for what you did, Smoke. The lady who delivers the food said you'd forced the sheriff to get it from the hotel dining room, and it sure as hell beats what I was getting before." He chuckled. "I even got her to promise to bring in extra helpings of dessert."

He paused for a moment, and then he asked, "You got any news 'bout who might've done in the doc?"

Smoke shook his head. "No, but we've found out there may have been a witness there that night, a lady name of Rule. Did you see anyone else in the house that night?"

Pearlie frowned and shook his head. "No, not that I can recall. Course, I was kind'a busy fighting for my life, and then I passed out, so she could've been standing right there in the room and I wouldn't've seen her."

Smoke reached through the bars and put his hand on Pearlie's shoulder. "Don't worry, ol' pal, we'll see that you're cleared of this and we'll have you back in Big Rock before you know it."

Pearlie glanced over his shoulder at the one window in the cell block down the corridor, and listened to the hammer blows of the men building the scaffold to hang him from. "I sure hope so, Smoke, 'cause I ain't exactly anxious to test those boys' work."

Smoke and Cal laughed, glad to see their friend still maintaining his sense of wry humor.

Cal couldn't resist a gibe. "I tell you what, Pearlie, if'n I was you, I think I'd give up on those second helpings of dessert from the hotel dining room."

"Why?" Pearlie asked, looking down at his waist to see if he was gaining weight.

"'Cause if'n you get any fatter, your hoss Cold ain't

gonna be able to carry your fat butt all the way back to Big Rock."

Tears brimmed in Pearlie's eyes at the thought that he might be going home soon and he just nodded, unable to speak.

CHAPTER 22

As Smoke and Cal walked out of the corridor after talking with Pearlie, Sheriff Tolliver said with a smirk, "You find out anything from your friend, Jensen?"

Smoke just looked at him. "We found out enough to know he didn't kill the doctor, and the man he did kill was trying to kill him."

Tolliver forced a laugh. "Now just why would someone want to kill a complete stranger to the town?"

"That's what I intend to find out, Sheriff," Smoke said, his eyes boring into Tolliver's. "You wouldn't happen to have any ideas on the subject, would you?"

Tolliver turned beet red. "What? That's preposterous! Why would I possibly know anything about that?"

Smoke grinned and continued to stare into Tolliver's eyes, which were now tinged with fear. "Well, the man Pearlie killed was not only a relative of yours, but it seems he occasionally worked as your deputy. That's a pretty close connection, wouldn't you say?"

Tolliver's mouth opened and closed, but he didn't have anything further to say. When his eyes dropped, unable to meet Smoke's gaze, Smoke tipped his hat and headed for the door. "We'll be seeing you again, Sheriff, you can count on it."

After they left the sheriff's office, Smoke told Cal they were headed over to see Sam Hemmings.

"Why are we going there?" Cal asked.

"I need to get a feel for what was said at the trial," Smoke said. "It may give us a hint about who really did the killing of the doctor, and why a man who was not only a relative of the sheriff but who also worked as a deputy might have been trying to rob Pearlie."

"You mean you don't think it was just 'cause the man was a footpad?"

Smoke shrugged. "I doubt it, Cal. If Pearlie was the sort to flash around a big wad of greenbacks or sport some fancy watch fobs or diamond stickpins, maybe. But Pearlie's just a cowboy, and not a particularly rich one at that." He shook his head. "I just can't figure why the man Pearlie stabbed would have taken such a chance of breaking into a popular town doctor's house to steal the few dollars and old pocket watch Pearlie had."

Even though the job of mayor of a small town like Payday wasn't a full-time job, Mayor Hemmings happened to be in his office when Smoke and Cal arrived.

He answered the door himself. "Yes?" he asked politely.

"Hello, Mayor," Smoke said. "I'm Smoke Jensen and this is my friend Calvin Woods. We're friends of Pearlie's and we're the ones who brought him to town."

"Oh, yes," Hemmings said, "I've heard of you, Mr. Jensen." He motioned them inside.

Smoke smiled. He heard that all the time when he introduced himself. It was the price of being famous, or rather infamous. Sometimes it was said with a smile and sometimes with a frown; just about everyone had heard of Smoke in some way or other, and it was often a toss-up which way they felt about him.

"Come in, gentlemen," Hemmings said, showing them to a pair of well-worn chairs in front of his desk.

He sat down, put his elbows on the desk, and rested

his chin in his hands. "Now, first let me say that I'm very sorry I didn't get your friend acquitted of the charges against him." He sighed. "The evidence against him was just too strong, I'm afraid."

"That's one of the things we came to talk to you about, Mayor," Smoke said.

Hemmings held up his hand. "Please, call me Sam," he said with a deprecating grin. "The job isn't all that important in a town this size."

"All right, Sam. First off, I would like to know something about this Blackie Johnson that Pearlie says he killed because he caught him robbing Pearlie. Pearlie also says he got the feeling that Johnson was going to kill him and that the theft of his things was just an afterthought."

Hemmings leaned back in his chair. "You know, I wondered about that myself. Blackie Johnson, though certainly not one of the town's leading citizens, has never really been in trouble before; at least not jail-type trouble. He was pretty much a drunkard, but he usually sobered up enough to hold down a job doing menial labor, and as far as I know, was never charged with stealing anything before." He elected not to mention the widow's egg money Hattie had told him about since it was only hearsay.

"So, you can't think of any reason he might have to try and kill Pearlie?"

Hemmings smiled sadly. "Mr. Jensen, you brought your friend into town less than a week before all this happened, and he was unconscious and lying in bed the entire time he was here. No one in town had ever heard of Pearlie before this, and no one could possibly have had any reason to want him dead that I can think of." The smile faded from his face. "Hell, far as I know, no one in town even knew anything about him until the killing. Doc wasn't one to shoot his mouth off about his patients." Hemmings hesitated. "In fact, that was one of the things that worked against Pearlie with the jury—there was just no motive to kill him that I could come up with."

Smoke nodded slowly. "That's right, Sam. I hadn't thought of that until you mentioned it. Just how would anyone have known Pearlie was in town if the doctor didn't talk about it?"

"That's what I'm trying to tell you, Smoke. Johnson would have had no reason to try and kill your friend. Even if he'd met him before and had some sort of grudge against him, which is highly unlikely, he wouldn't have known he was in town."

Smoke snapped his fingers. "What about the telegraph operator?" he asked. "Dr. Bentley and I kept in touch by sending telegrams back and forth. The operator would have had to know about Pearlie, and that it was me who brought him into town."

Hemmings shrugged. "Well, that'd be Bob Jacobson," he said. "He also owns the general store, but that don't help you much, Smoke. That means there were two men who knew Pearlie was in town, and Jacobson didn't have anything to do with the killings."

Smoke leaned forward in his chair. "Maybe not, Sam, but maybe Mr. Jacobson wasn't as closemouthed about the doctor's business as the doctor was."

Hemmings frowned. "Well, you may be right there, Smoke. Ol' Bob does like to gossip a bit, like all general store owners I've ever known. But so what? From what Pearlie tells me, he's just a cowhand on a ranch down in the southern part of the state. Unless he's got a past that's a lot more exciting than that, I still don't see where anyone would care if he was in town or not."

Smoke leaned back. "Pearlie does have a past, Sam. He used to hire his gun out to ranchers a long time ago, but I doubt that has anything to do with his present predicament. I think that just might have to do with the fact that he's my friend and employee."

"What do you mean?"

Smoke smiled grimly. "Sam, I'm sure you know I *do* have a past, quite a long and involved one, and I've made more than my share of enemies in that past. Now, I'm starting to wonder if one of them isn't behind all of this."

"Now wait a minute, Smoke," Hemmings said, his face skeptical. "Surely you don't think someone killed the doctor just to get Pearlie hung to hurt you? Isn't that rather . . . well, complicated?"

Smoke shook his head and his face too was puzzled. "You're right, Sam. On the face of it, that doesn't make a whole hell of a lot of sense, but it makes more sense than for me to believe that a man I know as well as Pearlie would kill two people to steal a few dollars worth of bills and jewelry, especially when he's just waking up from a serious illness."

"Maybe we ought to talk to Bob Jacobson after all," Hemmings said.

Smoke shook his head. "No, Sam. I think I'll do better talking to Mr. Jacobson by myself."

"You won't, uh, do anything rash, will you Smoke?" Hemmings asked, his face now worried. He *had* heard of Smoke Jensen and from what he'd heard, Smoke was not the sort of man to use half measures, especially where a friend's life was involved.

Smoke smiled. "Of course not, Sam. You have my word I won't lay a finger on Mr. Jacobson."

After he got up and shook Sam's hand, he added with a smile, "I won't promise not to scare him just a bit, though."

* * *

After they were out of Hemmings's office, Smoke stopped on the boardwalk to build himself a cigarette. Cal took the opportunity to do the same. As he was lighting his cigarette, Smoke glanced over at Cal. "I need for you to do me a favor, Cal."

"Sure," Cal said, squinting as smoke from his own cigarette irritated his eyes.

"I want you to mosey on over to the livery and have a talk with the boy that works there."

Cal frowned. "What about?"

"I got to thinking when we were talking to the mayor that there was someone else who knew we brought Pearlie into town."

Cal's eyes widened. "Of course, the boy at the livery who took care of our horses. You gave him money to take care of Pearlie's horse until he got well, an' you even told him Pearlie was over at the doc's."

"That's right, and we need to find out just who these two might have talked to that might have a reason to go after either Pearlie or me," Smoke said.

Cal let smoke trickle out of his nostrils as he said, "You can count on me, Smoke. If'n that boy told anyone about us, I'll find out."

"I know you will, Cal. I'm counting on it."

Smoke spent some time browsing in the general store until all of the other customers had left and he was alone with the proprietor. After a few minutes, the man walked over to stand behind Smoke while he fingered some fancy holsters.

"Can I help you, sir?"

Smoke put the holster down and turned around. "Are you Mr. Jacobson?" he asked.

"Sure am. Robert Jacobson, but everybody calls me

Bob." He stuck out his hand. "Pleased to meet ya'. Are you new to town . . . Mr. . . . ?"

Smoke took his hand. "Jensen, Smoke Jensen," Smoke replied. "And no, I haven't moved to town." He noticed Jacobson's face drain of blood and go as pale as the cotton sheets he had in aisle two.

Smoke cocked his head. "Something wrong, Mr. Jacobson?" he asked.

"Uh, no, why, nothing's wrong."

"Good," Smoke said, dropping his easy smile and moving to the door. He reached up and pulled the shade down, turning the cardboard sign in the door's window from OPEN to CLOSED.

"Here now," Jacobson said, holding up his hand and taking a step toward Smoke, until he saw the look in Smoke's eyes when he turned around to face him.

Jacobson stopped short and sweat suddenly appeared on his forehead. He turned as if to run toward the back door, but Smoke said harshly, "I wouldn't do that, Bob. You wouldn't get ten feet 'fore I dropped you like a bad habit."

Jacobson turned back around, raising his hands in the air. "Is this a holdup?"

"Oh, put your hands down, Bob," Smoke said, smiling grimly. "I just want to talk to you without any interruptions for a few minutes."

"What about?" Jacobson asked, slowly lowering his arms, his eyes fixed on the gun in Smoke's holster.

"I think you know what about, Bob. You were the one sending messages back and forth between Dr. Bentley and me about my friend Pearlie."

Jacobson's head bobbed up and down. "That's right. So what?"

Smoke eased his hip up on the counter and sat. "Well, I think you got to shooting your mouth off about those messages and told someone here in town I had a friend at the doc's place."

"No . . . no . . . I would never talk about any of my messages. The company would fire me for that."

Smoke cocked his head. "So, you never gossiped about me to any of your friends?"

"Certainly not!"

Smoke sighed. Maybe he was wrong. Maybe Jacobson didn't have anything to do with Pearlie's problems after all. He glanced back at the man and noticed his eyes wouldn't meet his. No. The man was definitely nervous about something.

Smoke thought back over the messages he'd sent and received, and then he had it. His eyes narrowed. "You know, Bob, just before I left Pueblo for here, I got a message from Dr. Bentley telling me there'd been no change in Pearlie's condition. Do you remember that message?"

Now the sweat fairly poured from Jacobson's face, and his shirt had dark spots under his arms that reached almost all the way down to his belt. "Uh, no. Why should I?"

Smoke eased off the counter and moved until he was less than a foot from Jacobson's face. "Because the doctor was already dead when that message was sent, and Pearlie had already been arrested for his killing."

Jacobson sobbed and hung his head. "You're right, Mr. Jensen, you're right."

"Now, what I need to know, Bob, is why would you do something like that?"

Jacobson looked up into Smoke's eyes. "The sheriff, Mr. Jensen, the sheriff made me do it. He told me he'd hurt me if I told anyone about it, even though I told him it was wrong and that I could lose my job over it."

"You mean Sheriff Buck Tolliver ordered you to

send that wire telling me that Pearlie was still unconscious so I'd hurry and come back to Payday?"

Jacobson nodded, his face flaming red with humiliation and shame.

"Now why would . . ." Smoke began, and a faint tickling at the back of his mind reminded him that Tolliver had looked somehow familiar when they'd first met.

He put his finger on Jacobson's chest. "We're going to forget this talk ever took place, aren't we, Mr. Jacobson?"

"Yes, sir!" Jacobson said, his head nodding up and down rapidly.

"And you're especially not going to tell the sheriff we talked, are you?"

"No . . . no."

"Good," Smoke said, reaching up to pat the man's shoulder. "Then I'll see you later, Bob."

"Uh, Mr. Jensen?"

"Yes, Bob?"

"You're not going to mention anything about that message I sent you to the company, are you? I really need that job. This store doesn't do all that well."

"Don't worry, Bob," Smoke assured him. "Like I said, this conversation is going to be our little secret."

After he left the store, Smoke decided to head on over to the saloon and have a beer and a smoke. Sometimes you could find out a whole lot about someone by simply asking about him in his local watering hole, and he fully intended to find out everything he could about Sheriff Buck Tolliver.

He knew there was something about the man, either his face or his name was familiar, but he just couldn't put his finger on it. If he could only remember, it might give him the reason Pearlie was in such deep shit.

CHAPTER 23

Cal walked into the livery and over to where the boy had put his and Smoke's horses, right next to the stall that held Pearlie's mount.

Cal busied himself with running a currycomb over his horse Dusty until the stable was empty of any other customers. He put the currycomb down and ambled over to where the boy was mucking out a stall with a pitchfork that looked as big as he was.

"Howdy," Cal said, forcing a friendly smile.

The boy looked up and leaned against the pitchfork handle, obviously glad of any excuse to stop work for a moment. "Howdy," he said.

"My name's Cal Woods," Cal said, sticking out his hand.

The boy looked startled, as if no one had ever been friendly before. He glanced at his own hand, wiped it on his trouser leg, which was only marginally cleaner than the floor of the stalls he was mucking out, and then took Cal's hand.

"I'm Jerome Stone, but everbody calls me Jerry."

"Well, Jerry," Cal began, glancing over his shoulder at his horse. "I see you have a good memory for faces."

Jerry looked puzzled. "Huh?"

"Yeah, my friend and I were here 'bout two weeks ago and left another friend's horse with you, an' this time when we come back I noticed you knew to put our horses next to our friend's bronc without us having to tell you which one it was."

"Oh, yeah," Jerry said, smiling and looking at the horses. "Well, it weren't so much. After all, ain't that many fellers come in here ridin' full-blooded Palouse studs." He scratched his head for a moment, and then he grinned widely. "Matter of fact, you three are the first ones I've seen ridin' that particular kind'a hoss."

Cal gave a small laugh. "Oh, is that all there was to it?" He leaned forward and lowered his voice as if he were going to tell Jerry a secret. "I thought maybe it was 'cause you recognized the fellow I rode in here with. He's kind'a famous most places."

"Well, no, not really," Jerry said, lowering his voice and looking around to make sure no one else could hear. "Actually, your big friend in the buckskins is kind'a hard to forget. He's probably the first real true-to-life gunslinger I ever seen."

Now Cal frowned. "What makes you think he's a gunslinger, Jerry, if you didn't recognize who he was?"

Jerry grinned and nudged Cal with his elbow. "Aw, come on, Cal." His eyes dropped to Cal's pistol, slung low on his hip and tied down to his leg. "Both of you wear your irons like gunslingers." He chuckled. "And don't try an' tell me I'm wrong neither, 'cause I read all of Ned Buntline's penny dreadfuls and he's pretty clear on that particular point."

"What point is that, Jerry?" Cal asked.

"'Bout the way gunslicks tie their pistols down low on their leg whereas regular cowboys wear 'em up high so they won't get hung up on brush and such."

Cal returned Jerry's smile. "Oh, you're not wrong really. It's just that Smoke gave up his gunslinging days a long time ago. He's just a rancher now, like me."

"Smoke?" Jerry asked, his eyes wide and his freckles

standing out against his skin, which had suddenly turned as pale white as a new-washed sheet. "Don't tell me that man was Smoke Jensen!"

Cal nodded. "Yep, but don't tell nobody, Jerry. He don't exactly like to advertise when he's in a town 'cause of all the men gunnin' for him."

"Jumpin' Jehosaphat!" Jerry whispered, his face turning even paler. "I can't believe I curried the horse of the famous Smoke Jensen." He reached into his pocket and took out the money Smoke had given him as a tip. "I'm gonna keep this here money and never spend it an' I'm gonna tell everbody my friend the famous Smoke Jensen gave it to me."

Cal began to grin when Jerry looked up from the money in his hand and added, "No wonder the sheriff almost fainted when I described your friend to him."

Cal reached out and grabbed Jerry's shoulder. "What did you say about the sheriff?"

Jerry stepped back, alarmed at the change in Cal's demeanor. "Nothin', I didn't say nothin'." Tears of fear brimmed in his eyes. "Don't hit me, mister, please."

"Oh, don't be silly, Jerry. I'm not going to hit you, but you did say something about the sheriff," Cal persisted, trying to soften his voice and not be so harsh.

"Well, after you was here a couple 'a weeks ago, the sheriff came by and saw that Palouse you left for your friend. He asked me about it an' I told him 'bout you and Smoke, though course I didn't know his name at the time. Well, when I described Smoke to him, the sheriff turned as white as my mamma's sheets and dang near passed out right there in the street." Jerry chuckled now that he saw that Cal wasn't mad at him. "Heck, I thought I was going to have to throw a bucket of water on him to wake him up."

"Did he say anything else?" Cal asked, pleased to have found out so much, and pleased that he might have found out how people knew that Pearlie and Smoke were connected in some way and that Pearlie was in town.

Jerry shrugged. "Not really. He asked what y'all were doing in town, an' I told him 'bout you leavin' your sick friend over at the doc's an' all."

"So the sheriff seemed interested in what Smoke and I were doing in town, huh?"

"Heck, yes," Jerry said. "After I told him what I knew, he turned and wandered off like his mind was off somewheres else. Dang near got runned over by a couple of hosses on his way to the doc's too."

"You mean he left here and went directly to the doctor's office?" Cal asked.

Jerry nodded. "Sure did. An' he was mumblin' somethin' 'bout he couldn't believe it, not after all these years, or somethin' like that."

Cal reached into his pocket and pulled out a dollar bill. "Here, Jerry. Thanks for taking the time to talk to me. See that our mounts get a little extra grain if you would."

"Jesus . . . uh, I mean, hey, thanks a lot, Cal," Jerry said when he saw Cal was tipping him more than he made in a whole day of mucking out stalls. "Oh, and Cal . . ."

"Yeah, Jerry?" Cal called back over his shoulder.

"You tell Smoke I said hello, would ya?"

"Sure thing, Jerry," Cal said, laughing as he hurried to find Smoke and tell him what he'd found out.

Cal didn't know exactly where to find Smoke, so he decided to wait for him in the saloon. Besides, all that talking and excitement had made him thirsty for a cool beer.

When he walked through the batwings, he immediately stepped to the side with his back to the wall like Smoke had taught him, and waited for his eyes to adjust to the gloom. Not that Cal had all that many people interested in gunning him down like Smoke did, but since he rode with the man and was known to be his friend, Smoke had told him to take the same precautions he did and he'd live long enough to grow whiskers.

As soon as his eyes were adjusted, Cal saw Smoke standing at the bar, his elbows planted around a shot glass of whiskey, and he started to walk toward him.

Smoke saw him coming and gave a minute shake of his head, cutting his eyes toward a nearby table that was empty.

Cal took the hint and altered his course to the table and took a seat, pretending not to look at Smoke. When one of the girls came over and asked him if he'd like some company, Cal shook his head. "No, but if you'll get the bartender to send over a glass of beer, I'll buy you a shot too."

She leaned down close to him and whispered in his ear. "I don't really like liquor all that much, but I'll take the money instead and get you your beer if you don't let on to the bartender about it."

Cal grinned, enjoying the view down the front of her dress, and said, "Sure thing, ma'am."

She noticed where his gaze was locked on and winked at him. "You sure you don't want some company? We got some awfully nice rooms upstairs where we could go and be alone while you drink your beer."

Cal blushed from the top of his head all the way down to his boots. "Uh . . . no, thank you anyway, ma'am." When she made a face and stuck out her lip in a pout like her feelings were hurt, he explained, "I'm just here waiting on a friend of mine. As soon as he gets here, we got to leave. Otherwise, I'd be right honored to go upstairs with you."

She smiled and tousled his hair. "All right, cowboy, it's your loss." And she strutted off to get his beer, looking back over her shoulder to see if he was enjoying the view of her hips as they swayed back and forth—which he most definitely was.

Cal was on his second beer when he saw Smoke pat the man next to him at the bar on the shoulder, throw some money down, and walk over toward Cal's table.

Smoke pulled up a chair and leaned back, building himself a cigarette as his eyes roamed the room as they did every few moments, checking for familiar faces or for danger. "Did you learn anything from our friend at the livery?"

Cal nodded and filled Smoke in on what Jerry had told him about the sheriff, his obvious interest in their business, and how he'd acted when he recognized Smoke from Jerry's description.

"What did you find out?" he asked Smoke.

Smoke tipped smoke out of his nostrils and said, "Pretty much the same as you. The sheriff seemed to show a lot of interest in our comings and goings, more than would be usual for a sheriff in a small town like this, especially since he didn't have any paper on me."

"Yeah, an' Jerry said he went right off to talk to the doc about what Pearlie was doing there an' to find out what he could 'bout us."

"You know, Cal," Smoke said, dropping the butt to the floor and squashing it with his boot, "I'm inclined to think the sheriff is hip-deep in this affair, and what worries me is I don't know why."

"Jerry seemed to think the sheriff knew you, or at least recognized who you were from your description," Cal said. "Does that mean anything to you?"

Smoke frowned. "Not really, but I've crossed paths with more than my share of hard men in the past, Cal, and it could be that Sheriff Tolliver is one of them." He inclined his head toward the bar and the man he'd been talking to. "Word around town is that the sheriff always has a pocketful of money and has a hell of a nice spread out of town stocked with some fine livestock, much better than what he makes as sheriff would account for."

"Where do they think he gets it?"

Smoke shrugged. "There's been rumors of miners turning up missing and friends of the sheriff turning up with signed bills of sale for their claims, but nothing definite anyone wants to get involved with. I get the idea everyone is pretty much afraid of Tolliver and his friends and no one wants to stand up to them."

"And they told you all this?" Cal asked, amazed that Smoke could get so much information being a stranger in town.

Smoke grinned. "Give these miners enough whiskey and before you know it, they're telling you their life stories and anything else you want to hear." He grinned. "But, like I said, most of it is just miners' gossip, so a lot of it can be discounted."

Cal laughed. "That's still strange that they would repeat all that to you since they don't know you."

"Not when you think about it," Smoke said. "Mining is a pretty lonely business. After working for months alone out in the mountains, when you come to town and someone buys you whiskey and offers a sympathetic ear, it's only natural to want to talk more than you should."

When Cal shook his head, Smoke added, "The two best places to pick up on gossip are a woman's quilting circle and the most popular bar in town, 'cause the only person who gossips more than women is a man who's drunk more than he can handle."

CHAPTER 24

Robert Jacobson's eyes widened when he translated the dots and dashes of the telegram that came in over his wire that afternoon. He sleeved at the sweat that suddenly appeared on his forehead as he sat and reread the wire.

"To Mayor Samuel Hemmings, Payday: Mr. Hemmings, please meet the five o'clock train at the station in Payday tomorrow afternoon. I will be in the last car, but I refuse to exit the train. I have important information about the killing of my nephew Dr. Bentley. Please tell no one of this wire, as my life will be in danger if news of my arrival gets out." It was signed Janet Rule.

Holy shit! thought Jacobson. The wire is addressed to Mayor Hemmings, but the sheriff told me to keep him informed of any information about Missus Rule that came in over the telegraph. Jesus, now what do I do? And then there's Smoke Jensen. Holy shit, maybe this job isn't worth all this aggravation after all!

Finally, he decided it wouldn't hurt to let the sheriff have a peek at the wire after he showed it to Hemmings. After all, the sheriff was the one investigating the murders, not the mayor. Besides, he reasoned, all Hemmings could do if he found out was get him fired. The sheriff, on the other hand, could and probably would do much worse if he ignored his orders to keep him informed, and he didn't even want to think about what Jensen might do—so he just vowed to make sure Jensen never learned of the contents of the wire or that he intended to let the sheriff know about it.

After discussing it for a while, Smoke and Cal decided about the only person in town they dared to trust with their new information about the sheriff was the mayor, Sam Hemmings, and only because he seemed to genuinely believe in Pearlie's innocence.

They met him in his office just after lunch. "What can I do for you boys?" he asked. "You come up with any evidence that might help clear Pearlie?"

Smoke and Cal looked at each other. "Well, it's not exactly evidence, Sam, but we've been talking to some people around town and we've come up with some rather strange behavior on the sheriff's part. We'd like to see what you think about it," Smoke said.

Hemmings shrugged. "I don't see what that has to do with the case, but go ahead. I'm willing to listen to anything at this point," he said, glancing out of his window and shuddering at the hanging scaffold that was almost completed. He certainly didn't want someone to go to the gallows because he hadn't done his job well enough.

Smoke began by telling Hemmings what Jacobson had said about how the sheriff had told him to send the fake wire to get Smoke and Cal back to town, and then Cal finished by detailing what the livery boy Jerry had told him about the sheriff's strange reaction to his description of Smoke and how he'd immediately gone to the doc's to investigate Pearlie.

Hemmings rocked back in his chair, stroking his chin and glancing longingly at a box of cigars on his desk.

"Go ahead and light one up," Smoke said, grinning. "It won't bother us if you smoke."

"Are you sure?" Hemmings asked, looking relieved. "It's a small office and the smoke can get pretty thick, but I think better when I'm chewing on a stogie."

Cal got up and opened the mayor's office window. "There, now the smoke can get out."

Hemmings struck a match on his trousers leg and held it under the tip of a long, black cigar until it was smoking like a train engine.

He flicked the match out of the window and leaned back in his chair, staring at the ceiling. "Now," he said contentedly, "I agree Sheriff Tolliver's actions seem a bit out of the ordinary, but they don't necessarily mean he had something to do with Dr. Bentley's death. It might just be that you two have crossed paths in the past, Smoke, and that as sheriff he was worried about having a . . . no offense . . . rather famous gunfighter in his town."

Smoke, who'd been thinking on the sheriff's actions for some time now, said, "Let me say something, Sam, and give me a little leeway on it until you hear all of it."

Hemmings looked at him. "All right."

"Let's assume, for the sake of argument, that the sheriff has a longtime, very strong grudge against me for some reason that I'm unaware of."

"Go on."

"And then, he comes into town one day and sees a strange horse. When he inquires of the livery boy, he's given a description of me, and it shakes him up so much that even the livery boy notices it."

"But how could he recognize you from a description that could fit dozens of men?" Hemmings asked, playing the devil's advocate.

Smoke smiled. "Sam, how many men do you suppose

run around in this day and time in buckskins, are over six feet tall, and have two guns and a knife on their holster tied down low on their legs? I agree, there are lots of big men with light-colored hair, but when you put that with the buckskins and the guns"—he shrugged—"it may have struck enough of a chord with Tolliver that he wanted to see the doctor and check it out to see if it really was me."

"All right, I'll grant you that you do present a rather unique appearance. Go on."

"Now, once he's determined that I might be in town, what is he to do? He has to go immediately to the doctor's house to see if it really is me and find out what the hell I'm doing in his town after all these years."

Hemmings nodded slowly. "I can see that. And I suppose that the doctor fills him in that it is indeed Smoke Jensen and that you've left your very good friend in his care."

Smoke agreed. "And not only that, but he probably tells Tolliver that we've been keeping in touch by telegraph from Pueblo, so his next stop is to see Jacobson and find out what else he can."

Hemmings leaned forward to tap his ash into his trash can, and then he said, "All right. Even granting all of that, how would you get from there to the killing of the doctor? Like I said, each and every one of his actions could just as easily be explained by the fact that he's sheriff here and it's his job to keep the peace. Maybe he just wanted to keep an eye on a notorious gunman, and that is all."

"Just suppose, again for the sake of argument," Smoke said, "that Tolliver decided to have Pearlie killed. That would do two things. One, it would cause me great grief and pain, and two, it would bring me running back to town."

"And that's where Pearlie's story starts to make sense," Cal said. "He says he woke up to find that Blackie man—the sheriff's cousin, remember—standing over him with a gun. It makes sense that the sheriff would have sent someone he trusted to do the dirty work, someone who'd never tell anyone who had ordered him to commit cold-blooded murder."

Smoke held up a finger. "According to his testimony, the sheriff was having drinks and dinner with the doctor when he and Blackie decided to make their rounds. What if in fact it was just Tolliver that walked the doctor back home, intending to be there when he found Pearlie dead, but instead he found Blackie dead and Pearlie lying unconscious near the body?"

Hemmings nodded, beginning to see how Smoke's story might explain some things about the case that had been bothering him. "That would put him in a devilish position, trying to explain what Blackie was doing in the doc's house and how he happened to get himself killed by a man in a coma."

"Exactly," Smoke said, leaning back and spreading his arms out wide. "His only way out would be to do what I think he did. Kill the doctor and try and put the blame on Pearlie."

"That would also work to get Smoke back to town, once we found out about Pearlie's arrest," Cal said. "And then he'd have him right where he wanted him if he intended to do him some harm."

"And what better way to hurt me than to make me watch my good friend being hanged for something I would be sure he hadn't done?" Smoke asked.

Hemmings smiled and held up his hands. "All right. You two have at least given one way things could have happened that would explain the sheriff's actions, but you still have not one shred of proof or evidence to back up your claim." He shrugged. "It could just as easily have happened just as the sheriff said it did, if we assume Pearlie is guilty."

Smoke's face fell. "You're right, Sam. But we're going to work on that. We just wanted someone in this town to know what we're doing and why."

Hemmings was about to reply when the door burst open and Robert Jacobson burst in. "Say, Mayor," he began, and then stopped, his face flushing bright red when he saw Smoke and Cal sitting there.

"Oh . . . uh . . . I didn't know you had someone here," he stammered, at a loss for words. "I'll come back. . . ."

"No, don't be silly, Bob. You can talk in front of these men. What is it?" Hemmings asked.

"I . . . uh . . . this wire came for you just now. I thought you might ought to see it right away." As he held out the wire, Jacobson said while keeping his eyes away from Smoke, "The wire specifically asks that the contents be kept strictly confidential, Mayor."

Hemmings took the wire and read it, being careful not to hold it where anyone else in the room might be able to read it. When he was finished, he immediately glanced at Smoke and Cal. "All right, Bob. Thank you. I'll take care of it." He folded the wire and put it in his pocket until Jacobson had left.

Once the door closed behind him, he said, "This may solve all of our problems, one way or another." He stubbed out his cigar. "The doctor's aunt, Janet Rule, was staying at his house at the time of the murders. She probably saw everything."

Smoke nodded. "We know, Sam. Our next step is to try and find her to get the evidence we need to clear Pearlie."

Hemmings grinned. "You won't need to find her.

She's going to come here and she says she has some information for me to hear about the killings."

"Great news!" Smoke said. "When is she going to get here?" he asked.

Hemmings's face turned serious. "I don't think I should divulge that information, Smoke. After all, if I'm wrong and Pearlie is guilty and you are trying to protect him, then you might be inclined to prevent Miss Rule from testifying, by fair means or foul."

"But . . ." Smoke started to argue, and then he saw Hemmings's point and nodded. "Of course. You can't be one-hundred-percent sure we're on the up and up, and you have to protect your witness. I can see that." He hesitated. "But don't you think it's strange that she sent that wire to you, and not to the sheriff? After all, he is the law in town, and I can think of only one reason she wouldn't feel safe in confiding her account of the murder to him."

Hemmings's face became thoughtful. "I agree, it is strange for her to send the wire to me, but I guess we'll just have to wait until she gets here for her to tell us her reasons for doing so."

When Smoke nodded, Hemmings smiled again. "Thank you, Smoke, for being so understanding of my need for secrecy, and I assure you, you'll be the first to hear what she's told me after we talk."

Smoke got up and held out his hand. "That's all we can ask, Sam. Thank you."

Hemmings rose and took Smoke's hand. "For me, my money's on her telling me that Pearlie had nothing to do with the doctor's death," he said.

"You and us both," Cal said enthusiastically, "and I'll also bet she tells you that the sheriff is up to his eyeballs in this mess."

CHAPTER 25

As soon as he left Mayor Hemmings's office, Robert Jacobson walked straight to Sheriff Tolliver's office, checking back over his shoulder occasionally to make sure Hemmings and Jensen didn't see him heading that way. Jensen hadn't *specifically* ordered him not to tell the sheriff anything about a *new* message, just not to discuss that he and Jensen had talked about a previous message, so he didn't think Jensen had any gripe coming, but with a man like Jensen, you didn't want to take chances.

When he entered Tolliver's office, he found the sheriff sitting at his desk staring off into space as if he were deep in thought. Uh-oh, he thought, maybe this isn't the best time to bother the man, what with all he's got on his mind and all.

"What do you want, Bob?" Tolliver asked irritably without looking at him.

"Uh . . . I got this wire from Pueblo a while ago, Buck. I thought you ought to know about it."

For the first time, Tolliver showed some animation. He sat up in his chair and leaned forward, his eyes now boring into Jacobson's. "What is it? Has the sheriff there located that Rule lady?" he asked, thinking it was too much to hope for that she'd died of old age or apoplexy or something suitable for a meddling old bitch.

Jacobson smiled slightly. "Better than that, Buck," he said, sure now that he'd done right in coming to see the sheriff. Now the sheriff would owe him, and he'd just have to try and think of some way to collect on the debt.

"Well, what is it? Don't just stand there grinning like a cat with a bird in its mouth."

"Oh, this is much better than a bird, Buck. But first you got to promise you won't tell nobody I told you about the wire. It wasn't addressed to you and if anyone finds out," he said, an image of an irate Smoke Jensen playing in his mind, "I could get fired."

Now Tolliver looked puzzled as well as irritated. "Well, who the hell was the damn thing addressed to?"

"Mayor Hemmings."

"Hemmings?" Uh-oh, he thought, that doesn't sound too good. "Who was it from?"

"It was from that Miss Rule herself you been looking for and it was sent to Mayor Hemmings. She said she's gonna be on the afternoon train tomorrow from Pueblo, but that she ain't gonna get off. She wants Hemmings to meet her on the last car in the train while it's stopped and she's gonna tell him something important about the killing of Doc Bentley, but she didn't say what it was she was gonna tell him."

Oh, shit, thought Tolliver. Please tell me you didn't already give the message to Hemmings. "Bob, am I the only one you've told this to?" he asked out loud.

"Why, no, Buck," Jacobson answered, surprised that he would ask such a question. "I gave the written message to Mayor Hemmings like it was addressed, but I thought you ought to know about her being in town 'cause you're the one investigating the crime."

Tolliver figured it was time he tried to disavow any interest in the matter. "No, that's not true, Bob," he said, leaning back in his chair and putting his hands behind his head. "I already got the killer in jail, and he's already been convicted, so nothing Miss Rule or anyone else has to say on the matter makes any difference to me."

"Then, you ain't gonna go and talk to her?" Jacobson asked incredulously.

"Naw, I don't think so, Bob. But, hey, thanks for filling me in. I'm sure the mayor will tell me all about what the old lady had to say next time I see him."

Disappointed that his news hadn't been received with more enthusiasm, Jacobson nodded. So much for Tolliver owing him one, he thought. "Sure thing, Sheriff, glad to be of help."

"Oh, and Bob. One more thing," Tolliver said as Jacobson moved toward the door.

He stopped and turned around. "Yeah?"

"I wouldn't go around telling anyone you told me about the wire from Miss Rule. After all, it wasn't addressed to me, and if the company found out you were giving me confidential messages, they'd not only fire you, but they'd probably prosecute you and put you in jail."

Jacobson's face paled. "Now, Sheriff, you asked me to. . . ." he stammered.

Tolliver held up a hand. "Yes, I did, Bob, and I appreciate the way you're cooperating with the law, so I won't tell anyone about it either. It's just that the company might not be so understanding, if you get my drift."

Jacobson shook his head and jerked the door open. "You can bet I won't tell nobody, Sheriff," he said, thinking if Hemmings or Jensen found out he'd talked to Buck, they'd probably do a lot worse than put him in jail.

After he left, Tolliver put his hat on and walked down the street to the livery, forcing himself to walk slow and easy and not seem to be in any hurry in spite of the fact he felt like running the entire way.

This entire matter was getting out of hand, and he knew he'd better put a stop to it before it went any further. Jensen was proving too hard to kill, so he figured he'd end the investigation another way.

Jerry Stone looked up from his usual job of mucking stables and smiled nervously when he saw it was the sheriff. He hoped that Cal feller hadn't said nothing to the sheriff about what he'd told him. If it was one thing Jerry didn't need, it was John Law on his back.

"Howdy, Sheriff. What can I do for you? You need your horse saddled?" he asked, knowing he was talking too fast but unable to control his mouth. He was also sweating like a pig, but that wasn't unusual when he was mucking stalls.

"Yeah," Tolliver said, flipping him a nickel. "And I need it quick."

"Sure thing, Sheriff," Jerry said, putting the nickel in his pocket and wondering why it was gunfighters and outlaws always tipped better than lawmen did. That sure said something about the way of the world, all right.

Tolliver turned the head of his dun gelding down the trail that led to the mining cabin where his men spent their time between jobs when they weren't in town. It was one of the first mines he and his men had "liberated" from its previous owners, now dead and forgotten, and it was still their best producer of gold ore. Except, of course, for his new acquisition, but they didn't know anything about that and if he played his cards right, they never would.

"Yo, the cabin," he called, not wanting to surprise the

boys or they might just shoot him before they realized who it was.

"Yo yourself," Jeb Hardy called back from the corner of the cabin, where he stood with a rifle in his hands.

Tolliver grinned. "You heard me coming, huh?" he asked as he stepped down off his mount and tied it up at the rail in front of the cabin.

"I heard that old horse of yours puffing and farting for the last quarter mile. He wouldn't be so windy if you'd give him a little grain instead of all that hay."

Tolliver snorted. How's that for a lawyer giving a rancher advice about how to take care of his horse! "The boys inside? I got some business to discuss."

"All but Bubba," Hardy said. "He ain't been here for two, three days. We figure he's staying with that Molly girl over at the saloon spending all his loot from the last job." Hardy shook his head and grinned. "I can't understand that boy, and that's a fact. If he wanted to lie down with a horse-faced female, we got plenty of horses up here at the cabin."

Tolliver stopped Hardy with a hand on his chest. "That ain't it, Jeb. Bubba's dead," he said, wanting to tell him before they got inside so the others wouldn't hear.

"Dead? Whatta you mean dead?"

"Dead, as in not breathing anymore. That kind of dead."

"What the hell happened?"

"You remember how he told us 'bout him and Hog bracing Jensen and his friend a couple of weeks ago and how Jensen took his gun away and dropped it in the dirt down the trail a ways?"

"Yeah, what of it?"

Tolliver shrugged. "I guess he nursed a grudge and

he tried to settle it last night with his pistol, and Jensen ventilated him."

"He manage to put a lead pill in Jensen?" Hardy asked, his eyes hard. He'd never particularly liked Bubba; after all, the man was dumb as a rope. But he was a sort of partner, and Hardy didn't like the fact that some out-of-town hard case could come into his town and kill one of his friends. Men just didn't let things like that pass without doing something about it, usually something deadly.

Tolliver shook his head. "Nope. Far as I could tell, Bubba never got off a shot."

"Please don't tell me the son of a bitch was dumb enough to draw against a man like Jensen?"

Tolliver smiled. "No, he walked into the bathroom over at the hotel and surprised Jensen and his friend while they were taking baths."

"And Jensen still managed to kill him?"

Tolliver nodded. "Nobody ever accused Bubba of being smart, or fast with a gun." He hesitated. "Let's not tell the others just yet, all right?"

Hardy shrugged. "Sure. All right by me, but I got to tell you, Buck. I ain't plannin' on letting Jensen get away with this. Bubba wasn't no prize, but he was still one of us, and Jensen has got to be made to pay."

"Count on it, Jeb," Tolliver said, and he went on into the cabin and greeted Kid Akins and Hog Hogarth. "Howdy, boys," he said.

"I see Jeb didn't shoot a hole in your ass with that big Henry of his," Kid said, laughing and putting his cards down on the table.

"Hey," Hog said, looking at the cards and the small pile of money in the middle of the table. "Let's finish this hand. I got a good one this time."

Kid inclined his head. "Take it, Hog. I was bluffin' anyway."

While Hog grinned and raked in the pile of bills, Kid looked at Hardy and then at Tolliver. "What brings you out to our happy home, Buck? You got some more miners lined up for us to skin?"

"Not this time, Kid. It's more important than that."

Akins gave a short laugh. "What could be more important than making a few bucks the easy way?"

Hardy pulled out a chair, and the three men sat and listened while Tolliver told them about the wire from Janet Rule and how she was supposed to meet Hemmings in the last car of the train while it was stopped in Payday. He also told them about how Jensen and Cal were going around asking a lot of questions about him and the night the doc and Blackie were killed.

Hardy grinned. "So, I assume you're here 'cause you sure as hell don't want the lady talking to Mayor Hemmings about what she saw that night."

"Or anybody else," Tolliver added grimly. "She needs to be eliminated from my life before that train gets to Payday, or I'm gonna be in deep shit."

"That might be difficult to manage, Buck," Kid said, leaning back in his chair with his hands behind his head. "That train goes over some pretty rough country 'tween here and Pueblo. There ain't hardly no place where it can easily be stopped." He looked around. "Especially by three or four men. Maybe if we had a dozen or more . . ."

"I got that figured out," Tolliver said, leaning down with his hands on the table. "You all know the train don't actually come into Payday, but just stops outside the town to let people on and off."

The men all nodded.

"Well, there's a grove of oak trees just before the train gets to its stop. I figure someone could hide in those trees and pitch a couple of sticks of dynamite into that car the lady's riding in, and that'd be the end of our problem once and for all."

Hog squinted his little pig eyes. "What do you mean 'our' problem, Buck? Seems to me this lady is your problem, not ours."

Tolliver straightened up, frowning. "I already told you once, Hog. Any problem I got is a problem for all of us, unless you got an aversion to keeping on getting rich off me."

Hardy glared at Hog and held up his hands. "We already agreed to help you, Buck, but dynamiting the whole train to kill one little old lady seems a mite . . . extreme, don't you think?" He stared at Tolliver. "A job like that would bring the federal marshals swarming down on Payday like locusts, and I for one can do without that sort of grief."

"You got a better idea, Jeb?" Tolliver asked. "Like the Kid said, there just ain't no good place to ambush that train and make it stop between here and Pueblo unless we had a dozen or so men, and I only count four here."

Hardy shook his head. "Don't need to make it stop," he said. "Since the lady was kind enough to tell us which car she was going to be in, it should be an easy matter to wait by that big clump of boulders right at the base of that last incline 'fore the train gets to Payday. When it starts up that hill, the train slows to almost a walk. It should be easy enough to ride up next to the windows in that last car and put a couple of slugs into one little old lady."

"Yeah, but we won't know which side of the car she'll be on," Kid said.

Hardy sighed. "That's why there's gonna be two of us, Kid. One on each side." He looked back at Tolliver. "Now, killing one little old lady, or even maybe a couple of others in that car, ain't gonna be big enough news to bring no marshals down here. So, since we got the local sheriff on our side, the investigation into the killings ought to pass on by easy enough without anyone getting fingered for it."

"What about me?" Hog said.

"You're gonna stay here, Hog," Hardy said. "Your fat ass is too distinct, even with a mask on. The other people on the train are liable to recognize you."

"Besides," Kid said laughing, "your horse would probably have a stroke if it tried to haul your lard ass up that hill to catch the train."

Hog gave Kid a flat look. "Keep it up, Kid, and this lard ass is gonna be sitting on your face 'fore you know it."

CHAPTER 26

After Smoke and Cal left Hemmings's office, they went to the hotel. "I want you to pack an overnight bag, Cal, and then we're going to put you on today's train to Pueblo."

"Why?" Cal asked. "I thought we were gonna look into the sheriff's dealings an' see what he's been up to."

"That's exactly what you're going to be doing in Pueblo, Cal. If the sheriff has been stealing claims around here, he's sure not going to file them in the local claims office where everyone knows who he is. They'd all know he doesn't have time to be out prospecting for gold with his job here in town as sheriff."

Cal nodded. "I see. You want me to check the claims office in Pueblo for any claims listed under Buck Tolliver's name."

"Not only claims listed under his name, Cal, but any claims he might be a partner in. I'm sure he's not working alone, but he's probably too smart and too cautious to let his partners have the claims in their names alone, so he could be listed as partners with them in the claims with his name second on the recorded deed."

"What about askin' around at the bank?" Cal asked. "If he's makin' all this money he's got to be stashing it somewhere, and like you said, it sure as hell wouldn't be here in Payday."

Smoke nodded. "That's a good idea, Cal, but I don't think the bankers in Pueblo would talk to you about one of their customers, especially if he's got as much money as I think he has."

"Oh," Cal said, disappointed his idea hadn't panned out.

"But," Smoke said, clapping him on the shoulder, "there's another way to get the information we need. As soon as you get to Pueblo, wire Monte Carson at our bank there and have him get the president to wire the bank in Pueblo for a credit report on Buck Tolliver. Have them say he's down there wanting to invest in some ranches and they need to know if he's good for the money."

"Why not just wire Big Rock from here?" Cal asked. "It'd be a whole lot quicker."

Smoke glanced toward the general store down the street. "I don't think Robert Jacobson is a man we can trust, Cal. I think the sheriff probably has him in his pocket, and the less Buck Tolliver knows about our business, the better I'll feel."

Cal's eyes widened. "Smoke, that reminds me. You don't think he might've told the sheriff about when Miss Rule is coming into town, do you?"

Smoke nodded, his mouth grim. "It wouldn't surprise me a bit, Cal, but I don't think bracing him about it would do any good. He's probably more scared of Tolliver than he is of me, so he'd probably just deny it and we couldn't prove a thing. But if he did, and if the sheriff is as dirty as we think he is, then he won't be able to allow her to talk to Hemmings. He'll have to try and do something to keep her from talking."

"What are you gonna do?"

"I'm going to stick close to the sheriff without him knowing it. If he does go after her, maybe I can stop him before he gets to her and prevents her from clearing Pearlie's name."

"You watch your back and ride with your pistols loose, Smoke. The sheriff is almost certain to suspect we're on to him, so the chances are pretty good he'll come after you too," Cal advised.

"Don't worry, Cal. I never turn my back on a snake, especially one as slippery as Buck Tolliver." He grinned. "Course, if he were to try something, it sure might solve all of our problems, 'cause he'd be planted six feet under boot hill."

"Come on, then, Smoke. Let's go get me packed and on that train."

As soon as Cal was safely on the train, Smoke went to the livery and asked Jerry to saddle up his horse. He wanted to be able to ride on a moment's notice if the sheriff decided to leave town.

Jerry just stood there, his mouth hanging open slightly with a dazed look in his eyes.

"Are you all right, son?" Smoke asked, wondering if the boy had eaten something that disagreed with him.

"It's just that I never met a famous gunfighter before, sir," Jerry said, his eyes wide.

Smoke laughed. "Well, we're just like everyone else, Jerry. We put our pants on one leg at a time just like you do."

"Uh, do you think you could sort'a sign your name on my hat, Mr. Jensen?"

Smoke shook his head. It was the first time he'd ever been asked to give his autograph. "Sure, if you'll get Storm saddled before it gets dark."

While Jerry was saddling his horse, Smoke casually asked him, "Which horse belongs to Sheriff Tolliver?"

"Oh," Jerry said over his shoulder as he tightened the cinch strap on Smoke's horse, "it ain't here now. The sheriff took him out about an hour ago."

"Is that so?" Smoke asked, handing him his hat with his name written on it. "You see which way he rode out of town?"

Jerry straightened up, a puzzled look on his face as he took the hat and stared at the name Smoke Jensen written on it. "Why you askin', Mr. Jensen?"

Smoke shrugged. "Don't worry, Jerry. I'm not gonna shoot him or anything like that. It's just that he's got my friend in jail, and I owe him for some extra food I had him order from the hotel dining room. I thought if he was around I'd pay him now and settle the bill."

"Oh, well, in that case, he took the north road up into the mountains like he usually does when he goes riding."

"He have a place up that way?" Smoke asked, trying to sound casual.

"Naw, his ranch is off to the south where the land is flat. Ain't no good ranch land up north, it's too hilly up in the mountains. Nothing up there but gold mines an' such."

"I see," Smoke said, realizing the sheriff probably had a camp up there that he used to meet with his accomplices.

He gave Jerry a gold two-dollar piece and climbed up into the saddle. "Thanks, Jerry."

Jerry's eyes shined as he turned the gold coin over and over in his fingers, thinking what a cheapskate the sheriff was. "If I see the sheriff, I'll tell him you're looking for him."

Smoke shook his head. He didn't want Jerry warning

the sheriff that he'd been asking around about him. He wanted the man off guard as much as possible. "Don't bother. I think I'll just leave the money in his desk at the jail where he'll be sure to find it. See ya' later, young man."

Smoke took the north road out of town and rode slowly, keeping a sharp lookout up ahead. He didn't want to run into the sheriff on his way back to town and have to explain what he was doing on the same road.

He figured he was pretty safe from being bushwhacked since the sheriff didn't know Smoke was tailing him, but he rode with his eyes searching both sides of the trail just in case.

There were too many tracks on the road, which was actually little more than a trail where the horses and wagons had worn down the grass, to determine which ones were the sheriff's. Smoke figured he'd have to check each trail or path that turned off the road and hope that sooner rather than later he'd find the one the sheriff took.

He'd gone up and down six or seven trails with no luck by the time the sun began to set. This was no job to attempt in the dark, and so he reluctantly turned his horse around and headed back toward town, hoping the sheriff wasn't already on the way to do harm to Miss Rule.

He considered trying to warn Hemmings that the sheriff might well know about Rule's plans, but finally decided against it. Hemmings just wasn't quite ready to think the sheriff was behind the killings, and Smoke didn't want to alienate him by pushing too hard. He'd just have to hope that Cal came up with something before Rule came to town and put herself in harm's way.

He decided if the sheriff wasn't in town when he got back, he'd get up early the next morning and check out the rest of the trails to the north of town and try to find his hideout.

He was just coming into town when he saw the sheriff leaving the livery. Smoke breathed a sigh of relief, and pulled his horse in and told Jerry to give it some extra oats and grain before bedding it down for the night.

When he left the livery, he saw Tolliver entering the batwings of the saloon down the street. Smoke loosened the rawhide thong on his Colt and decided to follow him in. No telling what he might learn, he thought, and after his long trail ride, he was more than ready for a cold beer and a couple of hard-boiled eggs.

Smoke timed his entrance to coincide with the entrance of several miners who were in town to spend some of the dust they'd dug out of the mountains. Ducking down so the other men hid him, he broke off, moved into a corner, and took a seat at a table where the lantern light didn't quite reach.

He pulled his hat down low on his head and slumped in his chair as he looked around the crowded room. After a moment, when his eyes adjusted to the relative gloom and smoke, he saw Tolliver sitting at a table across the room with three men.

Smoke grinned slightly when he saw that one of the men was the gent he'd beaten up who'd been with the man who'd later tried to kill him and Cal. "I see you're keeping bad company, Sheriff Tolliver," Smoke mumbled to himself.

The men had their heads down and close and were

talking earnestly, evidently in low voices so they couldn't be heard above the clink of glasses and the rowdy laughter that was normal in saloons after dark.

"I'll just bet those are your partners, Buck ol' man," Smoke said, nodding to himself and giving the men a good long look so he'd be sure and recognize them the next time he saw them.

Smoke ordered a beer and a plate of hard-boiled eggs when one of the waitresses came by, and drank and ate slowly, keeping his head down and watching to see what happened across the room.

In less than an hour, the sheriff and his men had finished their business and all four got up and walked outside. Smoke noticed the bottle of whiskey they'd had at the table was still over half full, so the talk must've been about something important for them to forgo drinking while they talked. He bet they were planning on how they could get to Miss Rule and keep her from talking.

Smoke quickly got up, left through the back door, and peeked around the corner of the building to see what they did. He was disappointed when the men waved good-bye to the sheriff and made their way toward the hotel instead of the livery stable. Evidently, they were going to spend the night in town since they didn't seem to be in any hurry to get their horses out of the stable.

Smoke wished Cal was with him. If the men separated in the morning, there was no way he could follow or watch all of them, and he figured the sheriff was probably enlisting their help in silencing the Rule lady.

Once they were all out of sight, Smoke made his way to the hotel and went up the rear stairs to his own room. He'd need to be on watch first thing in the morning in case the men decided to get on the move early.

Of course, he mused as he got undressed and flopped down on the bed, they might try to sneak out in the middle of the night, but there was nothing he could do about that. He had to sleep sometime, and since Miss Rule was an elderly lady, she most likely wouldn't be traveling at night.

If he couldn't find the men in the morning, he'd have no choice but to go to Hemmings and demand to know Rule's schedule so he could try to protect her. That was his last thought before he dropped into a deep, dreamless sleep.

CHAPTER 27

As soon as Cal got off the train in Pueblo, he went straight to the telegraph office. He sent the telegram to Sheriff Monte Carson in Big Rock as per Smoke's instructions, and even added a request that the sheriff inform everyone that Pearlie was all right physically and they were going to make sure he stayed that way.

"I'll check back in an hour or so for any reply," Cal said. "I've gotta go by the land claims office."

He could see the eyes of the man behind the counter light up with gold fever. "You struck it rich, mister?" he asked, his eyes measuring Cal to see if there was some way he could get some of Cal's new riches. The telegraph operator had been known to make a few extra dollars by tipping off some rough friends of his when men sent wires back home that they'd struck it rich. His friends would then waylay the men and rob them of their dust with no one making the connection to the telegraph man.

Cal grinned and shook his head. "Nope. Sorry, but I'm just gonna check on somebody else's claims. I'm not a prospector, I'm a cowhand."

"Oh," the man said, getting back to his work and ignoring Cal as if he didn't exist any longer now that he wasn't going to be rich. He'd never seen a cowhand with two nickels to rub together, much less enough to rob him for.

Cal chuckled to himself and wondered why so many men were eaten up with the prospect of getting rich. It was as if their own lives were meaningless unless they happened to find gold. He further mused that for most of the men who did strike it rich, their new-found wealth was probably more of a curse than a blessing. Smoke and Sally were about the only rich people he'd ever known who were completely happy, but of course, they didn't act like rich folks either.

Cal opened the door to the claims office and went inside. His heart fell when he saw stacks and stacks of folders arranged along both side walls and even all the way across the back wall. "Jimminy, I ain't never gonna get through all those files," he muttered to himself, taking off his hat and scratching his head.

A gray-haired, older lady who was puttering behind the counter must have heard him, for she gave a low laugh and cleared her throat to get his attention. "Excuse me, young man. I couldn't help overhearing you. Are you looking for a particular file or information on a particular mine?"

Cal walked up to the counter and leaned on it, his eyes still roving across the thousands and thousands of files. "Well, ma'am, I was going to, but seein' as how you got more claims in here than the number of people in the whole world, I'm sort'a rethinking my options. I need to find out if a certain man has filed any claims for mines and such here, and if he has, who his partners in the ventures are."

The lady chuckled. "Well, sonny, you look so cute standing there with your eyes big as melons that I'm going to take mercy on you and show you the easiest way through our little maze here."

"Gosh, ma'am," Cal said, "that'd be great. I'm in kind of a big hurry, and if I don't find out what I need to know a very nice lady might be hurt."

"Oh," the lady said, her eyes big and round. "That sounds very serious. All right, first off, let's get the formalities out of the way. If I'm going to slog through all those dusty files for you, I should at least know your name. Mine's Martha Jameson."

"Oh, excuse my manners, Missus Jameson. I'm Calvin Woods," Cal said, quickly taking off his hat and holding out his hand to her.

"I'll bet they call you Cal, right?" she asked, taking his hand and giving it a firm shake.

"Yes, ma'am, ever since I was a shavetail."

"And there ain't no Mr. Jameson, so just call me Martha instead of Missus."

"Yes, ma'am," Cal said, blushing scarlet.

She took a small pad of paper off the desk behind her and handed it to Cal with a pencil. "Now you just write down the names of all the men you're interested in and we'll get to work." She hesitated, still holding the pencil. "You can read and write, can't you?" she asked, not unkindly.

"Oh, yes, ma'am," he said. "I graduated high school and everything, and my boss's wife used to be a schoolteacher, so she's been helping me with some college courses during the winter at the ranch."

"You must be very lucky to have such a good friend and boss," Martha said, handing him the pencil.

"Yes, ma'am," Cal said, and he wrote "Buck Tolliver" on the paper and smiled ruefully. "This is the name I know, but I just don't know who else may be involved with him. I'd assume the mines would be in the vicinity of the town of Payday."

Her brows knit. "Involved? What do you mean involved?" she asked, opening the countertop to let Cal walk through and back toward the file shelves.

Cal began to tell her what he and Smoke suspected about the sheriff's nefarious activities, and she stopped and stared at him with wide-open eyes. "Why, it's like a great mystery, isn't it?"

"Uh . . . what do you mean, ma'am?" he asked, not understanding what she meant by "mystery."

She took his arm and leaned in close. "I've been reading the most delightful series of mystery stories by a British author, Conan Doyle, about a detective named Sherlock Holmes. They're all about how he uses deductive reasoning to solve crimes."

Since the only detectives he'd ever heard of were the Pinkertons, and since he had no idea whatsoever what the words "deductive reasoning" meant, Cal just smiled and nodded his head and hoped she'd drop the subject.

Within minutes, she was climbing up on a small three-step ladder and snatching various files off the shelves and flinging them at him.

By the time his arms were full, Cal was covered with dust and was sneezing fitfully from the dust that'd gone up his nose and clogged his mouth.

"Most of these claims are filed alphabetically by first letter of the last name and then filed by county, so we should be able to find some with your fellow's name on it if they're here."

Within ten minutes, they'd struck pay dirt. After that, it was relatively easy to follow Tolliver's trail through the maze of file folders. After they'd noted the names of men on the claims that had Tolliver listed first, they then went through the stacks and found lots of other claims with those other men's names listed first, though Tolliver's was always there someplace.

An hour and a half later, Cal folded up the paper on which he'd written the information they'd gathered and stuck it in his pocket.

"Can I offer you some money for helping me out, ma'am?" he offered.

"Of course not, young man," she said indignantly. "I did this to help you solve your mystery and free your friend from this sheriff's evil clutches."

Thinking Martha sure did talk funny, Cal thanked her again and left, hurrying toward the bank to see if the wire from the bank in Big Rock had done any good.

When he gave one of the tellers his name, he was immediately shown into an opulent office in the rear of the building.

A portly man wearing a full suit, vest, and a carnation in his buttonhole grinned at Cal like he was an old friend and got up from behind his desk to come around and shake Cal's hand. Cal didn't know what the bank president at Big Rock had written about him, but whatever it was, it sure as hell had impressed this man.

"Howdy, Mr. Woods. I'm Gerald McManus, the president of this bank," the man said, showing Cal to a plush armchair in front of his desk.

After he'd taken his seat, McManus stared at him from under bushy eyebrows. "My, but you look awfully young to have such impressive credentials."

"Credentials?" Cal asked, bewildered.

McManus's head bobbed up and down. "Yes. The president of your bank back in Big Rock tells me you're out here to purchase some large tracts of land and that you're interested in the financial status of one of the men you're going into partnership with, a Mr. Buck Tolliver."

So that was it, Cal thought. McManus thinks I'm some rich investor out here to spend a lot of money.

"Of course, we'll be glad to be of any assistance to you that we can here at my bank," McManus said, leaning over to offer Cal a cigar from a wooden humidor on his desk. As Cal took the cigar and struck a match on the bottom of his boot, the man frowned and asked, "Would you care for a snifter of brandy or a cognac, Mr. Woods?"

"No, thank you kindly," Cal said, not having the faintest idea what a cognac was. As he exhaled a thick blue cloud of smoke, he thought, this is the best cigar I've ever had.

McManus hooked his thumbs in the armholes of his vest and leaned back in his chair until Cal thought he was in imminent danger of tipping over. "Do you plan on keeping any of your investment capital in this town, Mr. Woods, or will you use your bank back in Big Rock?"

"Well," Cal said, thinking like crazy. "I'm sure Mr. Tolliver and I'll need a local bank to handle some of our money," he said, not knowing if he was making any sense at all. "That is, if Mr. Tolliver is as well heeled as he tells me he is."

McManus took a sheet off the top of his desk and handed it to Cal. "Here is a current financial statement on Mr. Tolliver's holdings in our establishment, which I'm sure will be more than adequate for almost any investment you two would care to make."

When Cal's eyes almost bugged out as he glanced over the paper, McManus leaned forward and whispered conspiratorially. "And I understand that Mr. Tolliver also has dealings with both of the other banks in town, though I can't imagine why he doesn't just put all of his money in one place. It would be so much more convenient for him."

And it'd mean a hell of a lot more money for you too, Cal thought. "Can I take this with me?" he asked.

"Certainly," McManus said expansively. "We here at

the First Territorial Bank of Colorado intend to please."

After he left the bank, Cal saw that if he hurried, he had time to get a wire off to Smoke and still be able to make the afternoon train back to Payday.

He kept the wire short and simple, not wanting to put too much in it for Robert Jacobson to read. "Smoke, got what I came for and it's going to knock your eyes out. Cal."

He paid the man for the wire and took off at a dead run for the train terminal, hoping he'd make it in time.

The train was already pulling out of the station, so he didn't have time to stop and buy a ticket. He ran down the tracks after the last car, and just managed to grab the rail and pull himself up, panting and sweating, as the train picked up speed.

"Golly, that was close," he muttered as he dusted himself off and entered the rear door of the last car.

"It certainly was, young man," an elderly, white-haired woman said from the next to last seat in the car. "I was afraid for a moment you weren't going to make it and that you might trip and fall under the wheels."

"Oh, no danger of that, ma'am," Cal said, wondering what it was about his face that made little old ladies want to adopt him and take him under their wings. "The train weren't going all that fast yet."

"Wasn't," the lady corrected him.

"Uh, yes, ma'am. Wasn't," Cal repeated, taking the seat across the aisle from her and leaning his head back to hopefully catch a few winks of sleep on the trip. If his luck continued to hold, the lady across the aisle wouldn't chatter the entire way to Payday.

CHAPTER 28

Smoke was waiting outside the hotel, standing well back in the alley so he wouldn't be seen, when the three men Tolliver had been talking to the previous night in the saloon walked out of the door.

Smoke had been there since just before dawn, and yawned widely as he watched the men walk down the street and enter a small café named Mom's. Glancing at his watch and seeing it was almost eleven o'clock in the morning, Smoke decided to stir up some action by following the men into the place and having himself some breakfast. Truth was, he was bored; he'd been standing in that alley for almost six hours and he wanted to make something happen.

As he entered, he chuckled to himself. Long ago he'd promised himself he'd never again eat at any place named Mom's. The food in such establishments was invariably terrible, bordering on inedible. However, present circumstances dictated that he give Tolliver and his men a push, so he guessed he'd have to make do.

He walked through the door and took a table in the rear of the rather small room, sitting so his back was to a wall and he had a clear view of the front door and the inhabitants of the place. The three men he'd followed had taken a seat near the front window, and were just giving their orders to a plump, matronly woman wearing a flour-stained apron and a kerchief tied on her head.

They hadn't seen him as yet, and he was interested to see what their reaction would be when they did. It could be that they were just friends of Tolliver's and not involved in his schemes or in the murders, but he didn't think so. The way they'd sat last night with their heads close together and their voices low bespoke of nefarious dealings, he'd bet his ranch on it.

After the waitress left their table, she stopped by his on the way to the kitchen and asked quickly, "Coffee?"

Smoke nodded, but kept his eyes on the men across the room. After a few moments, the youngest one of them happened to turn his gaze onto Smoke. Smoke almost grinned when the young man froze and his mouth dropped open and his eyes went wide.

He hurriedly lowered his head and leaned in close to his companions, speaking rapidly, and then all of their heads turned and all of their eyes were on Smoke.

Smoke grinned and dipped his head in greeting, as if he were just being polite to strangers whose eyes happen to meet across a room.

The young man's face turned beet red, his right hand went to the gun on his hip, and he started to stand up, until the oldest man at the table reached over and grabbed his arm, whispering something under his breath that made the young man sit back down.

Just as the waitress was setting Smoke's coffee on his table, Sheriff Buck Tolliver walked into the room. He started toward the table with the three men, until one of them gave a quick shake of his head and looked over at Smoke.

Tolliver followed his gaze, and quickly altered his course and walked over to stand before Smoke's table.

He tipped his hat. "Howdy, Mr. Jensen," he said. His voice was light, but his eyes were dark and suspicious.

"Hello, Sheriff," Smoke replied. "Care to join me for some breakfast? I know it's a bit late in the day, but I've been busy this morning talking to people about how things are here in Payday."

Tolliver started to look over his shoulder, then caught himself just in time, but not before Smoke saw the movement. "Sure. I don't normally eat breakfast this late, but since it's a bit early for lunch, I'll have a cup of coffee with you." He wondered what the mountain man was up to. Had he been following Hardy and the others, and if he had, how had he known they were partners with Tolliver?

He pulled out a chair and took a seat, setting his hat on a chair next to him. He glanced up at the waitress, who was still standing patiently waiting for Smoke's order. "Hey, Mom," he said, "bring me a cup of coffee, will ya'?"

She nodded and looked down at Smoke. "You gonna eat, mister?"

Smoke said, without taking his eyes off of Tolliver, "Three hen's eggs, scrambled, half a pound of bacon, crispy, fried potatoes, sliced tomatoes if you have 'em fresh, and biscuits and gravy."

Mom grinned. "That all for you, mister, or are you expectin' a wagon load of miners in here to eat with you?"

Smoke smiled and looked up at her. "It's all for me, Mom. I'm still a growing boy."

"Huh," she said, blushing down to the roots of her hair as she gave him a wink. "Growing, maybe; boy, definitely not!"

After she brought the sheriff his coffee, Tolliver leaned back in his chair and shook his head. "Now just what am I going to do with you, Mr. Jensen? I can't have you running all over town sticking your nose in where it don't belong. It won't look right to the citizens of this town that elected me to do that very thing."

Smoke shrugged and sipped his coffee, staring at Tolliver over the rim but keeping the men behind the sheriff in his peripheral vision at the same time. "First off, Sheriff, there's not a damned thing you *can* do about it, and I think you know it. But what I'm wondering is why it bothers you so much that I'm looking into the killings, unless it's the fact that you railroaded my friend into jail for something you or your friends over there did."

Tolliver's face flushed and his jaw clenched so hard his jaw muscles bulged and his teeth creaked. "I don't allow nobody to talk to me like that, Jensen!"

Smoke grinned and leaned back in his chair. This was what he'd been waiting for. Get a man mad enough and he'll often say things he'd wished he hadn't later. He said in an even voice, with no trace of anger or hostility, "Then fill your hand or shut your mouth, Sheriff, 'cause I'm going to say and do what I please."

Tolliver stared at him for a moment, and then he forced himself to take a deep breath and relax, an insolent grin on his face. "Naw, I don't think I'll kill you right now, Jensen. I'd rather wait until I see the look on your face when your friend dances on the air at the end of a rope. Maybe then I'll put you out of your misery."

Smoke knew then that he'd been right. Everything that had happened to Pearlie had been because of Tolliver. For some reason that Smoke still couldn't remember, Tolliver had a gutful of rage at *him* and he was using Pearlie to get his revenge.

"That's not going to happen, Sheriff," Smoke said,

his voice low and hard and the smile gone from his face.

"Oh, and why not?" Tolliver said, his grin showing he was enjoying making Smoke sweat.

Smoke leaned forward, his elbows on the table, and talked in a low voice that only Tolliver could hear. "Because you and I both know you're dirty, Sheriff. You've disgraced that badge you're wearing dozens of time over—and I'm going to prove it. And when I do, not only will Pearlie go free, but unless I miss my guess, you and your friends over there will be taking his place on that scaffold they're building down the street, only there'll be four ropes dangling from it, not one."

"Why you . . ." Tolliver said, half-rising from his chair and reaching for his gun.

His eyes widened and his mouth dropped open when he found himself staring down the barrel of Smoke's Colt before his hand had even touched the butt of his own pistol.

Across the room, Kid Akins was watching and exclaimed, "Holy shit!" He'd never seen anyone draw so fast in his entire life and vowed then and there that if he ever went after Jensen, it was going to be from the back, not the front.

Hardy, who'd also seen Smoke's lightning-fast draw, just nodded. His friends had been right when they'd told him Jensen was the fastest they'd ever seen with a short gun. He knew *he* was fast too, and the only question he had in his mind right now was whether Jensen was faster.

Sheriff Tolliver froze, his hand trembling over the butt of his pistol, but no longer making a move to draw. "Sit down, Sheriff," Smoke ordered, and he holstered his gun.

When Tolliver was in his seat, beads of sweat pooling

on his forehead, Smoke said, "I don't know what you have against me, Tolliver, or why you've gone to so much trouble to hurt my friend, but I'll find out sooner or later and we'll have a reckoning, you and me." Smoke took a drink of his now-cold coffee, made a face, and set it back down. He looked into Tolliver's eyes. "You do know, don't you, Buck, that only one of us is leaving this town alive?"

Tolliver tried to speak, but his throat was too dry, so he picked up his coffee cup and drank, spilling a little with his shaking hand. "You can bet on it, Jensen," he croaked. "And I'll make sure and tell you why you're going to die before I plant you in the dirt."

Smoke threw back his head and laughed out loud. "Well, from what I've seen so far, Sheriff, you'd better bring plenty of help, 'cause if you're not any faster than I've seen so far, you'll be dead and lying on your back in the dirt before you ever clear leather."

"Now, if you gentlemen are finished with your discussion, I'd kind'a like to put this food down on the table 'fore it gets cold," Mom said, her eyes moving back and forth between the sheriff and the stranger.

Smoke looked over and saw she'd been standing there during the entire incident with the gun.

He leaned back, still keeping his eyes on Tolliver and his friends. "Sure, Mom, put it down. I'm done with this snake for a while."

Tolliver flushed again, nodded once at Mom, and then he got up and walked quickly out of the café, followed close behind by the men at the table across the room.

As they walked down the street toward Tolliver's office, Jeb Hardy whistled. "Jesus, Buck, I been around and I've seen some of the best in the business handle iron, but I'll tell you true—I ain't never seen nobody as fast as Smoke Jensen."

Tolliver stopped and turned his reddened eyes on Hardy. "You telling me you're afraid of him, Jeb?"

Jeb shrugged. "Let's just say I've got a newfound respect for the man, that's all. But what I do want to say is that if you expect *this* man to go up against someone like that for you, then you're going to have to come up with a lot more money than we've talked about up till now." He grinned. "I still think I can take Jensen, but it'd be close and I'd probably take some lead in the deal, so I'm gonna need a pretty good incentive to even try."

"That goes for me too, Buck," Kid Akins said, moving a toothpick around in his mouth and looking back over his shoulder to make sure Jensen hadn't followed them out. "That man is snake-quick with a six-killer and I'd love to be the one that gets famous for putting him down, but like Jeb says, it'd be a mighty tall risk."

"Don't you worry none, Buck," Hog Hogarth said, sticking his thumb against his chest. "I ain't afraid of that bastard Jensen."

Hardy laughed. "That's 'cause you're an idiot, Hog. Jensen already chewed you up and spit you out once and the word is he didn't even break a sweat doing it."

Hog's face turned bright red and he squeezed his right hand into a fist and stuck it under Hardy's nose. "What'd you call me, Jeb?"

Before he could blink, Hardy had his pistol out and the barrel was punching up under Hog's chin, raising it until Hog was staring at the sky. "I said you're an idiot, Hog. Do you want to do something about it?" He eared back the hammer with a loud metallic click, making Hog blink and start to sweat.

"Uh . . . no, Jeb. That's all right," Hog said, his eyes rolling as he tried to look down at Hardy's gun. "Like you said, Jensen done took me once."

"Oh, for God's sake," Tolliver said, whirling around and heading for his office. He looked at the sky. "Why did you saddle me with such idiots for partners?" he asked in a plaintive voice.

The others followed him in and he closed the door behind him. After they'd all taken a seat and Tolliver had poured whiskey all around, he sat on the edge of his desk and said, "Now, you boys saw what Jensen did and you know what you got to do or he's gonna be on us from now on like a duck on a June bug.

"Hog, you're gonna head on back to the cabin, and Jeb, you and the Kid are gonna get your mounts and head on over to the hill coming into town and take out that meddling old lady in the last car of the train."

"Aw, why can't I go with them?" Hog asked.

"Because you're pretty near worthless with a short gun, Hog, and that express gun you carry won't go through the windows and walls of the train car. Besides, I want Jensen to follow you out of town so Jeb and the Kid can do their jobs."

"What makes you think Jensen will follow Hog to the cabin?" Hardy asked.

Tolliver smiled and drained his glass. "Because I'm gonna go with him. Jensen can't afford to let me out of his sight. My guess is that Hemmings hasn't told him when the Rule lady is arriving, so he'll have to follow me thinking I'm gonna be going to take her out. And so when the news comes that Rule was killed by two gunmen, Smoke Jensen is going to be my alibi that I was up in the mountains and nowhere near the train line when she was killed."

Jeb Hardy grinned and also drained his glass. "Good, now that we've got the plan outta the way, we need to do some more talking about money."

"What do you mean?" Tolliver asked. "We've already

discussed the fact that since we're partners, you need to help me to keep the money coming in."

"Yeah," Jeb said, "but we ain't exactly equal partners, Buck. And since we're gonna be pulling your fat outta your fire, I figure it's only fair that from now on all of the money we manage to liberate from the miners is split up into equal shares."

"But . . ." Tolliver began.

Hardy held up his hand. "And don't give us that 'I'm the sheriff' business, because if we don't help you, you ain't gonna be the sheriff for too much longer." He looked around the desk at the other men. "Far as I'm concerned, everything we take in from now on gets cut into equal shares. You boys agree with that?"

Akins and Hog both nodded, their eyes on Tolliver to see if he would agree.

Tolliver sighed. "All right, all right. Equal shares, but only after Miss Rule *and* Smoke Jensen are both dead."

CHAPTER 29

Smoke figured something was going to happen and probably happen fast after his confrontation with the sheriff in the café, so he got his horse from the livery stable and stationed himself at the end of an alley just down the street from the sheriff's office so he could see what went on.

About an hour after they entered, two of the men left the office and walked directly back to the hotel and entered. Smoke saw that it was the older man and the younger one, who dressed like he fancied himself a gunfighter, who went into the hotel.

Five minutes later, the sheriff and the big, wide man that Smoke had beaten up left the office and walked down to the livery stable. Smoke moved down the street and waited behind a large tent building where he could see the entrance to the livery. After about ten minutes, the two men rode out the door and turned left onto the main street of Payday.

The sheriff led the way and headed his horse north out of town the way he'd gone the night before when Smoke had trailed him up into the mountains.

Smoke hesitated. If the sheriff was heading up into the mountains, it probably meant Miss Rule wasn't arriving today for her talk with Hemmings, because she sure as hell wasn't coming into town over the mountain passes between Pueblo and Payday.

He knew he couldn't watch both sets of men, but he figured the most important one to keep an eye on was the sheriff, since he was almost certainly the leader of the gang.

As they moved on up the trail, Smoke let them get just out of sight, and then he walked his horse after them. The sheriff was sure to know Smoke would be tailing him, and so he reached down and loosened the rawhide hammer thong on both of his Colts, knowing that it wasn't unlikely that the sheriff might try to lead him into an ambush. Smoke grinned to himself at the thought. Men a lot more dangerous than Tolliver had tracked him and he was still alive. Besides, as soon as they got out of town, Smoke planned to ride his horse off to the side of the road and trail the men by moving along with them, not behind them, so an ambush would be impossible.

Hardy and Akins watched through the second-story window of their hotel room, and saw Smoke follow the sheriff and Hog as they rode out of town.

Hardy nodded as he peered through the binoculars in his hand. "I'll give Tolliver one thing," he said.

"What's that?" Akins asked.

"He knows his men. He was right about Jensen following him and Hog and leaving us alone to do what we got to do."

"You know," Akins said, looking back out of the window at Jensen as he rode down the street, "if I had my rifle up here, I could end all of this right now." He aimed with his finger and made a motion of pulling a trigger.

Hardy snorted. "Now you're sounding as dumb as Hog, Kid."

Akins glared around at him. "Why do you say that?"

Hardy shook his head. "Just what would you do after you shot Jensen? Walk out of the hotel with your smoking Winchester in your hand and say, here I am, arrest me for murder?"

Akins laughed a little, but his eyes were flat and his voice was hard. "Nope. I'd hightail it down the stairs and out the back door. By the time the crowd started looking for the killer, I'd be on my horse and headed out of town with no one the wiser."

"Bullshit, Kid," Hardy argued. "Our names are on the register downstairs along with our room number. You think none of those people on the street down there are gonna see where the shot came from?"

Akins started to reply, and then he just shut his mouth and looked back out of the window. "Well, it was just a thought anyhow."

"You let me and Tolliver do the thinking, and you'll live a lot longer," Hardy said, a mocking tone in his voice that went right through the Kid.

Akins whirled around and his right hand dropped to the butt of his pistol, his eyes flashing.

Hardy grinned and stepped back, his right hand too near his gun. "You sure you want to test me, Kid?" he asked. "You may be a tad faster, I don't know. But at this distance, I'll get off at least one shot and you'll eat some lead no matter who fires first."

Akins took a deep breath and moved his hand out away from his side. "What are we arguing for, Jeb?" he asked, grinning slightly. "After all, we're on the same side here."

"Glad you see it that way, Kid. Now, let's get our mounts and head on out to the hill where we're gonna ambush that train."

Akins pulled out a pocket watch and frowned. "But we got several hours yet 'fore the train's due in."

Hardy sighed, thinking the Kid really was dumb as

a stump. "I know, Kid, but I'd kind'a like to look around the area before we have to take down the train. We might have to clear some brush from alongside the track where we're gonna be riding, and that might take some time. Besides, it's better if the people in town don't see us riding off toward the ambush site right before the ambush occurs, all right?"

"Yeah, sure, Jeb. But if we're gonna hang around out there in the wilds all day, you mind if I get a bottle to kind'a keep my throat from getting dry?"

"As long as it's a short bottle, Kid," Hardy said with a laugh, trying to ease the tension between them. "It wouldn't do to get drunk an' fall off our horses when we're trying to kill somebody."

Mercifully, the little old lady across the aisle from Cal spent most of the trip knitting instead of talking, though Cal couldn't for the life of him figure out how she managed to make those tiny knots with the railroad car swaying and bouncing the way it did.

Anyway, by the time the train was nearing Payday, he was sound asleep and snoring like an engine himself. Smoke had always marveled at how Cal could fall asleep on the back of a horse while they were riding the trail and not fall off, and the train ride wasn't much smoother.

"Well, I swan, would you look at that?" the lady next to him exclaimed, bringing him out of a deep sleep.

"Wha . . . what is it?" he asked groggily, wiping at his eyes and trying to force himself awake.

The lady smiled at him and pointed out the window. "Looky there. Those men are trying to race the train up this hill," she said gaily, as if intrigued by the actions she was seeing.

"Race the train?" Cal asked, leaning forward and

glancing out the window across from her. Sure enough, a man with his hat pulled down low was leaning over his saddle horn and riding hell-bent for leather alongside the car as the train struggled up the incline and began to slow down.

"That's funny," Cal said, and he glanced out his own window and saw a different man doing exactly the same thing, only this man had a gun in his hand and his eyes were on the window Cal was looking out of.

"Shit!" Cal exclaimed, realizing what was about to happen. He drew his own pistol and hunkered down between the seats for cover.

"What did you say, young man?" the woman asked harshly, looking up from her knitting and glaring at him as if she'd never heard a man curse before.

"Everbody get down, now!" Cal hollered, trying to get the other people in the car to take cover.

When they just turned and looked at him like he was crazy, and when he saw the man outside the car raise his pistol, Cal aimed his gun at the roof and fired off two shots.

Men shouted and women screamed, but all of them dove out of their seats and hit the floor, some covering their heads with their hands. All except the old lady across the aisle from Cal, who just continued to glare at him as if he'd committed some terrible faux pas like farting at the dinner table.

Just as he was reaching for her to drag her down with him, both men opened fire. Bullets crashed through windows on both sides of the car sending shards of glass flying and showering sparks as the slugs ricocheted off metal struts.

The lady grunted once and her eyes opened wide in surprise as a bright flower of blood blossomed on her blouse just over her right shoulder.

Cal grabbed her, and her eyes rolled back and she

fainted and fell into his arms. He pulled her down and laid her gently on her back on the floor under the seats as more bullets thudded into the car.

Really pissed off now, Cal raised his head and aimed out the window and fired off shots as fast as he could pull the trigger until his gun was empty. He was rewarded by seeing the horse of the man on his side of the train swallow his head and somersault forward, sending the outlaw tumbling through the air to land hard in a sycamore bush.

Cal quickly began to reload, but by the time he'd filled the chambers, the other bandit had pulled up his horse and was riding across the tracks to help his friend.

It didn't matter anyway as the train had reached the top of the hill and was picking up speed and would soon be at the Payday stop.

Cal holstered his pistol, reached down, and slid the old lady out from under the seat into the middle of the aisle. He leaned over and ripped the lady's blouse open at the shoulder.

"Here now, young man," a woman from several rows ahead shouted indignantly, pointing her parasol at him like it was a rifle. "Just what do you think you're doing to that poor, unfortunate woman?"

Cal didn't answer until he'd taken his bandanna off and tied it tightly around the lady's shoulder, slowing the steady stream of blood pouring from her wound.

Then he looked up and said calmly, "I'm tryin' to keep this woman from bleedin' to death. Do you mind?"

The woman's husband, who was evidently much smarter than her, or at least had maybe seen gunshot wounds before, shushed her and came back to kneel next to Cal.

"You need any help, son?" he asked.

"Help me get her up on the seat. She'll be more comfortable there," Cal said. "We're gonna need to keep some pressure on that wound to slow the bleeding down as much as possible."

After they'd picked her up and laid her on the seat crosswise, the man helping said, "Sounds like you've seen a few gunshot wounds before, son."

Cal thought of the many scars on his body from similar wounds he'd suffered helping Smoke, and grinned. "A few, mister, so I know what we got to do."

He eased down on the edge of the seat next to the lady and said, "I'll stay here with her and as soon as the train stops, someone needs to get a wagon from Payday and we need to get her to a bed where someone can try and get that bullet outta her shoulder 'fore it festers up."

The man shook his head. "I don't know who that'd be," he said. "I'm from Payday and our only doctor was killed a few weeks back."

Cal grinned sourly. "I know," he said, hoping Smoke was still in town. He knew the mountain man had plenty of experience removing slugs from people's bodies, and to him it looked like this lady wasn't going to make it unless someone worked on her sooner rather than later. "I guess we'll just have to find somebody else to do it."

He glanced up at the man's wife, who was hovering over them, watching to make sure Cal didn't do anything inappropriate. "Ma'am, do you know this lady?" he asked.

She shook her head. "Why, no, I don't."

Cal inclined his head toward the lady's handbag, which was lying next to her knitting she'd dropped when she got shot. "Maybe there's something in her bag that'll tell us who she is. We need to notify her family she's been hurt."

The lady picked up the bag and opened it. She took a yellow piece of paper out of the bag. "Here's a telegraph receipt," she said, reading it. "It's a message to the mayor of Payday and it's signed Janet Rule."

Jiminy, Cal thought, this is the lady we've all been looking so hard for and she's right here on the train with me.

He looked down at the lady, struggling for her life. "She's got to survive," he said to the man leaning over her with him. "She's got some important news for the mayor, so we've got to get that bullet out of her and keep her alive."

The man shrugged. "Well, we got a sheriff here in Payday. He's had some experience with gunshot wounds. Maybe he can take the bullet outta her."

Cal glanced up at him. He knew the sheriff was probably the reason she had a bullet in her in the first place. "Over my dead body," he said, causing the man to look at him strangely.

Just then the train jerked to a stop and the conductor stuck his head in the door. "Is everyone all right back here?" he asked.

Cal looked up. "We need a wagon from town and some blankets and we need 'em fast!

CHAPTER 30

Jeb Hardy watched the train disappear in the distance and shook his head. What a colossal fuck-up this was, he thought sourly. He took his Stetson off and looked at the bullet hole punched neatly in the crown, about one and a half inches above where his head had been. He didn't know who the yahoo was who'd started shooting back at them from the train, but he was damned good.

He jerked his horse's head around and rode it across the tracks. He grinned for a moment at the sight of the very proud and self-important Kid Akins lying ass over teakettle in a sycamore bush, but he was careful not to let the Kid see his amusement.

He walked his horse over to the bush. "Hey, Kid. You all right?" he called.

"Hell, no, I ain't all right, you asshole," the Kid yelled back from among broken branches and limbs of the bush. Evidently, the fall hadn't improved his disposition any, Hardy thought wryly.

"What's wrong?"

"I think I broke my damned arm," the Kid called back, struggling to free himself from the limbs and branches he'd broken in his fall that were entwined all around him.

When he finally emerged from the tangled mess,

Hardy whistled softly. "Whew, that looks like a nasty break," he said sympathetically.

The Kid glanced down at where his left arm hung limply at his side. Between the elbow and the wrist, the arm took a bend that wasn't at all natural and was swollen to almost twice its size. The Kid's face was scratched and bleeding and screwed up in pain, and he just shook his head. "I hope I get my hands on the son of a bitch who was doing all that shooting," he groused, his voice harsh and almost a croak from the pain.

"Well," Hardy said, climbing down off his horse and pulling a large-bladed knife from the scabbard on his belt. "You can't hardly blame him none, Kid. After all, we started the shooting and he was just shooting back."

The Kid turned flat, dangerous eyes on him. "That don't matter none at all. If I ever find out who it was, he's a dead man."

When Hardy moved toward him, his knife extended, the Kid slapped at his empty holster with his right hand, and then he looked around wildly for his pistol, which had evidently fallen from his hand when he was somersaulting over his horse's head. "What are you doin' with that blade?" he asked, backing away until he was almost back in the sycamore bush.

Hardy grinned, pleased to see the Kid was frightened of him. It was a fact worth savoring, and remembering. "Hey, don't worry, Kid. I'm not going to hurt you. But I figure we're gonna need to cut some limbs off that there sycamore bush to make you a splint for that arm, 'less you want to ride back to town with it bouncing and flopping around all over the place."

After he cut four limbs about twenty-four inches in length, Hardy turned to the Kid, who was sitting on a rock cradling his left arm with his right, his face pale and covered with sweat and dried blood from all the scratches.

"Now for the fun part," Hardy said, laying the sticks at the Kid's feet.

"Whatta ya' mean?" he asked, his eyes widening in fear and pain.

"I'm gonna have to set that wrist, Kid, or you're gonna have to go the rest of your life with an arm as crooked as a dog's hind leg."

"Wait a minute," Kid said, looking around as if he might find someone to tell him he didn't have to go through with it.

Hardy took the Kid's arm. "No use fighting it, Kid. We done drank all the whiskey while we was waiting to shoot up the train. Now, just bite on this and I'll fix you right up." He handed Kid his leather knife scabbard.

Kid put it between his teeth and closed his eyes, and Hardy took his wrist in his hands and gave it a quick jerk.

When the bone snapped into place, Kid screamed once and then he leaned over and vomited into the dirt. When Hardy shifted his grip, the Kid looked at the arm, swallowed once, and fainted dead away.

Hardy looked down at him and shook his head. What a baby, he thought as he bent over and tied the four sticks to Kid's arm, holding the bone straight until they could get to town and put a proper splint on it.

While the train was stopped at the small platform that served as the Payday station, Cal waited by the old lady's side until someone had fetched a buckboard from the town, and then he climbed in next to her for the trip back to town.

Once there, Mayor Sam Hemmings directed the driver of the wagon to park it in front of Dr. Bentley's house.

"But Mayor," the man argued, "the doc's dead. He ain't there no more."

"I know that, you fool," Hemmings said irritably, "but he's got the only place set up for someone to be treated for a gunshot wound in."

Once the lady was lying on one of the doctor's beds, still unconscious, the mayor got a good look at her. "Well, I'll be damned," he said, shaking his head.

"I see you know who she is," Cal said from the other side of the bed.

"Sure I do. That's Janet Rule, Dr. Bentley's aunt," the mayor said. "I was supposed to meet her when the train came in this afternoon so she could give me some information about the doc's murder."

Cal nodded. "I know. We looked in her bag on the train and found the telegram she'd sent you with her name on it," Cal said, still astonished at the tricks fate can play on man. Here was the very lady Smoke and he had been trying to find ever since they found out about Pearlie's arrest and her maybe having knowledge that would clear him.

"Jesus, what a mess," Hemmings said. He took his hat off and scratched his head. "I just hope she comes around so she can tell me whatever it was she wanted to." He looked at Cal. "Otherwise, your friend is gonna hang."

"Speaking of friends," Cal said, "have you seen Smoke around this afternoon?"

Hemmings shook his head. "No, but when I went to get my horse out of the stable to come up here to meet the train, Jerry Stone said Smoke got his horse and rode out of town this morning and hasn't come back since."

"Damn," Cal said. "Isn't there someone in this town who can take that bullet outta her shoulder?" Cal asked worriedly. He knew that time was critical in gunshot wounds. If the bullet stayed in the flesh too long, suppuration was almost sure to set in and the patient would have little chance of surviving.

Hemmings shook his head. "No, I'm afraid not, son. Since we had the doc here for so long, none of us ever had to learn to take bullets outta people."

"Shit!" Cal said, rolling up his sleeves. "Get me a basin of water, boiled and hot, and some towels."

Hemmings's eyebrows shot up. "You gonna try to get that lead outta her?"

Cal nodded, his stomach doing flip-flops. "I will if you'll show me where the doctor kept his instruments. The last time I did this, I did it with a skinning knife heated in a campfire, but the doctor's probably got something better suited for it than that."

"You sure you know what you're doing?" Hemmings asked after he told one of the men standing nearby to get the water and the doc's bag of instruments.

Cal grinned sourly. "No, but I've at least done it a time or two before, and I've seen Smoke do it on me four or five times. You got any better ideas?"

"We could send someone to Pueblo. . . ." Hemmings started to say, until Cal cut him off.

"She'd be dead before he got there, much less before anyone could get back here. If we're gonna do this, it's got to be done now."

After a pan of steaming-hot water was placed next to the bed and Cal had the doc's instruments laid out on a side table next to him, he closed his eyes and whispered a silent prayer before he began. When he opened his eyes, he noticed Mayor Sam Hemmings doing the same thing, and chuckled. He was going to need all the help he could get, and a little divine intervention would be more than welcome.

Taking a long, slim knife off the table, he glanced up at Hemmings, who was standing behind him. "If you want to help, you can stand next to her and make sure she don't move."

Hemmings nodded and sleeved sweat off his brow. It was obvious that he'd had no experience with such matters in the past.

Cal took the knife in one hand and a pair of slim tongs in the other. He used the tip of the knife to open the wound a bit, and then he probed down deep with the tongs, trying to feel with the metal like it was his fingers. Immediately, blood began to ooze up out of the wound, but since it wasn't spurting, Cal tried to ignore it.

After a few moments, he felt a slight click as the tip of the metal tongs touched lead. Spreading the tong tips slowly, he gently pushed deeper, and then closed them around the butt end of the slug.

As easy as he could, he withdrew the tongs and sure enough, lying there between the tips was a slightly bent and crumpled lead bullet.

"Good God Almighty," Hemmings exclaimed, grinning as sweat continued to pour off his face, "you did it!"

Cal dropped the slug into a metal basin and put the knife and the tongs down. "It ain't over yet, Mayor."

He took a clean cloth, rolled it into a small cylinder, and dipped it in the hot water, and then, after wringing it out, he gently pushed it down into the wound, which was oozing blood a little faster now that he'd stirred things up inside her.

Once the flow of blood was stopped, he took a larger piece of cloth and asked Hemmings to hold her shoulder up off the bed while he wrapped the cloth around it in a figure eight, making it tight enough to keep pressure on the wound.

When he was done, Cal got to his feet and sighed deeply. "Now, it's up to her and how bad she wants to live," he said, feeling as bone tired as if he'd run several miles.

Hemmings glanced down at the sleeping lady. "Well, at least her color looks a mite better."

"Yeah," Cal replied, "but I'm worried that she didn't even move when I was probing her wound. She's still pretty deep asleep, an' that ain't exactly a good sign."

Hemmings put his hand on Cal's shoulder. "Well, at least she's got a chance now, son, thanks to you."

Cal nodded quickly and moved over to take a seat in a chair next to the wall. He leaned back against the back of the chair, loosened the rawhide thong on his pistol, and laid his head back and closed his eyes.

"Uh, what are you doing?" the mayor asked.

Cal opened one eye. "This lady's got some information that's gonna put some galoot's neck in a noose, Mayor. He's already tried to kill her once, and if he finds out she's still alive, it's my guess he's gonna try again." He closed his eye. "I aim to prevent that from happening."

"I was planning on asking the sheriff to stand watch over her until she woke up, Cal," Hemmings said.

Cal snorted without opening his eyes. "That'd be like askin' the fox to guard the henhouse, Mr. Hemmings."

"Oh, I don't. . . ."

Now Cal opened his eyes. "You're welcome to stay here if you want, or have some lady from the town stay here with us, but I'm not leaving this lady's side until she tells us who really killed the doctor."

Hemmings pursed his lips. "And what if she says your friend did it?"

Cal grinned. "That ain't gonna happen, Mayor."

"And just how are you so sure?"

Cal sighed. "Think about it, Mr. Hemmings. The trial was over and done with, and Pearlie'd been sentenced to hang. If this lady knew he was the one that done it, why would she come all the way down here to tell you about it? Hell, he was done for. All she had to do was keep her mouth shut an' he was gonna hang."

Hemmings narrowed his eyes and stroked his chin, thinking about what Cal said.

Cal smiled. "See? The only thing that makes sense is that she knew an innocent man was gonna die for something somebody else did unless she spoke up. That's the only thing I can think of that would make her come all this way to talk to you. And the fact that she wanted you to keep it a secret means the man she was going to accuse was still running around loose and might do her hurt if he found out she was going to talk."

Hemmings finally nodded. "By gum, you're right, Cal." He hesitated. "And like you and Smoke said earlier, the only reason she'd have to wire me instead of Sheriff Tolliver with her offer to testify is if she was going to accuse him."

Now it was Cal who nodded. "Now you're catching on, Mayor. As you know, my partner, Smoke Jensen, and I think it's definitely the sheriff that is somehow mixed up in all this. That's why I don't intend to let him near Miss Rule until she's had a chance to talk."

Hemmings shook his head. "I just can't believe that Sheriff Tolliver is a murderer, but what you say does make a lot of sense."

Cal measured the mayor with his eyes for a moment. He didn't know if he was mixed up with the sheriff or not, but he decided to trust him. "That ain't all either," Cal said. "What would you say if I told you that the sheriff and some other men named Hardy, Akins, Hogarth, an' Barkley are partners in over twenty mining claims in this county, and that the sheriff has over three hundred thousand dollars in one Pueblo bank and no telling how much in other banks in the city?"

Hemmings's eyes nearly bugged out of his head. "What? That . . . that's just not possible," he finally managed to say. "Why, the sheriff only makes a hundred dollars a month salary, and he hasn't spent any time prospecting or mining that I know about."

Cal closed his eyes and leaned his head back again. "Something to think about, huh, Mayor?"

Hemmings sat down across the room from Cal and did just that, turning things over and over in his mind until he was certain that Cal and Smoke had called it correctly—Sheriff Buck Tolliver was in this up to his eyebrows.

CHAPTER 31

The next day, Smoke was up at dawn after sleeping only fitfully in the woods near the cabin Sheriff Tolliver and his companion stayed in. Smoke had made a cold camp, not daring to light a fire lest he give his location away. He felt sure the sheriff knew he was out there following him, but he didn't want to make it too easy in case the man decided to do something about it and came looking for him after dark. The thought made him grin in anticipation, for the dark and the woods and the mountains were Smoke's elements, not the sheriff's.

When the sun rose and there was no sign the two men in the cabin were even awake yet, Smoke said to hell with it and made himself a hat-sized fire. He used only small, very dry sticks so there'd be little or no smoke, and he cooked bacon and beans and used the grease to make the rock-hard biscuits in his saddlebags soft enough to eat without the danger of breaking a tooth.

By the time Smoke was on his last cup of boiled coffee and his second cigarette of the day, he saw signs of life in the cabin. Tolliver walked out the door and into the old outhouse out back.

Smoke used the time to pack up his breakfast fixings, and was ready to go when Tolliver and his companion finally got onto their horses and headed back toward town. He hadn't seen any smoke coming out of the small stovepipe on the roof, so he knew the men hadn't cooked themselves any breakfast or made any hot coffee.

After a while, Smoke decided to have some fun, so he walked his horse out of the thick brush alongside the trail and got into line a hundred yards or so behind the sheriff, only keeping pace with the two men and not catching up, but making sure they knew he'd been following them.

Other than glancing over his shoulder and grinning a few times, Tolliver didn't look like Smoke's being there bothered him at all.

Smoke began to wonder if he hadn't been suckered; if the sheriff hadn't guessed he'd be following him and sent the other two men off to do his dirty work. If that were true, then Miss Rule had probably already been sent on to her reward in the afterlife and he was going to have to find some other way to prove Pearlie's innocence. Oh, well, Smoke thought, shrugging, there wasn't anything he could do about it. He could only follow one of them, and the sheriff had been the logical one to keep an eye on.

After years living in the High Lonesome with Preacher when he was younger, Smoke had developed the ability to live in the present while preparing for the future and all without dwelling on the past. What was done was done, and there was no changing it, so there was rarely the need to worry excessively over it. If mistakes had been made, he just tried harder not to make them again. It was a good philosophy to live by, but it was small comfort when a friend's life depended on you making the right choice the first time, because you weren't going to get another chance.

When they got to town, the sheriff and his fat friend

walked their horses straight to the café they'd eaten at the previous day. The men had obviously been too lazy to make themselves breakfast, so they were going for an early lunch, Smoke figured.

No need to follow them there. He'd do better checking in with the mayor to find out if he'd heard anything from Miss Rule since Smoke had last talked with him. It was about time for Smoke to put his foot down and make the man divulge when and where she was going to show up so that he and Cal could make sure she lived long enough to testify.

When he got to the mayor's office, Smoke found a note tacked to the door saying the mayor was over at Dr. Bentley's house.

"That's strange," Smoke said to himself. "What would he be doing at a dead man's house?"

Smoke tied his horse to the hitching rail out front and knocked on the doctor's door. A haggard-looking mayor answered; his hair was askew, his face was unshaven, and his eyes were bleary and bloodshot.

"Oh, hello, Mr. Jensen," he said, stepping to the side and ushering Smoke inside.

"Good morning, Mayor Hemmings," Smoke said, taking his hat off and hanging it on a peg near the door. "You look like the north end of a southbound mule."

The mayor grunted and nodded. "Yeah, it comes from staying up all night jumping at every sound 'cause you're sure someone's gonna shoot you in the head while you're asleep."

Smoke raised his eyebrows, and was just about to ask what Hemmings meant when Cal walked into the room. "Hey, Smoke," he said. Cal looked considerably fresher than the mayor, as if he hadn't had any trouble sleeping at all. In fact, Smoke thought, he looked quite chipper.

"Hey, Cal. Now just what have you two been up to?" Smoke asked, looking from one to the other.

"You tell him," Hemmings said to Cal, waving a limp hand. "I'm going to shave while you make us some fresh coffee."

He turned and shuffled into the doctor's bedroom, looking for a razor and shaving soap and water to scrape his beard off with.

"Come on in the kitchen and I'll make us all some coffee while I tell you what's been happening," Cal said.

Half an hour later, the mayor had shaved, the coffee'd been made and drunk, and the men were standing in the clinic room looking down at Janet Rule.

Smoke leaned over and put his palm on her forehead. "If she's got a fever, it's very slight," he said. He peeked under the bandages on her shoulder, and then he glanced at Cal and smiled. "You did a good job getting that slug out of her, Cal. You probably saved her life. There is absolutely no sign of festering or suppuration around the wound."

Cal frowned. "Yeah, maybe. I just wish she'd wake up and tell us what she knows that might help Pearlie. That way no one would have any reason to kill her and we could relax a little bit."

"So, you two sat up with her all night?" Smoke asked, an appraising glint in his eye.

The mayor nodded, glancing at Cal. "Yes. Your friend here thought her life might be in danger, so we both elected to guard her during the night."

"He was obviously correct, Mayor," Smoke said.

"From what Cal said, the outlaws who attacked the train only fired into the last car. That means they weren't trying to rob the train, and it also means they knew beforehand when Miss Rule was arriving and exactly where she was going to be seated."

Hemmings snapped his fingers. "Of course, I hadn't thought of that." He shook his head. "I was so busy worrying about whether she was going to live or not, I plumb forgot to think through what her attack meant."

"Who else besides yourself knew of Miss Rule's plans?" Smoke asked.

The mayor thought for a second. "Only myself and Robert Jacobson, the man who took the telegraph message."

Cal snorted. "Huh. We already know Jacobson's got a big mouth and that he's pretty friendly with the sheriff."

Smoke looked at Hemmings. "What do you think about what Cal found out in Pueblo, Mayor?"

The mayor shrugged, looking uncomfortable. "It doesn't sound too good for the sheriff," he said. "It probably means he's been stealing claims from miners for some time, but it does not necessarily mean that he had anything to do with Dr. Bentley's death. The two things may not be connected, and while it certainly puts him on the hook for a lot of crimes, it won't help clear Pearlie unless the sheriff confesses to the murder of Bentley too."

"You're right, Mayor," Smoke said, moving to the window and staring out of it. "What we found out about the sheriff means he's most probably a killer and is certainly a crook and a thief, but it doesn't prove he killed the doctor."

"But, Smoke!" Cal said. "We both know he's guilty as can be."

Smoke looked over his shoulder. "Knowing it and proving it are two separate things, Cal."

Then, Smoke surprised them both by grinning.

"Why have you got that shit-eating grin on your face, Smoke?" Cal asked, smiling himself because he knew that expression meant Smoke had figured out a way to get to the sheriff.

"I've got an idea," Smoke answered. He looked at Hemmings. "What was the name of that woman who helped treat Pearlie's wounds? The ex-nurse?"

"Why, uh, Hattie Monroe," Hemmings replied, blushing slightly.

Smoke smiled in return. "And you two are, uh, close friends, I take it?"

The mayor's blush deepened. "Yes, you could say that. Why?"

"Do you trust her completely?" Smoke asked.

The mayor shrugged. "I guess so. As far as I know, Hattie is an honorable woman in spite of her profession, but you still haven't answered my question. Why?"

"I told you," Smoke said. "I have an idea. . . ."

Jeb Hardy and Kid Akins were riding into town, doubled up on Hardy's mount since Akins's horse had broken his leg in the fall and had been put down.

"Hey, Jeb," Akins said, "isn't that Buck's horse over at the café there?"

"Yeah," Hardy said. "You feel up to eating something this afternoon?"

"I guess so, but I was kind'a hoping for something a little stronger to drink than coffee. I need something to ease this pain in my arm, and just about every other bone I got feels like it's been stomped on by a mule."

"We'll get to that," Hardy said, thinking to himself

what a crybaby Akins was. "Let's see what Buck has to say first and then we'll head on over to the saloon."

They dismounted and went into the café, Akins still cradling his broken left arm and its splints with his right hand.

Buck raised his eyebrows when he saw them, and then he scooted over to make room for them in the booth where he and Hog Hogarth were sitting.

As soon as they'd ordered some coffee and food from the waitress, Tolliver leaned over and whispered harshly, "What the hell happened? I didn't see any commotion when I rode into town like somebody'd been killed. Did you get the old lady?"

Hardy shrugged. "I think so. We put about a hundred rounds into that rail car, and I think I heard her scream just before she dropped outta sight."

"What happened to you?" Hog asked, looking at Akins and grinning. None of the group particularly liked the brash young man, and Hog especially had no love for the boy since Akins was always riding him about his weight and sloppiness.

"Some asshole in the train started shooting back at us, an' he got lucky and plugged my hoss."

Hog nodded. "And so then you fell off and broke your little arm?" he asked, sarcasm dripping from his voice.

Akins's eyes narrowed. "Yeah, but it's not my gun hand, so don't go getting any ideas, fat man."

Hog gave a short laugh. "I don't care if'n your gun hand is good or not, little man. If'n I wanted to take you I'd take you, guns, fists, knives, or teeth," he growled.

"Shut the fuck up!" Tolliver snapped in a low, hard voice. "I'm trying to get some work done here and you two keep acting like little kids fighting all the time."

They all shut up while the waitress brought their

coffee and food. Once she'd left the table, Tolliver leaned back and smiled at Hardy. "So, you think you got it done, huh?"

Hardy nodded around a mouthful of bacon and eggs. "I said I think so, Buck. Won't know for sure till we go on into town and listen to what everyone is saying. Hell, train ought'a have been here by now."

Tolliver craned his neck around to look out of the window. "I don't see no crowds around my office, nor anyone gathered in the street. Maybe the train just kept on going and didn't stop to let anybody off since they'd been attacked."

Hardy nodded down at Tolliver's empty plate. "I see you done finished your meal. Why don't you head on over to the mayor's office and see what he's heard? We'll wait here for you."

"The hell we will," Akins said, shoveling food into his mouth one-handed, his injured left arm propped up on the table. "Soon as I finish this here grub, I'm headin' for the saloon to get me some whiskey to kill the pain."

"Crybaby," Hog muttered.

Tolliver gave him a flat look and held up his hand before Akins could respond to the gibe. "All right, all right. I'll mosey on over to Hemmings' office and I'll meet you men at the saloon in half an hour."

He stood up and stared down at Hardy and Akins. "And for you two's sake, I'd better find out that train pulled into the station with at least one dead body on it."

CHAPTER 32

Mayor Sam Hemmings was sitting in his office going over some paperwork when the door opened after a short knock. Sheriff Buck Tolliver walked in and took his hat off before sitting down, a sign that usually meant he intended to stay and chew the fat for a while.

"Howdy, Mayor," he said.

"Hello, Buck," Hemmings replied, feeling the sweat begin to gather under his armpits. Even though they'd been casual friends for a long time, Tolliver was a dangerous man when crossed, and Hemmings was about to cross him in the worst way, thanks to Jensen. Being a natural-born politician helped Hemmings keep the fact that he was lying through his teeth hidden from Tolliver.

"Haven't seen you around for a couple of days," Hemmings said, trying to keep his tone light as if he had nothing important on his mind.

Tolliver nodded and yawned, as if bored. He too was trying to keep the fact that he was lying hidden. "Yeah, well, I had to do my weekly ride around to the mining camps in the county and make sure they weren't having any problems with poachers or claim-jumpers."

I'll bet, Hemmings thought, but didn't say. "Well,

you sure missed some excitement here while you were gone."

"Oh?" Tolliver asked, trying to sound mildly interested, but Hemmings could tell it was the real reason he came by the office.

"A couple of desperadoes shot up the afternoon train from Pueblo yesterday," Hemmings said. "Probably just a couple of drunken cowboys 'cause they didn't try to rob it or anything, just shot the hell outta one of the cars as it was slowed down coming up that big hill just outside of town."

Tolliver attempted to sound casual, but his eyes gave his excitement away. "Is that so? Anybody hurt?"

"Yes, matter of fact. Miss Rule, you remember, Dr. Bentley's aunt, was shot up."

"Oh, I'm awful sorry to hear that," Tolliver said, leaning back in his chair and pulling a cigar out of his vest pocket. As he struck a match on his pants leg and held the flame under the tip, he glanced up through the smoke at Hemmings and asked, "They gonna have a funeral for her here or in Pueblo?"

Hemmings smiled. The son of a bitch is taking the bait, he thought. Now to pull him in. "Well, now, that's the good news," he said. "She wasn't killed, just wounded. That friend of Pearlie's, Cal Woods, happened to be on the train, and he took the bullet outta her and she looks like she's gonna be all right."

Tolliver gave a tiny gasp, choked on cigar smoke, and coughed for a minute like he was trying to heave up a lung. When he could breathe again, he asked, "She able to tell you anything about the night the doc got killed?"

Hemmings put a disappointed look on his face. "No, not yet. Unfortunately, she's still unconscious from loss of blood and hasn't been able to tell me anything as of yet. But we expect her to wake up anytime now and as soon as she does, I'm going to go over there and see what she has to say."

"Where . . . where are you keeping her?" Tolliver asked, trying to sound disinterested. "I might ought'a go on over there an' see if I can get a statement from her."

"She's over at the doc's house in that little room where he kept his sick patients when they had to stay overnight. I've got Hattie Monroe staying with her, but she says we ought not bother her for a few more days till she gets her strength back. Hattie said she'll let me know as soon as she wakes up and is ready to talk."

Tolliver raised his eyebrows. "Hattie the only one staying there?"

Hemmings tried to look shocked. "Well, after all, Buck, Miss Rule is a proper lady. We can't hardly have any townsmen staying in the same house with her while she's unconscious. It just wouldn't be right."

"Of course, you're right. I wasn't thinking," Tolliver said, a speculative glint in his eye. "Besides, the only man who'd have any reason to not want her to tell about that night is already in jail waitin' to be hung."

"That's right," Hemmings agreed. "I suspect that when Miss Rule wakes up, she's gonna tell us that Pearlie killed the doc and that'll be the end of it."

"I'm sure you're right, Mayor," Tolliver said, getting to his feet and stubbing his cigar out in the ashtray on Hemmings's desk. "Well, I'd better be on my way. The good citizens of Payday don't pay me to sit around jawing all day."

"See you later, Buck," Hemmings said, lowering his head as if he were getting back to his paperwork.

After Tolliver left, Hemmings went to his window and took a handkerchief out of his pocket. He stuck his hand out of his window and waved the cloth a couple of times as if he were dusting it off, and then he went back to sit at his desk and worry about how things were going to play out.

This was a very dangerous game he and Jensen were playing, and he hoped that the right people got caught in the trap, and not the ones setting the trap.

Tolliver could hardly keep from running as he made his way straight toward the saloon down the street from the mayor's office.

He burst through the batwings and looked frantically around for his friends. Sure enough, Hog and Jeb and Kid were sitting at a corner table across the room. As he made his way toward them, Tolliver noticed that the whiskey bottle in the center of the table was already half empty. Damn, he thought, they sure as hell weren't wasting any time getting plowed.

Hardy glanced up and saw Tolliver making his way through the crowded room, and shook his head when he saw the expression on Tolliver's face. "Uh-oh, boys," Hardy said, pouring himself another drink from the whiskey bottle in preparation for what he knew was going to be a hell of an afternoon. "Looks like we got storm clouds ahead." And he winked and inclined his head toward Tolliver.

"He looks mad enough to piss nails," Kid said, wincing as his movement caused a stab of pain in his injured arm that ran all the way past his shoulder and straight into his head.

Tolliver took a seat and without speaking, grabbed the whiskey bottle and a spare glass and filled it to the brim. He set the bottle down, upended the glass, and drained half of it in one long, convulsive gulp.

"Uh, bad news, I take it?" Hardy said, though his face showed little concern.

Tolliver turned red, bloodshot eyes on him and growled, "Damn straight there's bad news. It seems you and the Kid here didn't do too good a job yesterday."

He looked over at Kid and sneered, "In fact, about the only thing you got killed was the Kid's horse."

Hardy frowned. "Hey, Buck, I saw the lady go down with my own eyes. I know she was hit."

"Yeah, she went down but not out, you fool," Tolliver spit back at him. "You only managed to wound her, and that damn kid with Jensen was on the train, and he fixed her up good enough that the mayor says she'll be good as new in a few days and talking her fool head off."

"Did she tell him what she saw the night you . . . uh . . . the doc was killed?" Hog asked. He was on his third glass of whiskey and his words were slightly slurred because his lips were numb and weren't working right.

"Not yet, thank God," Tolliver said, finishing off his glass and pouring himself another one. "But according to Hemmings, it won't be too long 'fore she's able to send us all to the gallows."

"Hold on there, Buck," Hardy said, his voice low and hard. "None of us had anything to do with the doc's killing. That was yours and Blackie's mess, so don't be talking no gallows talk to me."

Tolliver gave a short laugh and took a deep swig of his whiskey. "I done told you once, Hardy, it don't make no never mind about who did the doc. If it looks like I'm gonna swing from the end of a rope, I can guarantee you I won't be dancing alone."

Hardy's hand dropped to the butt of his pistol. "It's beginning to look like the simplest thing for us to do is to plant you forked-end-up, Buck. That'd solve all of our problems."

Tolliver sneered. "Yeah, but my lawyer in Pueblo has all the information he needs to make sure every last one of you sons of bitches will be convicted of dozens of murders, Jeb, so you'd better get shut of that idea right now."

"Hey, fellas," Kid said, laying his good hand on Buck's forearm. "Let's not fight among ourselves. Remember, we all got a good thing going here. There's no need to let a little old lady fuck it up for us."

Hog nodded. "For once, the Kid's right, men." He upended his glass for another drink before he realized it was already empty.

Tolliver looked around the table. "All right then. Here's what we have to do. The mayor has the old lady being kept in the doc's house. She's being watched over by Hattie Monroe, and there's no other guards."

Hardy grinned evilly. "Then there should be no problem sneaking in there tonight and putting a lead pill in both their heads."

"Hold on, Jeb," Tolliver said, sipping his drink now instead of gulping it. "It would raise a lot of questions if they're killed like that. People might start to wonder who has something to hide."

Hog sighed heavily. "Well, then, Buck. Just what do you want us to do? Take her out to the cabin and hold her until she dies of old age?" he asked, giggling a little at his lame joke.

Tolliver laughed, more from nervousness than from amusement. "No. I just need someone to slip into the house without being seen, cut their throats, and then set the house on fire."

"But people will still know they been killed," Hog argued. "Won't they?"

Tolliver shook his head. "No, they won't, Hog. The fire will destroy the bodies so no one will know their throats were cut. Everyone knows Hattie smokes like a chimney. They'll just assume she fell asleep and set the place on fire." He looked around the table. "Matter of fact, it might be a good idea to take an empty bottle of whiskey and lay it next to her body like she'd been drinking all night and passed out while smoking a cigarette."

"Who do you want to do the job?" Kid asked.

"Not you, Kid," Tolliver said, looking down at his broken wrist. He glanced across the table at Hog. "I think Hog's the best one here with a blade, so he should do it."

"Yeah," Kid said sarcastically, "and even he ought to be able to kill a couple of women and start a fire without messing it up too bad." He paused. "Unless he's too drunk to walk by then."

Hog's eyes flashed. "I ain't drunk, Kid, but I tell you what I *am* gonna do, an' that's start a fire under your ass when I get done with them two ladies."

The men were all so intent on their discussion, they didn't see Smoke Jensen and Joshua Banks standing on the second-floor landing watching them cold-bloodedly plan the murder of two women.

Smoke had thought it might be best to have an impartial witness to the sheriff's meeting with his henchmen just in case it came down to his word against the sheriff's, and Banks, the lawyer who'd acted as judge during Pearlie's trial, was the logical choice.

Banks looked at Smoke as the sheriff and his men got up and left the saloon. "I see your point, Jensen," Banks said. "Now that Mayor Hemmings has given the sheriff and only the sheriff the information about Miss Rule, and if subsequent to this meeting one or more of those men try to do her harm, we'll have an excellent prima facie case for conspiracy to commit murder against the sheriff."

Smoke grinned. "I take it all that highfalutin lawyer talk means we'll have him dead to rights."

Banks grinned. "Deader than a hog on a spit!"

CHAPTER 33

Scudding clouds raced across the night sky and blotted out the moon, making the main street of Payday as dark as the inside of a black cat at midnight.

A heavyset, rotund figure moved from the alleyway just south of the late Dr. Bentley's house, and moved slowly along the boardwalk with his back pressed up against the buildings.

From the second floor of the hotel across the street, Mayor Sam Hemmings and Joshua Banks had to cover their mouths to keep from laughing at the sight of the fat man tiptoeing down the boardwalk, looking back over his shoulder every few feet or so.

"Jesus," Banks said under his breath, even though they were over a hundred yards away and couldn't possibly be overheard. "He might as well wear a sign painted on his back saying I'm up to no good—arrest me."

Hemmings returned Banks's chuckle. "Well, Joshua, if crooks were smart, the law'd never catch them and then they wouldn't need high-priced flatheads like you to defend them."

"Yeah, lucky me that most of them are as dumb as dirt." He sighed. "That's one of the reasons I thought I'd give up the law and try my hand at mining." He grinned and his teeth showed in the semidarkness. "You don't get near as dirty that way."

Hemmings cocked an eyebrow at Banks. "How are you doin' with that, Joshua? Making enough money to stay 'retired' from the law?"

"Sure," Banks replied, smiling sardonically. "If I only eat once a week, and if I don't mind sidling up to a mule instead of a lady on the rare occasion I'm not too tired to think of female companionship."

Hemmings laughed, and then he quickly covered his mouth and looked out the window to make sure Hog hadn't heard them. When he saw the fat man was still making his way down the boardwalk, he turned and asked Banks, "So, I take it you'll be adding Esquire after your name again in the not-too-distant future?"

Banks nodded. "Yeah, but not until after these assholes are hanged." He glanced at Hemmings and said earnestly, "I wouldn't want to be in practice and find myself being asked to defend one of the bastards."

Down on the street below, Hog Hogarth felt as if his heart was going to hammer itself right out of his chest. It wasn't that he was afraid of breaking the law; he'd been doing that ever since he was tall enough to slip into shop windows in town and steal what wasn't tied down. And it wasn't the thought of killing one, or even, two women—dead was dead, he figured, and it didn't matter a hill of beans whether you were a man or a woman; you hated being killed as much as anyone. No, he thought. It was the fact that he was supposed to slip up on them and do Hattie quick before she had time to raise an alarm, and then he was supposed to kill the Rule woman, who was lying unconscious according to Buck Tolliver.

Hog just didn't take with slitting the throat of someone who wasn't awake to possibly have a chance to fight back. As big as he was, Hog had never been a bully. He'd never had to be, and all the time he was growing up, his daddy had preached to him that he should never hit anyone smaller than him. This posed somewhat of a dilemma for Hog, as just about everybody in town when he was growing up was smaller than him.

He'd solved his problem by never fighting anyone his size or smaller with two hands—he'd just licked them all one-handed and been done with it.

Now, however, he was being asked to kill not only a woman, but a woman who was asleep at the time. This was sticking in Hog's craw, and he didn't know how he was going to deal with it, and wouldn't know until the very moment the knife was in his hand and he was standing over the lady.

When he was halfway across the last street between him and the doctor's house, the moon came out from behind the clouds and exposed Hog in full moonlight standing almost on the doctor's porch.

"Damn!" Hog exclaimed, and then he clamped a hand over his own mouth and ran up onto the doctor's porch. Stupid shit, he told himself. Now just grit your teeth, Hog old man, and get the job done so you can go back to the saloon and pick up the money Tolliver promised you.

Hog reached out and tried the doorknob. It was locked. That was no problem for him. He stuck the empty whiskey bottle he was carrying under his arm, pulled out a thin-bladed stiletto, and inserted the point between the door and the jamb. He gently probed until he felt the tip of the knife up against the bolt. He pressed the point into the metal of the dead bolt and twisted. The bolt screeched once, and then it moved back into the door, leaving the door unlocked.

Careful not to make any more noise, Hog folded

the stiletto blade back into its handle and stuck the knife in his pocket. He withdrew a large-bladed bowie-type knife from a scabbard on his belt, enjoying its heavier weight and more substantial feel than the stiletto. Stilettos were all right to gut-punch someone with, but to do a good job on the throat with all its tendons and blood vessels and muscles, a man needed a real knife like the bowie. One whose blade wouldn't snap like a dry twig and whose point wouldn't get stuck in a bone or something.

Holding the knife in one hand, Hog reached down, slipped his boots off, and left them on the porch. He would be as quiet as a mouse pissing on cotton, he thought as he tiptoed into the darkness of the parlor.

He stood there for a moment in the dark, letting his eyes adjust to the gloomy atmosphere. Off to his right he could see light coming from under the door of the doctor's clinic room. That must be where they are, he thought, holding the knife out in front of him as he shuffled his feet along the floor so as not to make any boards creak as he moved toward the light.

As he eased the door to the clinic room open, he vowed to try to wake Miss Rule up before he cut her throat. He'd look into her eyes and give her a chance to try to fight him off. It wouldn't do her any good, but it might salve his conscience a little bit anyway.

He peered around the edge of the door and saw a woman sitting in a rocker with her back to the door, her long, blond hair hanging down her back. She had her hands in front of her, and it looked like she was knitting to pass the time.

On the bed in front of her, turned so her back was to the room, was the sleeping form of a white-haired lady. The covers were pulled up to her ears so he couldn't see her face, but how many grannies could there be lying in the doctor's old house, he thought, suppressing the urge to giggle at the thought.

Slowly, he crept toward the woman in the rocking chair, and as he neared her he reached out with his left hand to grab her hair and jerk her head back, exposing her neck to his bowie knife.

He was close enough now. He reached out and grabbed the hair and yanked it toward him.

He fell back and stumbled and almost went down on one knee when the hair came off in his hand. He almost screamed at the eerie feeling it gave him to yank a woman's hair plumb outta her head, but then he glanced at the rocking chair and saw Smoke Jensen turn around and grin at him. The mountain man was wearing a shawl over his buckskins and had a Colt .45 in his hand, and the hole in the end of the barrel that was pointed at Hog's head looked big enough to fall into.

The woman on the bed stirred, and Hog saw the young man who was riding with Jensen take his white wig off and sit up in the bed, yawning. "Good thing it didn't take him much longer to get here," Cal said to Smoke. "I was about to fall asleep right there in the bed."

Smoke waved the barrel of the Colt around in a little circle. "You want to drop that bowie knife, Hog? Or do you want me to shoot it out of your hand?"

Hog hesitated, trying to figure his chances of throwing the knife before Jensen could get a round off.

"Course," Smoke added, grinning, "it's kind'a dark in here and I might miss the knife and blow a couple of your fingers off instead, and they'll be calling you Lefty in the state prison for the next twenty years if you manage not to get hanged."

Hog blinked, hardly able to follow the humor in Smoke's comment, but he did hear "blow your fingers off," and that convinced him to drop the knife and raise his hands in the air.

"What do you mean hanged?" he asked, trying to force a shaky grin onto his lips. "I saw the light in the window and I knew the doc was dead and I thought I'd make sure nobody was trying to rob his place."

Smoke threw back his head and laughed. "That's a good one, Hog," he said, nodding appreciatively. "Did you think that up all by yourself?"

"Whatta you mean?" Hog asked, wondering who else was there to tell him what to say.

"Well, I thought since we have witnesses to you and Sheriff Buck Tolliver and your other friend cooking up this little assassination attempt, they might've helped you with that little story about you just being a civic-minded citizen worrying about a dead man's property."

Hog was dumb enough that he didn't realize Smoke was joking with him. He gave a lopsided grin and shook his head. "No, Jensen. For your information I thought that up all by myself. Didn't nobody help me at all."

He was so stupid he actually smiled while Smoke and Cal laughed at him. He was still smiling when Mayor Hemmings and the lawyer Joshua Banks walked into the room.

"I heard that, Smoke," Banks said, "and if I have to I'll so testify in court that Mr. Hogarth freely admitted he was lying about just checking out the place."

Hog's grin faded and he hung his head, shaking it slowly. He was thinking his daddy had been right all along—he was as dumb as a stump.

"All right, so what do we do now?" Hemmings asked, looking from Banks to Smoke.

"Well, we got one of the rats in our trap," Smoke

said. "Now it's time to see if we can't entice the rest of them to join him."

Smoke put his pistol in his holster and bent over to pick up the knife Hog had dropped on the floor. As he lowered his head, he heard Hog give an inarticulate grunt. Knowing what was coming, Smoke hunched his shoulders and ducked his head just as a ham-sized fist slammed into the side of his head and he found himself wrapped inside Hog's meaty arms in a bear hug's death grip.

Smoke's vision blurred and his head swam as he heard Cal give a shout and saw out of the corner of his eye Cal's pistol being aimed at the back of Hog's head.

"No!" Smoke shouted through laboring lungs, and shook his head, causing stars to glisten and swim across his vision. "I'll handle this," he finished with a croak.

Hog grunted again and squeezed with all his might, trying to take his frustration at being not only caught in the act but also tricked into confessing out on Smoke. Smoke turned his head to the side where he could look into Hog's bloodshot gaze. He grinned at the fat man, whose face was turning red with his exertion as he tried to squeeze the life out of Smoke.

Smoke took a deep breath, flexed his own considerable muscles, and slowly moved his arms out away from his body, breaking Hog's grip and causing the big man to stumble backward a step or two.

Hog's eyes opened wide in amazement; he'd never had anyone be able to break his bear-hug grip like that, and the mountain man hadn't even seemed to have to strain to do it.

Smoke felt the lump that was already forming on the side of his head, and grinned good-naturedly at Hog. "That was a pretty good shot, Hog. You want to dance some more while I'm ready for you, or are you just good at surprising a man who's not looking?"

Hog swallowed audibly. Truth be told, he'd just as soon not test the big man any further, remembering how it'd turned out the last time they fought, but he was no coward. "Sure, I'll go a couple of turns around the dance floor with you, Jensen, but you won't like the ending."

Smoke held out his hands and wriggled his fingers at Hog in a gesture saying, "Come on and show me what you've got."

Hog made another mistake to add to the several he'd already committed that day. He ducked his head and charged Smoke, his arms out-flung, hoping to catch the mountain man unawares.

Smoke simply stepped one step to the side and popped Hog in the left ear with a wicked right jab as the big man stumbled by.

Hog yelped and grabbed his ear, whirling around just in time to catch a left hook Smoke threw from his heels on the point of his chin.

Hog's eyes crossed, he moaned, and then he went down like he'd been hit in the head with an ax handle.

"Jumping Jesus," Banks exclaimed, shaking his head. "I don't think I've ever seen anyone hit so hard in my entire life." He looked at Smoke. "You lifted his feet plumb up off the ground when you connected with his chin."

Smoke shook his hand and grimaced. "I usually take the time to put on padded gloves before hitting someone like that. It's tough on the knuckles otherwise."

"Damn, I hope you didn't kill him," Hemmings said, stooping to put his hand in front of Hog's mouth to see if he was still breathing.

"Oh, he'll live, but he's gonna have a helluva

headache when he wakes up," Smoke said, kneading his bruised knuckles with his other hand.

"How are we going to get his carcass to the jail?" Banks asked, shaking his head. "He looks like he weighs three hundred pounds."

"Who said we're taking him to the jail?" Smoke asked, grinning. "I don't think there's any need to let the sheriff know that we have Mr. Hogarth in custody. It'll be more fun to see what he does when Hog doesn't return to the saloon to tell him his mission was accomplished."

"Yeah," Cal said, nodding and smiling. "Let the dirty bastards wonder what happened when he doesn't show up."

Smoke smiled slyly. "It might just be that they'll come looking for their lost friend."

"Which will seal their fate for once and for all," Joshua Banks said, rubbing his hands together and grinning from ear to ear.

"Let's roll Hog's fat butt under that empty bed over there," Smoke said, "and then you can get back into this one, Cal."

Soon the mayor and Banks were out of sight behind an armoire against a far wall, and both Smoke and Cal were back in their assigned places. The lantern was turned down low so shadows covered Smoke and Cal's faces and the trap was once again set.

CHAPTER 34

Sheriff Buck Tolliver looked at the big Regulator clock on the wall of his office for at least the hundredth time since they'd sent Hog off to kill the Rule woman and Hattie Monroe.

It'd been an hour and a half since Hog had snuck out the back door of the jail and disappeared into the night to do his dirty work.

"I'm telling you, Buck, something's gone wrong," Kid Akins said, nervously fiddling with the sticks still strapped to his left wrist as a brace. "Even as slow as that fat ass Hog is, he's had plenty of time to get into the doc's office and kill two ladies."

Hardy's eyes followed Tolliver's to the clock on the wall. "I'm afraid he's right, Buck," Hardy said reluctantly.

"But," Tolliver said, still clinging to some hope that things might turn out for the best, "there's been no alarm raised. No one's called for the sheriff and there's been no shots fired, so maybe he just got lost or passed out drunk or something."

Hardy snorted through his nose. "Well, as dumb as Hog is, I guess anything's possible, but one thing we do know for sure is there ain't no fire at the doc's house," he said, getting up and peering out the window toward the house in question.

"Do you think he could've killed them and forgotten

to light a fire?" Akins asked hopefully. "Maybe that's it. Maybe he just forgot, or the fire went out or something, and he's over at the saloon getting piss-drunk while we sit here worrying our fool heads off."

Tolliver turned angry eyes on Akins. "If he is, then he's a dead man 'cause I'm gonna kill him with my bare hands," he said harshly.

Hardy continued to look up and down the street. "Like you said, Buck, the good news is there hasn't been any alarm raised. If Hog had fucked up and gotten caught, then I'd expect the street to be full of men hell-bent on finding out what was going on, but it's quiet as a church on Monday out there."

"I'll tell you what, men, you two go on over to the saloon and see if Hog is there," Tolliver said. "If he is, keep him there and make sure he don't get so drunk he shoots his mouth off."

"What are you gonna be doing?" Hardy asked, his voice suspicious.

Tolliver got to his feet and hitched up his belt and holster. "Like you always said, Jeb, I started this mess, so I guess it's up to me to finish it. If Hog didn't kill the women, then I'm going to. I'll start the fire and then hightail it to the saloon. By the time someone reports it, you two can say I was there with you all the time."

"Sounds good to me," Kid said, his mouth already watering at the thought of more whiskey to ease his aching hand and arm.

Hardy stared at Tolliver for a moment. "All right, Buck, but if you ain't at the saloon in half an hour, I'm going to get on my horse and ride like hell to Pueblo, and hope I can get my money out of the bank before the marshals come looking for me."

"What? You think this is all some kind of trap, set to

catch us and make us admit what we did?" Tolliver asked, his voice incredulous.

Hardy shrugged. "I don't know what it is, Buck, but something ain't right. I can smell it."

Tolliver laughed. "Hell, Jeb, Jensen ain't that smart. He's a washed-up old gunslick, that's all."

"You can laugh at me when you show up at the saloon and the fire's eating that building down, Buck. Until then, I'm keeping my options open."

Fifteen minutes later, Tolliver was easing into the back door of the doc's house, his gun in one hand and a skinning knife in the other.

He could see the light from a lantern turned low under the door to the patient's room, so he made his way quietly through the darkness, his eyes looking back and forth for movement in case this was a trap.

When he got to the door, he used his knife hand to ease it open a couple of inches, and peeked through the slit. Sure enough, there was Hattie with her hair hanging down and her head slumped to the side in a rocking chair in front of the bed where she'd fallen asleep.

Janet Rule's gray hair was sticking out from under the covers on the bed in front of Hattie. This was perfect, Tolliver thought. He didn't know where Hog was or why he hadn't done the job, but he was damn sure going to do it himself and right now.

He holstered his pistol and held the knife out in front of him as he moved across the room. His heart almost stopped when Hattie stirred and turned around in her chair.

Suddenly he was staring into the pale eyes of Smoke Jensen and the dark hole of Jensen's .45 Peacemaker.

"Good evening, Sheriff," Jensen said, and his friend

Cal sat up in bed and grinned at him from under a gray wig. "Howdy, Buck," Cal said gaily, taking the wig off and dropping it on the bed.

Tolliver's mouth hung open as Mayor Sam Hemmings and Joshua Banks stepped out into the light from behind an armoire against the far wall.

Hemmings just shook his head sadly. "Why, Buck, why did you do all this?"

Tolliver grinned and dropped the knife. He was kind'a glad it was over. The strain of living a double life was gone, and it was like a weight had been lifted from his shoulders.

"Why, Mayor; you ask me why?" He moved to the side and took a seat on the edge of a bed there. "Robbing the miners was for the money, of course." He grinned. "You can't get rich off a hundred dollars a month, Mayor." And then he sobered and looked over at Jensen, his eyes filling with hate.

"The doc was just in the wrong place at the wrong time, like I told him before I shot him." He sighed and hung his head. "I hated that, 'cause I really liked him. But Blackie fucked up. He was supposed to kill Jensen's friend, and then when Jensen came back to town I was gonna kill *him*."

"Why, Tolliver?" Smoke asked, lowering the barrel of his pistol but not putting it away. "What did I ever do to you to make you want to hurt me?"

"You remember a man named Jack Tolliver?" he asked.

Smoke thought for a moment, and then he shook his head. "No, I don't."

"You and your Preacher friend shot him down in cold blood twenty years ago, him and four of his friends. It was right after you'd had a fight in a bar. They came out shooting and you and your friend killed every one of them."

Smoke's eyes lit up with memory. He stared at Tolliver. "You were the kid who shot me—the one with the peppermint stick in his mouth."

Tolliver sneered. "Yeah. Jack was my big brother and I watched you shoot him down like a dog in the street."

Smoke shook his head. "He didn't give me any choice, Tolliver. You had to know that."

Tolliver's eyes brimmed with tears. "It didn't matter then and it doesn't matter now. You took him from me and I wanted you to pay for that with your life."

Before Smoke could answer, Hog rose up from behind the bed, the stiletto from his pocket in his hand. He grabbed Hemmings from behind and stuck the knife against his neck.

Smoke raised his pistol, but didn't fire for fear of hitting the mayor in the low light of the room.

"Quick, Buck," Hog said, blood smearing his lip, "let's hightail it outta here."

As quick as a flash Buck was up and off the bed and running out of the room, with Hog stumbling along behind him dragging the mayor with him.

When he got to the doctor's back door, Hog shoved the mayor inside and slammed the door. Then he turned and ran as fast as he could after Tolliver toward the saloon down the street.

By the time Smoke and Cal and Banks picked the mayor up and got out the door, they could just see Hog and Tolliver entering the saloon.

As they ran toward it, men and women began streaming out of the batwings, screaming and hollering as shots were fired over their heads to make them scatter.

Smoke slowed to a walk, and calmly opened the loading gate on his pistol's cylinder and began to check his loads. "Looks like they're going to hole up in the saloon and wait for us to come in after them," he said.

Banks and Hemmings stopped cold in their tracks. "Hell with that," Banks said. "I'm a lawyer, not a lawman. I'm not going in there and getting myself shot."

Smoke glanced at Hemmings, who held up his hands. "I'm not a gunman, Smoke. I don't even carry a pistol."

Smoke smiled. He was used to this. He'd been here before, many times. "I'll tell you what, Mayor. You go let my friend Pearlie out of jail, give him his gun, and we'll clean up your town for you."

As he finished talking, the lights in the saloon went out, leaving the place as dark as a tomb.

"All right, Smoke. I'll do it right away."

"You might want to send him out with an express gun and some shells too, Mayor," Cal added without looking up as he too checked his pistols.

"Getting to be quite the expert at storming buildings, huh?" Smoke said to Cal with a laugh.

"It's the company I keep, I guess," Cal replied, grinning back. "I was taught by an expert."

Half an hour later, Pearlie and Cal and Smoke stood outside the saloon and discussed their options. "We could just burn the place down," Pearlie said, squinting his eyes to try and see better in the dark of the night.

Smoke shook his head. "I never held much with burning men alive," he said. "It shows no respect for your opponent."

"You think Tolliver deserves our respect after all he did?" Cal asked.

Smoke nodded. "I remember a boy of no more than ten or twelve, so small it took both his hands to ear back the hammer on a Colt. He stood there in that street with his brother and all of his brother's friends dead all around him and he tried to shoot me down while still sucking on a peppermint stick."

Smoke looked at Cal and Pearlie. "His brother had just been killed and he was man enough even at that age to try and do something about it, so, yes, he does deserve our respect. If not for the man he came to be, then for the boy he once was."

Pearlie nodded. "So, how do you want to handle it?" he asked.

"Let's give him another chance to be that brave little boy," Smoke said.

He walked up the street until he was standing in front of the saloon, well within pistol range if they tried to shoot from inside.

Hair standing up on the back of his neck, Cal joined him, as did Pearlie.

"Tolliver. Buck Tolliver!" Smoke yelled.

"Yeah, what do you want, Jensen?" came a voice from out of the darkness.

"None of you can get away, Tolliver. You got two choices. You can stay in that saloon until the marshals get here and root you out to die at the end of a rope, or you can come out here and face me and my friends in the street."

He looked around and saw several horses tied to rails nearby. "There are horses tied up out here," Smoke yelled again. "If you get by us, there's no one else to stop you from getting on those broncs and heading into the mountains. Who knows? You might even get away clean."

After several minutes went by with no reply, Smoke called again, "It's your choice, Tolliver. Stay and die for certain, or come out here and take a chance on living. Either way, a bullet is better than a long fall on a short rope."

Seconds later, four men walked out of the saloon side by side. Three of the men had pistols on their belts, and the fourth was carrying a short-barreled express gun cradled in his arms.

"Jensen," Tolliver yelled, "this is for my brother, Jack."

Smoke nodded and all of the men went for their guns.

Jeb Hardy's eyes opened wide in surprise as he saw all three of the men in front of him draw and fire while his gun was barely out of its holster. He'd known it was going to be close between Jensen and him, but he had no idea Jensen's friends would also be faster on the draw than he was.

The first slug took him square in the chest and made him pull his trigger while his gun was still pointing down. He glanced down in amazement as his own bullet plowed into his right foot, taking three toes clean off. He grinned through the pain in his chest until a second bullet took the top of his head off and put his lights out for good.

Kid Akins never even cleared leather before two slugs knocked him backward to land spread-eagled on his back staring up at the stars in the night sky. "I'll be damned," he muttered through the blood bubbling from his mouth, "my arm don't hurt no more." Those were his last words, and the stars were the last thing he saw before he was sucked into an intense light from the sky.

Hog Hogarth got off both barrels of his express gun, firing from the hip without aiming before he was hit, and hit hard. One bullet punched a hole in his belly button, doubling him over so that the second slug went into the top of his head, exploding it into a fine red mist as he toppled over into the darkness at his feet.

Tolliver surprised even himself by drawing and getting off one quick shot at Jensen before Jensen's slugs took him in the chest and belly, spinning him around to fall face-first in the dirt in front of the saloon.

Moments later, he felt himself being turned over, and he looked up into the face of Smoke Jensen. He looked down and saw a red stain on Jensen's shoulder, and he grinned. "Got you in the wing again, huh?" he asked.

Smoke smiled down at him. "Yeah, and as I recall, it's the same arm, Buck."

"I got no right to ask, Jensen, but I need a favor."

"Yeah?"

"Take the money I got in the banks in Pueblo and have my body sent to Homestead, Colorado. There's a little cemetery there with all of my family in it. Plant me there, Jensen, next to my brother, will you?"

Smoke nodded. "I promise, Buck."

"So long, mountain man," Tolliver gasped, blood oozing from between his lips. "I gave it a good try, but came up short . . . ." And then he died.

Smoke stood up and turned, his heart aching when he saw Cal slip to his knees, the front of his shirt covered with blood.

He ran back and knelt next to Cal along with Pearlie.

"Damn," Cal said, grimacing in pain. "I'm so tired of getting shot all the time."

Smoke quickly ripped Cal's shirt open and saw four holes in Cal's chest and stomach oozing blood. Just under the skin, less than half an inch deep, he could see the outline of buckshot from the express gun Hog had fired.

Smoke took a quick breath, relieved to know Cal's wounds weren't life-threatening.

Pearlie just shook his head. "I told you, Smoke, the boy's a lead magnet. It happens every time we get in a gunfight. The bullets just automatically head for ol' Cal."

Cal looked up and saw the blood on Smoke's shoulder, and he grinned weakly. "I'll take yours out if you'll take mine out."

Smoke nodded and laughed. "Since I heard you've been getting plenty of practice lately, it's a deal!"